SWEET HARMONY

HARMONY FALLS
BOOK ONE

ELIZABETH KELLY

EK PUBLISHING INC.

Edited by
L. Nunn Editing

Cover art by
EK Designs Inc.

SWEET HARMONY

(HARMONY FALLS BOOK ONE)

Faking it just got real.

Kira is desperate...

A decade of unrequited love will do that to a girl.

Dead set on making local hottie firefighter Daniel jealous, she proposes a fake relationship with Connor... her unexpectedly sexy dentist.

Connor is done with relationships.

He moved to Harmony Falls to escape his past and make a fresh start... one that doesn't include a girlfriend—fake or real.

Faced with the prospect of an awkward reunion with his ex and a family determined to bring them back together, he makes an agreement with Kira. He'll help make Daniel jealous if she poses as his girlfriend at a family wedding.

The relationship isn't real... but their sizzling attraction is.

As they grow closer, the lines blur between make-believe and reality until Kira realizes that it's Connor she wants.

Will Connor's past doom them from the start? Or are Connor and Kira meant to be?

CHAPTER 1

"Kira!"

The front door slammed, and heavy footsteps tromped down the hallway. Her heart pounded, and she ignored the look Grace gave her.

"What?" She hoped she sounded casual – wait, did she sound too casual?

"Can I use your shower?"

He popped into the kitchen, already beginning to strip off his shirt, and she soaked in the sight of his sweaty, naked chest as he grinned at her best friend. "Hey, Grace."

"Hi, Daniel. Why are you always half-naked?" Grace asked as Kira set the knife down and tried not to lick her lips. Or drool.

"The ladies love it," Daniel said with another grin. He wiped the sweat off his chest and perfect abs with his shirt before shifting the duffel bag on his shoulder. "Do you mind, Kira? The guys and I were playing ball, and I lost track of time. I need to be at the firehouse in twenty minutes, and your place is on the way."

"They have a shower at the station," Grace said.

"Yeah, but there's no line-up for Kira's shower."

"Maybe she's already got someone in her shower."

Daniel laughed before crossing the kitchen and slinging his arm around Kira's shoulders. "You bring some guy home from the bar last night, doll?"

Her traitorous body was already trying to lean into him, and Kira forced herself to stand perfectly still as Daniel stared at her. She could feel the heat of his body against hers, and she wanted to rest her head against his shoulder. At 5'10", he was only a few inches taller than her, and their bodies fit together perfectly. She wouldn't have to crane her neck to kiss him, and it would make having sex in the shower super easy.

Do not start thinking about sex in the shower with Daniel. Do not start thinking about –

"Well, do you?" Daniel said teasingly.

"No, of course not," she replied. "Go ahead and use it. You know where the towels are."

"Thanks, doll." He gave her a playful slap on the ass before leaving the kitchen.

Kira's cheeks flushed, and she stared down at herself, mainly to avoid Grace's gaze.

"Shit," she muttered. Watermelon juice stained her shirt, and her yoga pants had a grease spot. Why did she always look her worst when Daniel was around?

"You really shouldn't have given him a key," Grace said as Kira left the half-cut watermelon on the counter and sank into a kitchen chair.

"He's my friend," Kira said. "You have a key to my place."

"Yeah, and I don't use it to take advantage of you and your shower, your fridge, your sixty-inch TV, your -"

"He's not taking advantage of me." Kira ran a hand through her blonde hair.

"Honey," Grace leaned forward and took her hand, "Daniel's been taking advantage of your crush on him since high school."

"Keep your voice down." Kira glanced at the doorway.

"Honey, if he isn't interested by now, he'll never be."

Kira gave Grace a hurt look. "Why would you say that? You're supposed to be my friend and -"

They both looked up as the front door slammed again, and another set of heavy footsteps trod down the hallway. "Kira, did I leave my wallet here last night?"

Her brother Gideon appeared in the kitchen. Seven years older than her, his height, dark hair and large body were the complete opposite of her short and slender body, blonde hair and blue eyes. He favoured their father in looks, while Kira took after their mother's side.

"Yeah, it's on top of the fridge," Kira said.

"Thanks." Gideon grabbed his wallet and stuffed it into his back pocket. He was wearing his uniform, and she studied the gun at his hip as he grabbed a juice from the fridge. He didn't typically work on a Sunday, and she gave him a puzzled look.

"Why are you working today?"

He took a drink of the juice. "Ian's nanny is out sick. Talk to you later."

"Aren't you going to say hello to Grace?" Kira scowled at him when he ruffled her blonde hair.

"Hey." Gideon gave Grace a stiff smile.

"Hello, Gideon. How are you?"

"Can't complain. You?"

"I'm good, thanks."

3

Grace was staring at the table, and Kira reached across and poked her arm. "Grace, what's wrong?"

"Nothing," Grace mumbled.

Gideon cleared his throat. "I need to get to work. Bye, ladies."

"Bye, Gideon," Kira replied.

He left before Grace could say anything, and Kira poked her again. "Tell me what's wrong, Gracie-Lou."

"Don't call me Gracie-Lou, and nothing's wrong," Grace said. "What were we talking about?"

"You were telling me how Daniel would never be interested in me."

Grace raised her head and stared at her. Her bright green eyes were solemn looking, and she studied Kira for a few moments before saying, "Fuck it."

"Fuck what?" Kira gave her a bewildered look.

"You want Daniel Moore, right?"

"You know I do." Kira made another quick peek at the doorway.

"Then you're going to have him."

"What's gotten into you? Just a minute ago, you told me he'd never be interested, and in the last few months, you've become increasingly irritable about my love for Daniel."

"I haven't been irritable," Grace said.

"Oh, please," Kira said. "You've been super bitchy about almost everything. Even Addie said something about your mood, and she never says anything negative about anyone."

Grace crossed her arms over her ample chest. "First – sorry I've been a bitch. Second – as your best friend, I'm making it my mission to get Daniel Moore into your bed. A woman should have the man she wants."

Kira cocked her head and studied Grace for a moment.

"I'm not sure if I'm impressed or terrified of this new version of Grace."

Grace just grinned at her. "Okay, we need a game plan. Operation 'Bang Daniel' has officially begun."

Kira couldn't help but laugh. "Could we come up with something less crude?"

"What's wrong with crude? I like crude." Daniel strolled back into the kitchen, his blond hair wet from the shower and his t-shirt sticking to his perfect chest. Kira gave Grace a look of dismay.

"Um…"

Daniel stared expectantly at her.

"Are your arms bigger, or is it just my imagination?" Grace said.

Daniel flexed both his arms. "I've upped both my weights and reps at the gym, Gracie-Lou."

Grace smiled sweetly at him. "We can tell."

"Thanks!" He opened the fridge and peered into it. "Mind if I snag a juice?"

"Help yourself." Kira stared at his ass in his stupidly tight jeans.

He straightened and winked at her before sticking the bottle of juice into his duffel bag. He planted a kiss on her cheek. "Thanks for the shower and the juice, doll."

"Anytime." She wondered if anyone else heard the shakiness in her voice. The touch of Daniel's warm lips felt like it was branded into her skin.

"Later, Gracie-Lou!"

"Bye, Daniel!" Grace wiggled her fingers at him, but her sweet smile dropped from her face when he disappeared from the kitchen.

She waited until the front door closed before leaning

forward and taking Kira's hand. "You sure he's the one for you?"

"Yes." Kira touched the spot on her cheek where Daniel had kissed her. "I'm sure."

"Okay. Then let's do this." Grace leaned back and tapped her fingernails on the kitchen table. "You're going to win Daniel Moore's heart by making him jealous."

"I'm sorry, what?" Kira said.

"You're going to date someone else and make Daniel jealous."

"That's your big plan? I thought I'd take some cooking lessons and make him dinner a few times a week. My mom always said the way to a man's heart was through his stomach."

"Maybe back in the sixties. Now? Now, you need to force him to see what he's missing. You need to make him jealous. And what better way to make him jealous than by banging another guy?"

"I don't want to sleep with someone else," Kira said immediately.

"Fine, fine." Grace waved her hand. "We'll just pretend that you're having sex with another guy."

"What guy will pretend to date me to make another guy jealous?" Kira grabbed her phone and started scrolling across the screen.

"What are you doing?" Grace asked.

"Looking up cooking classes."

"Give me that!" She grabbed Kira's phone and wouldn't give it back. "This will work. Just let me think for a minute."

"There isn't anyone who -"

"Preacher."

Kira gaped at Grace. "Preacher?"

6

"Why not? Gideon saved his life. He'd do anything for him."

"One – he's my brother's best friend, and he's *old*."

"Oh my God, he's like thirty-five, Kira. That's not old," Grace replied.

"Too old for me," Kira said. "Two – it's Preacher."

"What's that supposed to mean?"

"It means he's so not my type. Even if he agreed to help me by fake dating me, no one - including Daniel - would ever believe it."

Grace tapped her finger thoughtfully against her cheekbone. "Hmm, you make a good point. Preacher is kind of... rough looking."

"That's an understatement," Kira said. "Do you think there's any part of him that isn't covered in tattoos?"

"Some girls like that look."

"Well, I don't," Kira said. It was Daniel's body she was thinking of. That smooth, perfect, tanned skin not marred by ink or piercings.

"Preacher is a good guy," Grace said.

"Yes, he is," Kira replied. "You think I don't know that? I've spent plenty of time with him and Gideon. But he's not my type, and besides, Gideon would freak out if I was dating his best friend. You know how he is."

"He's not your guardian. He can't make decisions for you."

"No, but he is the damn sheriff. Preacher might be his best friend, but that doesn't mean Gideon won't arrest him if he thinks he's being inappropriate with me."

Grace rolled her eyes. "Okay, fine. Preacher's off the table."

"Give me back my phone," Kira said as Grace stared

7

thoughtfully into space. "There isn't anyone else who'll fake date me. I appreciate your help, Gracie, really I do, but -"

"I've got it!" Grace suddenly declared. "I have the perfect man for you."

Kira gave her a suspicious look. "Who?"

"Connor."

"Your boss? Dr. MacMillan?"

"Yes."

"No."

"Why not?"

"He's a dentist."

"So?"

"What do you mean, so?" Kira said. "Dating a dentist isn't," she fumbled for the word, "cool."

"Oh, for God's sake. You're twenty-five years old and a real estate agent, Kira, not a damn rock star. This isn't high school anymore, and no one cares if you're 'cool'. Dating a dentist is perfectly acceptable."

"He's from Willington."

"He hasn't lived there in a while."

"He's still an out-of-towner," Kira said. "What would people say if they knew I was sleeping with an out-of-towner?"

"You're not actually going to sleep with him," Grace said.

"Yeah, but people don't know that. My dad would roll over in his grave if he knew I was dating an out-of-towner. Especially a Willington whiner."

"He's a really good guy. Just because he's from Willington doesn't make him a whiner," Grace said. "This town's stupid rivalry with Willington has always driven me batty."

"Why would he fake date me?"

Grace leaned forward and lowered her voice. "Okay, so

you can't say a word because Connor told me this in confidence one night when he'd had a little too much to drink, but -"

"A little too much to drink? How close are you to your boss?"

"We're friends," Grace said a bit impatiently. "We've gone for drinks a few times. He'd never admit this, but I think he's lonely. I keep wanting to invite him out with the gang but I'm not sure how it would go over. The good town folk of Harmony Falls aren't always friendly to outsiders."

"You're telling me," Kira said. "Honestly, I'm surprised his office is still open."

"Well, it helps that his business partner is a Harmony Falls lifer. But, he's also an excellent dentist," Grace said. "You know that – he's your dentist, for God's sake. So, what do you say? Do you want to fake date him? He's handsome."

"Is he?" Kira said. "He's always wearing a hospital mask when I see him. I couldn't pick him out of a lineup. Besides, you still haven't told me why he would fake date me."

"Right. So, he confessed one night that he's going to Willington next month for his cousin's wedding, and he's dreading it because his ex-fiancée will be there. His family is still upset that they called off their engagement and will spend the entire time trying to get them back together."

"Okay," Kira said. "So, how does this help me?"

"Think about it," Grace said. "If you guys are fake dating, you can go with him to his cousin's wedding. His family isn't going to push his ex on him with his new girlfriend sitting right there."

"I guess it could work," Kira said slowly.

"Great! I'll talk to Connor tomorrow and see if he's in," Grace said.

She reached across the table and squeezed Kira's hand again. "You'll be banging Daniel before you know it, honey."

"That's romantic," Kira said.

Grace grinned at her. "That's me. Romantic as fuck."

"GRACE? WHAT ARE YOU STILL DOING HERE? THE OFFICE closed half an hour ago." Connor stared in surprise at the curvy dental hygienist in the staff room.

"Just finishing up," she said. "Busy day, huh?"

"Yes." He shrugged out of his lab coat as Grace dropped onto the couch. They'd hired Grace right out of hygienist school last year, and it was one of their better decisions. She was fantastic with clients, reliable, and intelligent. She was also very pretty with her full curves, long, curly dark hair and green eyes, but he didn't feel a lick of sexual interest. He tried to tell himself it was because he knew it was a bad idea even to consider dating an employee, but that was a lie. He wasn't interested in his pretty employee because he had no desire to have his heart ripped out of his chest and stomped on right in front of him for a second time.

Crybaby, his inner voice mocked grumpily. It was more than willing to risk a heart stomping if it meant he got laid again on the regular. He had slept with exactly two women since he and Lisa broke up. Both were one-night stands when he was attending out-of-town work conferences. He hadn't gone on a single date since the night Lisa broke off their engagement.

He sat on the other end of the couch. "Big plans for tonight?"

She shook her head. "No. How about you?"

"Going for a run and then dinner," he replied.

She stared thoughtfully at him, and he raised his eyebrows. "What?"

"Dinner alone?"

"Yes," he replied. "Why?"

"So, you're not dating anyone yet, right?"

He grinned at her. "Are you asking me to dinner, Grace?"

"God, no." She looked so horrified at the idea that he burst into laughter.

"Shit, I didn't mean for it to come out like that," she said. "It's just – dating my boss is not a great idea."

"Right. It has nothing to do with your crush on our surly sheriff?"

"I told you that in secret," she said.

"I know, and I haven't told anyone. Do you regret sharing it with me?"

"Honestly? No. It felt good to tell someone. Besides, it seemed only fair since you had just told me your secret about your ex-fiancé."

He shrugged. "It's not really a secret, I suppose."

Grace cleared her throat. "Then you wouldn't be upset if I had told someone else?"

"It's not a secret, but that doesn't mean I want to be the town's gossip."

"You're not," she said hurriedly. "I only told one person."

"Who?" he asked.

"Kira Walker."

He frowned in thought. "The name is familiar."

"She's a client," Grace said. "Short and slender, long blonde hair and blue eyes. She's Gideon's baby sister."

"Right. Still has her wisdom teeth, only one cavity."

Gracie laughed. "Your ability to remember people by their teeth status is weird and impressive."

"Why did you tell her?" he asked.

"Because she has a similar problem, and I think you can help each other. She's in love with a guy named Daniel Moore. He's a firefighter in town."

"I know who he is," Connor said. "He plays on the fire-fighter's baseball team."

"Kira's been in love with him since high school, but he's got her in the friend zone," Grace said. "I promised her I would help her win his love, and I need your help to keep that promise."

"Mine."

"Yes. I want you to fake date Kira to make Daniel jealous."

"No." He stood up to leave. "Good night, Grace. Make sure you set the alarm before you leave."

"Connor, wait!" She stood and grabbed his arm. "Just hear me out."

"I'm not getting involved in that drama," he said.

"If you help Kira, she'll help you," Grace said quickly.

He stared at her. He felt like he should know what the hell his hygienist was talking about, but the answer danced just out of his reach.

"If you pretend to be her boyfriend, she'll pretend to be your girlfriend at your cousin's wedding. Your family won't try to get you back together with Lisa if you have Kira with you."

He wanted to tell her it was the stupidest idea he'd ever heard, but he was getting desperate. Mandy's wedding was a month away. If he didn't take a date with him, he'd be forced to listen to his family extol Lisa's virtues before pushing him into her arms. It would be awkward and uncomfortable, and he couldn't even hope that Lisa had found someone new. His aunt sent him regular emails filled with family news. The email contained all the information about Lisa, too. She was also still single – a fact that thrilled his entire family and gave them all hope of a reunion.

They were deluded, he thought bitterly. Lisa would never want him back. Not when she couldn't stand the failure he'd become or the way he'd ruined both their dreams.

"Connor?" Grace touched his arm, and he gave her a blank look.

"What?"

"Will you meet with Kira? Just talk to her about it?"

He sighed and rubbed at his knee. It was throbbing like a bitch, and he decided a run tonight wasn't a good idea. "I'll talk to her. Is she busy tonight?"

Grace shook her head. "I don't think so, but I'll text her. If she isn't, I'll tell her you'll drop by and then text you her address."

"Okay," he said.

Grace grinned at him. "Thanks, Connor."

"Yeah. Hey, does this Daniel guy even have any interest in Kira?" he asked. "There's no point in doing this if it won't make him jealous."

"I think so, but in the interest of full disclosure – I don't know for certain. Daniel is a total flirt with every woman he sees, but he could secretly be into her and isn't making his move because he's afraid of her brother."

Connor raised his eyebrows. "So, I would have to deal with an overprotective brother who just happens to carry a gun? You're not really selling this, Grace."

"Gideon isn't going to shoot you for dating Kira," Grace said. "You know the firefighters and the sheriff's department all have a rivalry/competition thing going on. Daniel probably isn't afraid of Gideon, but he dislikes him, and he knows Gideon isn't fond of him either. It might be why Daniel hasn't made a move on Kira."

"Then me dating her won't help," Connor said.

"It might. Daniel is super competitive, so if he has a thing for Kira and she's suddenly unavailable, it might spur him to do something. If it doesn't, and Daniel isn't jealous, then maybe Kira will finally realize he isn't nearly good enough for her and give up on her silly -"

She stopped abruptly. "Forget I said that."

"You don't like Daniel?"

She sighed. "I don't dislike him. I just don't think he's the right guy for Kira."

"Then why are you doing this?"

"Because she loves him," Grace said, "and I love her and want her to be happy. She's been obsessed with Daniel since she was fifteen. Besides, who am I to say who the right person is for someone?"

"What if it doesn't work? What if we fake date for a couple of weeks and no signs of jealousy. Then what? Kira," he made air quotes with his fingers, "dumps me, and I'm still on my own for my cousin's wedding."

"She'll still go with you to your cousin's wedding," Grace said. "Just make that part of the agreement."

He didn't reply, and she pulled out her phone. "I'll text her now and see if you can drop by. This is a great solution for both of your problems, Connor. I promise."

CHAPTER 2

When the doorbell rang, Kira smoothed down her blonde hair and checked her reflection in the toaster. Not that it mattered what she looked like. This wasn't a first date, for God's sake.

She headed out of the kitchen and down the hallway. Two long windows flanked the front door, and she could see one tanned arm and hand through the right one. Her dentist had big hands.

You know what they say about big hands.

She flushed and tossed that errant thought out of her head before opening the door. She smiled at the dark-haired man standing on her front porch.

"Hello, Dr. MacMillan."

"Hello, Ms. Walker," he said.

There was a moment of awkward silence, and then she stepped back. "Call me Kira. Please, come in."

He stepped into the house, and she shut the door before squeezing past him. "Would you like something to drink? I have water, iced tea and soda. Or I can make coffee."

"An iced tea would be fine," he said.

As he followed her toward the kitchen, she wondered if he was checking out her ass in her yoga pants. She knew she didn't have a great body. She was on the thin side, and she secretly coveted Grace's full curves. She scoffed inwardly. Who was she kidding? Forget Grace's curves, she'd take Addison's very respectable C-cup boobs if given the chance. She was barely a B-cup, and her cleavage was thanks to the miracle invention of the century – the push-up bra.

Why she even thought her dentist would check out her ass was ridiculous. It was flat and –

Hey, Kira? Maybe you should stop thinking about your own damn tits and ass and get the man his iced tea.

Dr. MacMillan was hovering in the kitchen doorway while she stood blankly next to the fridge, and she gave him an embarrassed smile. "Sorry. Have a seat, and I'll get that iced tea."

"Thank you," he said.

She poured each of them a glass of iced tea and perched on the edge of the chair across from him. He drank some iced tea before saying, "It's good. Thanks."

"I like it a little on the sweet side," she said. "My brother says it's way too sweet and that I'll rot my teeth right out of my head, but I guess that's why I go to see you, right? To keep my teeth from rotting out of my head when I eat too much sweet stuff?"

Kira! Enough!

She shut her mouth with a snap. Fuck, what was wrong with her? Why was she so damn nervous? Sure, Dr. MacMillan was handsome enough, but he wasn't Daniel. She closed her eyes for a moment and conjured up an image of

16

Daniel. It calmed her a little, and she took a deep breath. Daniel's blond hair and dark blue eyes were what she wanted.

Dr. MacMillan's eyes might be blue, but they were so light they were almost transparent. She could see none of the warmth and humour in them that Daniel's gaze had. In fact, her dentist was currently staring at her like she was some new and interesting species of bug he had discovered crawling up his leg.

She cleared her throat. "Sorry, I babble when I'm nervous."

He took another drink of iced tea. "You have a nice home."

"Thank you. It was my childhood home. It belongs to my brother now, but he didn't want to live here. My parents died a few years ago, and being in the house brought on too many sad memories for him. I love living here, though. It makes me feel closer to my mom and dad, you know?"

She closed her mouth again. Holy shit, she was making the worst first impression ever.

"I'm sorry about your parents." His voice was a low rasp, and the sound of it sent the weirdest shiver down her spine.

"Thank you," she replied. "So, um, Grace said we could help each other with our problems."

He nodded. "Possibly."

She waited and tried not to sigh with frustration when he said nothing else. His silence was beginning to unnerve her. Daniel was chatty and always the life of the party. She could barely get a word in edgewise when she was with him, and she loved that. She loved his bold brashness and how he lit up a room when he walked into it.

Her dentist hardly made an impact. Hell, she'd met him how many times in his office, and she had no impression of him at all. He was just a masked guy who came in and checked her teeth at the end of the cleaning.

"So, you need a date for your cousin's wedding?" she asked.

"Yes," he said, "and you need a boyfriend to make Daniel Moore jealous."

His voice had the slightest hint of derision, and she immediately blushed. It was evident that he thought she was an idiot.

"You know what? Never mind, Dr. MacMillan." She stood and dumped her iced tea down the sink. "This isn't going to work. I'll show you out now."

She stalked toward the front door. She could hear him behind her, but before she could open the door, he wrapped his long fingers around her wrist. The touch of his skin against hers made another one of those little shivers zip down her spinal cord. She froze and turned to stare up at him.

"I'm sorry," he said. "I'm being an ass."

"Yes, you are."

He sighed and dropped her wrist before raking his hand through his dark hair. "I apologize. Also, if we're going to fake date, you should call me Connor."

"Why are you even here, Connor?" she asked. "It's obvious you think this is a stupid idea."

"It isn't," he said. "I'm just -"

He paused and rubbed at one temple. "What if this doesn't work?"

"What do you mean?"

"What if our fake dating doesn't make Daniel jealous?

18

Will you still go with me to my cousin's wedding? Still pretend to be my girlfriend?"

"Yes," she said.

"What if it does work? Then what? You start dating Daniel, and I'm headed to Willington alone."

"Well, your cousin's wedding is in a month, right?"

"Yes."

"We don't have to start fake dating right away. We can give it a couple of weeks and use that time to learn more about each other. It's probably a good idea if we know more than each other's names. It'll be more believable if we know personal stuff about each other. That leaves only two weeks until your cousin's wedding. I think it'll take more than a couple of weeks to make Daniel jealous," she said.

"Do I have your word that you'll attend the wedding with me?" he asked.

"Yes," she said. "I'll be there, no matter what."

Then we have an agreement," Connor said. "You'll pose as my girlfriend at my cousin's wedding, and I'll help you make Daniel seethe with jealousy and realize that you're his soul mate."

She gave him a dirty look. "You don't have to make it sound so juvenile."

He just shrugged, and she reached for the front door. "Thank you. I'll get your number from Grace and text you in the next few days about meeting to go over personal stuff."

"There's just one more thing," Connor said.

"What?"

"This." He gripped the back of her neck and pulled her forward. She made a decidedly stupid-sounding squeak when he bent his dark head and pressed his mouth against hers. She stood stock-still with her eyes wide and unblinking as he slid his other arm around her waist and pulled her against his hard body.

When he sucked on her lower lip, a strange tingle went through her lower body, and another small sound escaped her lips. This one, embarrassingly enough, sounded like a moan, and she tried to step back. His hand tightened around her neck, holding her completely immobile. When his tongue slid across her upper lip, she heard another of those odd moan-like noises as her eyes drifted shut.

God, he smells so good, she thought bewilderedly as he tilted her head back. He kissed her again, his lips warm and weirdly persuasive, and it took her a minute to realize she was returning his kiss.

Kira! Stop kissing your dentist!

It was solid advice, but her body was completely and blissfully betraying her. She pressed up against Connor and put her arms around his neck. He was so tall that it was a real stretch to do it, but she liked the way it forced her breasts against his chest.

His tongue licked the seam of her mouth. Her head whirling and her pussy suddenly throbbing, she parted her lips. He slid his tongue between them and tasted her with slow, long licks that made Kira shudder with pleasure. He tasted sweet, like the iced tea he had been drinking. When she pushed her tongue into his mouth with a decided lack of finesse, he slid his fingers into her hair and tugged her back.

"Slow," he whispered.

She blushed fiercely. For roughly a nanosecond, she thought about telling him to stop, but then his warm mouth returned to hers, and he was urging her tongue back into his mouth with slow licks of his. She slowed down and mimicked the slow strokes of his tongue.

He groaned quietly. Besides his low whisper, it was the first sound he had made since kissing her. It flamed the lust in her belly even higher. She had a feeling that the icy Dr. Connor MacMillan never lost control. The idea that kissing her could make that control slip, even a little, was deliciously intoxicating.

She arched her back and rubbed her abdomen against the hardness pressing into it. Connor was hard. He was hard for her, and that sent another flickering flame of excitement through her nerve endings. She rubbed her small breasts against him and wondered what she could do to get him to touch them. Her nipples were almost painfully hard and poking against her bra. A sudden vision of Connor sucking on them brought on a gush of liquid that soaked the crotch of her panties.

He pulled away abruptly, and she would have fallen in a boneless heap to the floor if he hadn't steadied her. She stared dumbly at him before reaching up and touching her trembling, swollen lips.

"Why-why did you do that?" she whispered.

"If we're posing as boyfriend and girlfriend, it's going to require physical touching and kissing," he said.

She felt like she'd been through the wringer, but he wasn't even out of breath. If it hadn't been for the way his dick still strained at the front of his pants, she would have thought he was completely unaffected by the kiss between them.

"O-only when we're around other people." She couldn't seem to stop stuttering or touching her swollen mouth.

He gave her an impatient look. "It won't look very realistic if we kiss each other like it's the first time we've ever kissed. And I wanted to see if we had chemistry."

"Do we?" she asked like an idiot.

A brief smile crossed his face, sending a weird tingle down the base of her spine. "Yes. I think so, anyway."

She didn't reply, and he patted her shoulder like he was his sister. "That's a good thing, Kira. It will make it appear more real."

"Uh, right," she said.

He studied her. "How many men have you kissed before?"

"Why?"

"You're not," he paused, "great at kissing."

Her face was so red she was nearly sweating, and she gave him a furious look. "That's a really rude thing to say."

"No, just honest. We'll need to practice some more."

She wanted to tell him to take his idea of practice kissing and stuff it up his piehole, but strangely the thought of kissing him again wasn't entirely unpleasant. Besides, as much as it was a blow to her ego, he probably had a point. She'd kissed two men before him, and neither of them had provoked the type of reaction that her dentist's kiss did.

He opened the front door and asked, "What time do you work tomorrow?"

"Uh, I need to be at the office by nine."

"I'll stop by at eight, and we'll practice." He left, shutting the door quietly behind him, and she sank against the wall, her fingers still tracing her lower lip. What the hell just happened?

KIRA STARED OUT THE KITCHEN WINDOW AND SIPPED HER second cup of coffee. It was just before eight, and her insides were quaking with nerves and anticipation. She patted her hair self-consciously as she strained to hear a vehicle.

She was tired and on edge. It took her much longer than usual to fall asleep last night. Every time she closed her eyes, she relived the touch of Connor's mouth against hers. The way his tongue had stroked and tasted, the feel of his erection against her belly.

She abruptly dumped her coffee down the sink and grabbed a mint from the jar in the cupboard. She crunched it down as she checked her phone for the time. Grace had texted her last night to see how it went with Connor. She couldn't bring herself to tell her about the kissing, at least not over text, so she had simply said it went well and she would tell her more later. Now, she wished she'd mentioned the kiss, if only to get Grace's reaction. Maybe her dentist went around kissing random women all the time.

Idiot.

Yeah, she was.

The doorbell rang, and she jerked wildly. She left her phone on the counter and hurried to the door. She took a moment to smooth her blue pencil skirt before opening the door.

"Hello, Dr. – I mean, Connor." Her voice was too loud.

"Good morning, Kira."

"Come in, please."

He stepped into the house, and she licked her lips. He was wearing a blue t-shirt with jeans, and he smelled delicious.

"Do you always wear cologne?" she blurted out.

He gave her an odd look, and she grimaced in embarrassment. "Sorry. You smell, uh, nice."

"Thank you," he said.

He didn't say anything about how she smelled, and she waited stupidly for him to tell her she smelled good. He stayed silent, and her embarrassment grew.

"Uh, why don't we go into the kitchen." She turned and walked away before he could reply. Her stomach was churning with nerves, and her hand shook when she reached for a coffee mug.

"Can I get you a cup of coffee?" She turned, staggering back into the counter with a nervous squeak. Connor stood directly behind her, and she stared wide eyed at him.

"I have a root canal at nine and can't stay very long. Let's get started, shall we?" He plucked the coffee mug from her hand and set it on the counter.

Before she could even lick her lips in anticipation, his arm was around her waist, his other hand on the back of her neck, and his mouth on hers.

Don't moan, she thought fiercely as he brushed his lips against hers in a light, gentle caress.

Be cool, Kira. It's just a kiss, be cool.

She returned his kiss tentatively, once more mimicking the movement of his mouth, and tried to ignore the heat of his hand cupping her hip. He didn't move his hands or his body at all, just kissed her repeatedly with those same gentle movements. After what felt like hours, she made a noise of impatience and parted her lips. She wanted his tongue in her mouth, wanted it so badly she was nearly shaking, and she couldn't figure out why he wasn't reading her signals.

She pulled back slightly and said, "Please."

She was a little appalled at how needy and desperate she sounded.

"Please, what, Kira?"

His low voice sent shivers of lust down her spine. Without stopping to think about why she should be this desperate for another man's kisses when she was in love with Daniel, she said, "I want a real kiss."

A small smile crossed his face, and when he sucked on her bottom lip, she could no more stop the moan from escaping then she could stop the sun from rising. He sucked again, and she put her arms around his waist, her hands digging into his firm back as he licked first her upper lip and then her bottom lip.

"Now you," he said.

She licked his bottom lip with the tip of her tongue and then sucked on it. His soft moan made her pussy pulse with need, and she pressed her lower body against his growing erection.

"Good," he said.

Like a damn puppy eager to please, she traced his lips with her tongue before sucking on his lower lip again. It brought forth another low moan, and tendrils of excitement wove in her belly.

A girl could get addicted to the sound of her dentist's moans.

Before she could think about how stupid that was, his tongue slid into her mouth. She pushed her body against his, trying not to rub against him and remarkably succeeding as he licked and tasted and flicked his tongue against hers. Feeling both bold and unsure, she sucked on his tongue. His hips jerked against hers - only a little - but her entire body tingled with delight at his reaction.

His hand tightened around the nape of her neck, and he pulled her head back until she was staring up at him. He studied her mouth before nibbling on her lower lip. She gasped and moaned, her hands fisting into his shirt as he slanted his mouth over hers and kissed her deeply. He took control of her mouth, feasting on her lips and dipping his tongue between them repeatedly.

When he sucked on her tongue, it sent an answering pull of pleasure to her pussy. She rubbed herself frantically against him, trying to find some relief from the ache. He was too tall for his cock to fit where she needed it, and she was just considering hooking her legs around him and trying to worm her way up his body when he pulled away.

"Don't stop!"

She blushed immediately at her begging and looked at the floor in confusion as Connor reached down and tugged at the crotch of his jeans. She stared at the bulge, feeling both stupidly proud of the reaction she had invoked and oddly ashamed that she would be so pleased by it.

She loved Daniel – seeing another man's lust for her shouldn't make her proud.

"I have to go." There was a slight hoarseness to his voice.

"What? It's only…" She glanced at the clock on the microwave. It was eight-thirty. They had been kissing for a solid half hour, and she'd had no idea.

He stepped back, adjusting the front of his jeans again. "Are you available to meet tomorrow night to review personal information?"

"I – what?" she said.

"We need to get to know each other. I can drop by around seven if you're available," Connor said.

"Oh, right. Yes, that's fine."

"Good. Have a nice day, Kira."

"You too," she replied.

He left the kitchen without another word. When the front door slammed, she immediately headed upstairs to her bedroom. She needed to get to work, but the crotch of her panties was soaking wet. Her face flaming, she peeled off the damp ones and slipped into a fresh pair.

CONNOR STARED AT HIS BUILDING. HE WAS SITTING IN HIS CAR in the parking lot, and even though it had been nearly twenty minutes since he'd left Kira's house, he was still as hard as a rock. He looked around and then adjusted the crotch of his jeans. Shit. Maybe he needed to go home, rub one out, and then return to the office.

Have you lost your mind? You have a root canal in ten minutes. Get your shit together!

He closed his eyes. It was a mistake. Immediately, an image of Kira rose in his mind. He could almost hear her sweet moans and begging for a real kiss. The way she was rubbing her tight little body against him this morning had tempted him to cancel his appointments and spend the day tasting and teasing every inch of Kira's soft skin.

He groaned and stared fixedly at the steering wheel. He hadn't expected to be so turned on by Kira. She wasn't his usual type.

How do you know she isn't your type? Because she doesn't remind you of Lisa? That's a good thing, you idiot. Besides, you don't know anything about her. You're too busy sticking your tongue down her throat.

Good point. He needed to focus. Making sure they looked and acted like a couple when they touched and kissed was important but pointless if he didn't know anything personal about her.

Kira was already much more natural at kissing him this morning, which meant they didn't need to practice anymore. It was more than obvious they had chemistry, and it wasn't like they'd be making out in public anyway. He was against PDAs in general, never mind that he didn't want current or potential clients seeing him sucking tongues with or grinding away against Kira in a damn coffee shop or something.

His phone buzzed, and he grabbed it off the seat. Six minutes until his appointment. He considered letting the call go to voicemail before answering it.

"Hey, Mom."

"Hey, honey. How are you?'

Like always, his mother's voice sent warmth and guilt through him.

"Good. Just about to go into a root canal." He climbed out of the car and locked it before walking toward the clinic. "What's up?"

"I won't keep you long. I'm having coffee with Mandy, and she's reminded me that you haven't RSVP'd for the wedding yet. I told her you'll be there and don't have a plus one, but she's insisting I confirm with you."

There was a muffled sound, and his cousin's voice squeaked into his ear. "Dude, you're killing me over here. RSVP's were due two weeks ago!"

"I'm sorry, Mandy." He yanked open the door to the clinic and stepped inside. His client was already there, but his gaze was fixed on his phone, and Connor hurried past him, giving Keisha, the receptionist, the five-minute signal. She nodded, and he walked down the hallway toward his office.

"It's fine," Mandy sighed. "I know you're busy, but I need to give the caterer the final numbers. I'll put you down for one chicken, yeah?"

"Uh, actually," he sank behind his desk, "I'll be bringing my girlfriend."

There was silence. Faintly, he could hear his mother talking to someone else in the coffee shop. Not surprising.

She'd lived in Willington her entire life and knew pretty much everyone by name.

"Girlfriend?" Mandy's voice was even squeakier when it was surprised. "You have a girlfriend? That you're bringing to my wedding?"

Before he could reply, his mother was back on the line. "Connor? Why is Mandy talking about a girlfriend?"

He should never have answered the phone.

"Because I have a girlfriend, and I'm bringing her to the wedding."

"But," his mother's voice lost some of its oomph, "honey, what about Lisa?"

"What about her?" Connor's voice was harsher than he intended. "We aren't together anymore and haven't been for a long time. I have a girlfriend, her name is Kira, I'm bringing her to the wedding. End of story."

There was silence, and a fresh wave of guilt washed over him. "Mom, I have to go. Can you tell Mandy I'll text her with Kira's dinner choice this afternoon?"

"Sure." His mother disconnected the call before he could say anything else.

He tossed his phone into his desk and slammed the drawer shut before grabbing his lab coat and yanking it on. Grace stepped into his office and gave him a cheerful smile. "Good morning, Connor."

"Morning."

She checked behind her before lowering her voice. "So, I hear your wedding problem is solved."

He stared blankly at her, and she said, "Kira's going to the wedding with you, right?"

"Uh, yeah, right. Yes." Connor took a deep breath to clear his head. Disappointing his parents wasn't anything new for him, so why was his guilt still clinging to him like a fine layer of dust he couldn't shake off?

"Hey, you okay?" Grace asked.

"Fine. Just running late. I'll talk to you later."

"Sure," she said.

He brushed past her, ignoring her look of concern.

CHAPTER 3

"A dentist? You're going to make my brother jealous by dating a dentist?" Addison sat down on the couch with a graceful motion Kira knew she would never be able to imitate.

She studied Addison for a moment. In contrast to Kira's navy-coloured business suit, Addison wore a pastel pink, sixties style A-line dress that hugged her upper body and stopped just above her knees. Like always, her auburn coloured hair fell in soft, perfect waves to her shoulders, and her make-up was flawless.

Her manicure matched the colour of her dress exactly, as did – Kira took a quick peek at Addison's feet clad in peep-toe sandals – her pedicure. Addison toyed with the pearl necklace, a permanent fixture around her slender throat. "Why are you looking at me like that, Kira?"

"How is it that you've been teaching seven-year-old kids all day, and you look like you just stepped out of a modelling shoot, and I've done nothing more strenuous than sit at a desk, and I look like this." Kira pointed to her wrinkled skirt and the stain on her jacket.

"Oh, please. You're beautiful, and you're rocking those power suits. Don't change the subject – are you really going to date Dr. MacMillan to make my brother jealous?" Addison said.

"Fake date," Kira said. "You're missing an important key component. It's not real."

"And this was Gracie's idea?"

"It's a good idea." Grace walked into the living room wearing jeans and a scrub top embroidered with her name. She held two bottles of beer in one hand and a half-full glass of wine in the other. She handed Kira a bottle of beer and Addison the wine glass before sinking into the couch next to Addison. "These were the last two beers in your fridge, Kira."

"Okay, but what happens if Daniel does get jealous and realizes he wants to be with you?" Addison took a sip of her wine. "This wedding that you're going to be Dr. MacMillan's date for isn't for like a month, right? You know how my brother is just as well as I do. He's not exactly the patient type."

Kira nodded. "I know. Connor and I will take a couple of weeks to get to know each other first and then announce we're dating, which will only give us two weeks until the wedding. If we want to sell this whole 'we're dating' thing, we need to know each other's background, likes and dislikes, and... other stuff."

"Other stuff?" Grace lowered her beer bottle. "What kind of...other stuff?"

Kira knew she was blushing, but if she was honest with herself, she wanted to tell Grace and Addie what happened.

She'd wavered between giddiness and guilt about kissing Connor all damn day.

"Kira? Spill your guts, girl," Grace said.

"Okay, so, the first night I met with Connor to talk about dating, he kissed me."

Addie paused with her wine glass halfway to her mouth. "He kissed you?"

"Yes. He said he wanted to find out if we had chemistry before we tried to sell this whole dating thing."

Grace took a swig of beer. "Makes sense."

"Or he just wanted an excuse to grope Kira." Addison gave her an affronted look.

"You say that like it's a bad thing," Grace replied. "Nothing wrong with a little mutual groping from time to time…"

Addison made an unladylike snort. "Go on, Kira."

Kira took a big swallow of beer. "So, we did have chemistry, which is good, but I was bad at the kissing part."

Addison frowned. "He told you that?"

"Not in a mean way," Kira said. "More in a… practical way."

Addison gave her a blank look, but Grace laughed. "Yep, that sounds like Connor."

"Still, if some guy tells you that you're bad at kissing," Addison said, "he isn't worth your time."

"But what if he's right? I've only kissed two guys before, and neither of them kissed me like Connor kissed me, so…"

"What do you mean?" Addison asked.

"I mean," Kira tried to think of how to explain it, "when I kissed a guy before, it was pleasant and, um, fun, but mostly, I just kept thinking about how wet it was and how their tongues felt big and gross in my mouth and the one guy had terrible breath and just... it wasn't exactly the fireworks I expected, you know?"

"Well," Addison said delicately, "not every kiss can be fireworks."

"What?" Grace gave her a mock look of surprise. "Not every kiss with Harrison is full of sexy sparkles?"

"My love life with Harrison is perfectly fine, thank you," Addison said.

"Perfectly fine? That's not exactly a roaring endorsement for his bedroom skills," Grace said.

Addison flushed before throwing one of the couch pillows at her. "Hush, Gracie. Harrison is fantastic in bed, and that's all I'll say on the matter."

Grace grinned at her. "Good for you, honey. You deserve fantastic in bed."

"Anyway, back to Kira. Sorry, sweetie," Addison said. "You were saying that kissing Connor is different."

"Yes." Kira fidgeted with the buttons on her suit jacket. "He's a good kisser, I think. I definitely wasn't thinking about it being too wet or gross or anything like that. In fact, I wasn't really thinking at all."

"That's definitely the sign of a good kisser," Grace laughed.

"Anyway, because I wasn't great at it, Connor said we should practice. He came by this morning before work, and we practiced kissing for half an hour. It went better, only..."

"Only what?" Grace asked.

"I feel kind of guilty over how much I liked it. I mean," Kira took another swallow of beer, hoping it might help cool her flaming cheeks, "it turned me on, you guys."

"That's the point of kissing," Grace said.

"Yeah, but I'm in love with Daniel. Kissing Connor shouldn't turn me on. It should feel like a chore, right?"

Addison gave her a reassuring smile. "No, I don't think so. Heck, I'm engaged to Harrison, but I still have the occasional fantasy about kissing another man."

"Anyone we know?" Grace gave her a lecherous grin.

"No, of course not. It isn't anyone in particular, Gracie, just, you know, a random guy." Addison's face was bright red, and her gaze flickered to the left when Grace studied her more closely.

"Kira? I think our Addie-girl has a dirty little kissing fantasy about someone we know. Do you agree?" Grace said.

Kira grinned. "I am in total agreement."

"I don't," Addison snapped. Her fingers played restlessly with the engagement ring on her hand. "I love Harrison and can't wait to marry him. Anyway, this isn't about me. This is about Kira. I'm trying to say that you shouldn't feel guilty about being turned on by kissing Connor. I know you love my brother, but you're not in a relationship with him yet. There isn't anything wrong with kissing another guy and liking it."

"She's right." Grace pointed her beer at Kira. "In fact, you might even want to think about actually banging Connor. Nothing makes a guy jealous faster than thinking you've got some other guy between your legs."

"Crude but accurate," Addison said.

"I am not having sex with my dentist!" Kira gave Grace an indignant look. "This is a fake relationship, and just because I like kissing him a little bit, doesn't mean that I'm going to… to just… spread my legs and let him have a go at me."

Grace shrugged. "Sounded to me like you enjoyed kissing him more than a little bit."

"I love Daniel," Kira said. "I want him to be my first."

"Ugh," Addison said. "Sorry, honey, I'm trying to be supportive, but thinking about my brother having sex is making me feel sick."

"Kira," Grace said, "I know we've talked about this before, but are you sure that giving your virginity to Daniel is what you want to do."

"Yes. It's special, Grace."

"No, it isn't," Grace said. "A woman's virginity isn't some prize to be won or given away. It's just a thin piece of flesh, Kira."

"It's special to me," Kira said. "I want my first time to be sweet and loving and tender."

"Then you're barking up the wrong tree with ole Danny boy," Grace said.

Kira scowled at her, but Addison nodded in agreement. "It's true, Kira. I love my brother, but he isn't known for his tenderness or sweetness."

"He is with me," Kira said.

"When he wants something from you," Grace replied and then winced. "Sorry, Kira, I promised to be supportive, and that was a dick thing to say."

"I think," Addison was still toying with the engagement ring on her finger, "that you need to consider whether saving yourself and sleeping with just one man for the rest of your life is what you really want. You don't want to look back in a few years and regret not experimenting or at least trying out a few different items on the menu, do you?"

"Addie?" Grace's voice had turned serious. "Honey, do you want to talk about anything with you and Harrison?"

"What?" Addison gave her a startled look before shaking

her head. "No, of course not. I'm not talking about me, Grace. I have no regrets when it comes to Harrison."

"Okay," Grace said gently. "Just checking."

"Just be sure this is what you want. Okay, Kira?" Addison said.

"I'm sure." Kira took a sip of beer. "Anyway, Connor is coming by tomorrow night so we can learn about each other."

"As well as more kissing lessons?" Grace asked.

Kira blushed. "Uh, yeah, probably."

Grace sat back in her chair and stretched her long legs out. "Connor was super distracted when he came into work this morning. I guess I know why now."

"Was he?" Kira wondered if that was pride she was feeling. "Distracted, how?"

"Just distracted, not really into talking. Probably because he still had a raging boner."

"Gracie!" Kira said.

Grace just grinned at her. "What? You're telling me he wasn't affected by kissing you?"

"No, he was," Kira hesitated before forging ahead, "he was really affected by it. If you know what I mean."

"No," Addie gave her a teasing look, "I'm not certain I do. Describe it, Kira... and don't be stingy with the details."

"Ew, this is my boss we're talking about," Grace said.

"Suck it up, girl," Addie said. "We were just talking about my brother and his sex life, remember?"

"He, um, was just hard while we were kissing, and even when we stopped, and he left, you could still see that he was, uh..."

"Wishing he could have a little 'afternoon delight' with you?" Grace said.

Addison laughed, and Kira flushed again. "No, of course not. He knows it's fake, and this is so that we can make it look more realistic."

"All right," Grace said, "but I still think you should consider, as Addie puts it, 'tasting off the menu' with Connor before committing yourself completely to Daniel."

"I don't want to," Kira said. "I love Daniel and want to be with him, and only him."

"I LOVE DANIEL AND WANT TO BE WITH HIM, AND ONLY HIM," Kira murmured as she watched Connor park on the street and climb out of his car. "Dr. MacMillan is attractive, sure, but I'm not interested in him or his kissing abilities."

Of course, if she wasn't interested in him, how did she explain the way she'd sped home from work? Or why she'd had a second shower as soon as she got home, or why she was wearing a full face of makeup and her favourite pair of skinny jeans with that knitted top that Gracie always said made her tits look fantastic?

Or why you're wearing a matching set of lacy bra and panties?

She flushed at the knowing tone of her inner voice before smoothing her top down. She just felt like looking pretty tonight, no big deal, no particular reason. Lots of girls liked to feel good about themselves, especially in front of their weirdly hot dentist.

The weather was unseasonably warm today, even for April, and Connor wore just a fitted dress shirt and a pair of jeans. She studied the lean length of him before her gaze landed on his crotch. Warmth infused *her* crotch, and she looked away hurriedly.

"It's fine," she said. "Everything's fine. You're doing this to win over Daniel." She checked her reflection in the mirror hanging on the wall in the hallway before opening the front door.

Connor climbed the porch steps and gave her a polite smile. "Hello, Kira."

"Hi. Come on in."

He stepped inside and shut the door before following her down the hallway.

"Uh, I don't know if you're hungry, but I picked up a meat and cheese platter and some crackers." She stepped into the kitchen and pointed to the table where she had laid out the food platter and the cracker boxes.

"Thanks," he said. "I worked late tonight and haven't had a chance to grab dinner."

"Okay, well, sit down. Can I get you a beer or wine or…"?

"An iced tea would be good." He sat down, and she busied herself getting drinks for them as he helped himself to some food.

She set his drink in front of him before sitting down and grabbing some food for herself. She hadn't eaten supper either, and they ate silently for a few minutes.

"So, um, how was work?" she asked.

"Busy." He drank some iced tea.

"Do you like being a dentist?"

"I do."

He didn't say anything else, and feeling a little frustrated, she said, "You realize it's like pulling teeth trying to get you to talk, right?"

A slight grin played on his lips, and she made a little 'pfft' sound when she realized what she'd said. "I can't believe I just said that to a dentist. But it doesn't make it any less true.

We're trying to learn more information about each other, right?"

"Yes. Sorry, I'm not great at small talk or talking about myself. Never have been."

"Fair enough," she said. "Maybe it's best if I go first? My dad always said I could talk the hind legs off a horse. I never really knew what that meant, but I am excellent at talking."

He smiled …whoa, was that a dimple in his cheek, God help her… and said, "It's a British idiom from the 1800s. Basically, it means you talk so long the horse becomes exhausted and collapses."

She laughed. "How do you know that?"

"My dad always says the same thing to my mom."

She smiled a little before nibbling on a piece of cheese. She was trying to decide where to start. When she glanced up at Connor, he gave her an expectant look, his pretty blue eyes filled with amusement. "Cat suddenly got your tongue?"

Her gaze dropped to his mouth. Man, maybe they should forego the chitchat and get straight to the kissing practice.

"Kira?" he prompted.

"Sorry, just trying to decide where to start." She decided not letting herself get distracted by Connor's mouth was probably the best place to start.

"How about with your birthday," Connor said. "That seems like something I should probably know."

She smiled a little. "Yeah, probably. My birthday is October twentieth. I'm twenty-five, and, as you know, I have an older brother, Gideon."

"The youngest sheriff ever to be elected in the history of Harmony Falls," Connor said.

"That's right. I'm incredibly proud of him. He's done very well for himself. He's eight years older than me, but we've always been close. When he moved to New Cassel, I missed him a lot. We all did."

"He went to the police academy there?" Connor asked.

She nodded. "Yeah. Well, he first got his criminology degree and then joined the police academy. He worked as a cop in New Cassel until my parents died, and then he moved back to Harmony Falls."

She fell silent for a moment. It'd been three years since her parents boarded the plane for their annual winter vacation in Jamaica. She'd driven them to the airport in New Cassel but hadn't waited with them. She'd just dropped them off at the curb, hugged and kissed them goodbye, told them she'd see them in a month, and then left.

She didn't go to the city often and was anxious to check out a few clothing stores, tired of the same old options at Harmony Falls. Looking back, she would give anything to have had even a half hour extra with her mom and dad.

"You okay?"

She made herself smile at Connor. "Yeah... my parents died in a plane crash three years ago, and it's still really tough. I miss them."

"I'm sorry for your loss." His voice had softened with sympathy.

"Thank you. Anyway, where was I?"

"Your brother moved back."

"Right. I don't think he intended to return to Harmony Falls, but after our parents died, I wasn't doing so well and, long story short... he moved home and got a job with the Harmony Falls police. Just under a year later, Sheriff Walton retired, and Gideon became the new sheriff."

Her throat was dry from talking, and she sipped some iced tea. "In grade eleven, I got a job at Walgreens on Main

Street. I worked there until about nine months ago. I went to real estate school, and after I passed the licensing exam, I started working for Rose and Ray Armstrong. They own Rose and Ray Realty."

"I know them," he said. "Well, sort of. They're clients."

"Oh, okay."

"They seem like they're good people," Connor said.

"They are. Rose came into the Walgreens regularly, and after my parents died, she and Ray did a lot for me and Gideon. Anyway, Rose was the one who suggested I become a real estate agent, so I did."

"Do you like it?"

"I do," Kira said. "Except I've been working for three months and still haven't made my first sale. That's not... great. But Ray and Rose are supportive, and I'm lucky that Gideon lets me live in the house for free. I have some savings to live off of, but if I don't sell a house soon, I'll have to admit defeat and hope they'll hire me at Walgreens again."

She could hear the depression in her voice, and she made herself smile at Connor. "Let's see, what else... my favourite colour is green, I'm allergic to codeine, I took piano lessons from age five to eighteen, um... I love romantic comedies, hate eggplant, and like dogs more than cats."

She took another drink of iced tea. Connor was studying her, and she tried not to fidget.

"How long have you been in love with Daniel Moore?" he asked.

"Oh, uh, since forever."

"Define forever."

"High school," she said. "He's a couple of years older than me, but we were in high school at the same time for a while.

He's an amazing athlete. He was the number one player on the school baseball team in his senior year."

"Was he?" Connor's voice was weirdly neutral.

She nodded. "Yeah, he was a pitcher. He still pitches for the Harmony Falls Flames."

"I know. I play in the league."

"Do you?" Her brows drew down. "I don't think I've ever seen you play, and I go to almost all the games."

"Oddly enough, a baseball team full of dentists and doctors doesn't get nearly as much attention as the team of firefighters."

She laughed. "No, I guess not."

"So, why do you love Daniel?"

"Why does that matter?" she asked.

He shrugged. "Just curious, I guess."

"He's a good guy. He's smart and funny, and everyone loves him. Sometimes, he can come across as selfish and self-absorbed, but it's not who he truly is."

"Isn't it?"

She scowled. "No. He's a firefighter, for God's sake. He risks his life every day for people he doesn't even know. He makes a difference in his job. His job is important, and what he does matters. He's not just out there selling houses – or rather, trying to sell houses."

"What you do is important, too," Connor said.

"Not in the same way," she said impatiently. "Why are you asking me this, anyway?"

"It seems strange that you're in love with him."

"Why?" she asked.

"You don't seem like the type of woman to be in love with a man like Daniel Moore."

Feeling vaguely insulted on Daniel's behalf, she said, "Yeah, well, you don't know me at all."

"But Daniel does?"

"Yes, he does," she said. "I've known him since I was a kid. His sister is one of my best friends."

"Knowing someone for a long time doesn't mean they know who you are," Connor said.

She folded her arms across her chest and glared at him, trying and failing miserably not to look like a pouty little kid.

Connor glanced at his watch before standing. "That's probably enough for tonight. It's getting late."

Kira stood. "It's only ten after eight. That's not that late."

"It's been a busy day," he said.

"But I thought…"

"You thought what?" he asked.

Despite being a little pissed at him for his questions about Daniel, she said, "We would practice, uh, some more kissing."

He didn't reply, and mortified, Kira said, "Never mind. I'm being -"

"Tomorrow morning." His voice was a little terse. "I'll come by at eight-thirty, and we can… practice. If that works for you?"

"Um, yes, okay. That works."

"Good." He gave her a brisk, almost business-like nod. "Thank you for the food. I'll see you tomorrow morning."

CHAPTER 4

"Just for practice," Kira whispered to her reflection. "It's just for practice and nothing more."

She could see Connor parking on the street in front of her house through the side window. A nest of butterflies woke in her stomach. She clenched her thighs together and tugged her top away from her boobs before glancing at them. Shit, her nipples were hard and more than noticeable.

She snagged a cardigan from the hallway closet and hurriedly yanked it on, leaving it unbuttoned but pulling it across her tits to hide her stupid nipples. She smoothed down her hair and checked her makeup as Connor walked up the steps. He wore a t-shirt with his usual jeans, and she checked out his crotch as excitement burned in her belly. She opened the door and stepped back, hoping her smile looked more natural than it felt.

Connor walked inside and shut the door. "Good morning, Kira."

"Uh, good morning." She was ashamed to realize she was already wet and aching for him.

He followed her into the kitchen. There was a moment of awkwardness, and Connor slid his arm around her waist. He cupped the back of her head and dropped his mouth onto hers.

She moaned at the contact and parted her lips instantly. To her surprise, he immediately dipped his tongue into her mouth, and she sucked at it, hoping to make him moan.

He did, a low sound in the back of his throat that set her aflame. His fingers threaded through her blonde hair, and he angled his mouth over hers, taking the kiss deeper, demanding more that she willingly gave.

Time passed. She had no idea how long it was and didn't care. Her damn dentist was a master at kissing, and she didn't even realize she was rubbing herself against him until his hand squeezed her hip.

"Stop," he rasped.

"Please," she whispered before clinging more tightly to him. "I need it."

"You make the sweetest little sounds when I kiss you. Did you know that?" He nuzzled her ear, and she moaned when he traced the edge of it with his tongue.

"Am I – am I better at kissing?" she asked. It was stupid, but she wanted to know. She was oddly humiliated by not being a good kisser.

"Yes," he said. "You're a fast learner, little Kira."

"Please," she repeated before rubbing her flat stomach against his erection. "I need more."

"What do you need?" he asked. "This?"

He boosted her up onto the counter. It pressed his cock directly against her aching core, and moving on instinct, she wrapped her legs around his waist and dry humped him shamelessly.

"Better?" he asked.

"Yes! I mean, no... I don't know," she moaned.

He laughed, another low sound that made her shiver, and brushed his long fingers against the underside of one small breast. She arched her back and made an inarticulate pleading noise. When he slid his hand inside her cardigan and cupped her breast, his hand squeezing her gently through her shirt and her bra, she mashed her mouth down onto his. She kissed him desperately, and he returned her kiss before pinching her erect nipple.

She gasped, and he rubbed it with the ball of his thumb before groaning, "You have no idea what you do to me, Kira."

"You're driving me crazy," she whispered.

He kissed her again, and when she tentatively tugged at his shirt, he stripped it over his head and dropped it on the counter beside her. She stared at his chest. Unlike Daniel, who was as muscular and smooth as a bodybuilder, he had a lean build, and his chest had a light layer of dark hair. She touched the hair, a little surprised at the coarseness of it, before studying his abdomen.

"What?" he asked.

"I didn't expect a dentist to have a six pack," she said.

He grinned at her, and she traced the hard ridges of his stomach before smoothing her fingers over the v-line she could see just peeking out from his waistband. He inhaled sharply before sliding the cardigan down her arms. She twisted out of it, and he folded it and set it on the counter before reaching for the buttons on her shirt.

"Your turn," he said.

He had her shirt unbuttoned before she quite knew what was happening.

"Beautiful," he muttered.

She wasn't sure what was so beautiful about her smaller-than-average breasts, but her push-up bra did do a fine job of making them look larger than they were. She hoped Connor wouldn't take off her bra. Ignoring the fact that no guy had ever seen her half-naked, she rather enjoyed having him think they were beautiful.

He bent his dark head and kissed the tops of her breasts, brushing his lips over them with barely-there caresses that inflamed her senses. She realized with a vague feeling of embarrassment that her nipples were hard and protruding against the silk fabric of her bra. She tried to place her hands over them, and he tugged her hands away immediately, studying the outline of her nipples.

She gasped when he tugged on her right nipple through the fabric of her bra. It sent an aching pull of need straight to her pussy, and she was helpless to stop from arching her back. He made a low mutter of approval and toyed with her nipple as she gasped and moaned. But when his fingers reached for the front clasp of her bra, she stiffened and pulled away.

"What's wrong?" he asked.

"Nothing," she said. "I've just never, you know…"

He took a step back and gave her a cautious look. "Never what, Kira?"

"I've never had a guy, uh, see my…"

She stopped again, her embarrassment growing when his gaze narrowed.

"What exactly have you done?" he asked.

She cleared her throat. "Well, I've kissed guys – not very well, obviously – and done some other stuff."

"What other stuff?"

"You know - stuff."

"Tell me."

"I've done a bit of, um, groping. Uh – under the shirt but over the bra, sort of thing."

His look of surprise made her feel about three feet tall. "What?"

"You're twenty-five years old, Kira."

"So?"

"So, you're telling me you've never even taken your shirt off in front of a guy before?"

"You're making me sound like a freak," she retorted. "Stop it."

He grasped her chin and forced her gaze to his. "You're a virgin."

"Yes," she said.

"Why?"

"What do you mean, why?"

"Why are you still a virgin? You're smart and gorgeous, and I'm sure you've had plenty of opportunity. Why haven't you had sex?"

"Because I'm..."

She was suddenly ashamed to tell him the truth, but he made a low curse under his breath and released her chin. "You're saving yourself for Daniel."

She didn't reply, and he gave her a dark look of disapproval. "Daniel hasn't done the same for you. You can't possibly be that naïve to think he has."

"I know that," she snapped. "I just – it's special to me, okay? I want him to have it."

He shook his head in disgust. "He doesn't deserve it, Kira."

She glared at him. "Yes, he does."

"No, he doesn't."

"Let's agree to disagree." The exasperation was evident in her voice. "Can we just, uh, do some more kissing? We've still got some time."

He grabbed his t-shirt. "No. I need to go."

"Why are you angry with me?" she said. "This is fake, remember? We're only doing this so that we look like we're dating. What do you care if I'm a virgin or not?"

He just shook his head again before walking away. "I have to go."

He left the kitchen, and she stared blankly at her still-hard nipples. She was angry as hell at Connor for making her feel like an idiot, but she was also, stupidly, still incredibly horny. It was only a quarter after eight, and she'd apparently grown used to at least half an hour of kissing. What the hell had Connor done to her?

Before she could button her shirt or hop down from the counter, Connor strode back into the kitchen. He was still shirtless, and her eyes widened when he dropped his shirt to the counter, and his big hands grasped her thighs through her dress pants. He pushed her legs apart and crowded up against her until his crotch was snug against hers.

"Connor, what -?"

He kissed her, devouring her mouth with hard licks and nips. She moaned and returned his kisses enthusiastically. He cupped her right breast with one large hand and kneaded it roughly.

She had no idea why he'd returned, and she didn't care. It felt so good to kiss him, even if she could feel his anger with her through his kisses. She dug her nails into his back, wrapping her legs around his waist again and rocking her pussy against him. If he tried to undo her bra, she would let him this time. Her nipples were aching and throbbing in a way she'd never felt before, and she knew instinctively that letting him suck on them would help ease the ache.

"Kira? Hey, Kira?"

The front door slammed, and she tried to pull away. Connor made a low growl of disapproval and tightened his grip on her. He kissed her deeply, stealing both her breath and her instinct to stop.

"Kira? Can I borrow your phone charger? My phone died at the gym, and I ..."

She heard Daniel make a loud grunt of surprise. Connor pulled his mouth from hers and stared over his shoulder. "Can I help you?"

"What the hell is going on?" Daniel stared wide-eyed at them.

Kira felt a thin thread of irritation toward Daniel for the first time. If he hadn't interrupted, Connor would be sucking on her nipples right now and –

"Kira? Are you okay?" Daniel gave her a look of alarm.

She made herself concentrate on Daniel. He stood in the kitchen doorway, his phone in one hand.

"I'm fine," she said. "Connor and I are, uh...."

Shit. What did she say? They weren't supposed to be dating for another couple of weeks.

"You're what?" Daniel's face was a mask of confusion.

"We're dating," Connor said.

Daniel's gaze flickered to Connor and then back to her. "You're dating the doc?"

"Yes," Kira said.

"Since when?"

"A few weeks now. We've been keeping it quiet," Connor said smoothly.

He was blocking Daniel's view of her upper body, and he dropped his gaze to her breasts for a moment before raising one eyebrow at her. She blushed and scrambled to button her shirt. When she was fully covered, he lifted her down from the counter before pulling his shirt over his head.

"The two of you are dating," Daniel repeated as he drifted toward them.

Kira nodded, searching his face for any signs of jealousy. If he was jealous, it was effectively hidden by surprise and confusion.

"How did you two meet?" Daniel said.

"I'm her dentist."

"Isn't that, like, illegal to date your patients?" Daniel asked.

Before Connor could reply, the front door opened again, and she heard the tell-tale tap of dog nails on the hardwood. She immediately braced herself against the counter, already wincing in anticipation.

"What's wrong?" Connor asked.

"Kira, incoming!" Her brother hollered from the hallway as the giant fawn-coloured dog scrambled into the kitchen.

"Holy shit," Connor breathed. "It's a goddamn horse."

"Tank, no," Kira said as Tank, his tongue hanging from his mouth and a giant doggie grin on his face, lumbered toward her. "Stop! Down! Sit!"

It made her a terrible person, but she almost hoped that Daniel, standing in Tank's path toward her, would be the one knocked over by the friendly but overly enthusiastic dog. After being slammed into, stepped on, and knocked over by Tank for the last three years, she was over it.

Unfortunately, Daniel's good qualities didn't include taking one for the team in the form of being trampled by a one hundred-and seventy-five-pound Great Dane with a zest for life and no comprehension of personal space. He made a quick side-step just before Tank could close in on him. The big dog wasn't graceful enough to turn, so he settled for a swift and sloppy slurp across Daniel's forearm as he skidded by him.

"Tank, sit," Kira repeated, then steeled herself for impact when Tank didn't slow his enthusiastic race toward her.

To her surprise, the bone-rattling impact never came. Just as Tank reached them, Connor stepped neatly in front of her. The dog slammed into him in a tangle of long limbs, a madly wagging tail and a slobbery tongue. Connor grunted but bore the impact well, his body only lightly pressing against hers as he fended off the giant dog.

Her brother appeared in the doorway and barked out a command. "Tank, sit!"

Tank sat obediently at Connor's feet, his tail sweeping back and forth across the floor and his sides heaving with exertion.

"You okay?" Connor asked over his shoulder.

"Yes, uh, thank you. That was really nice of you to throw your body into harm's way like that."

He gave her a grin that showed off his dimple before turning back and letting Tank sniff his hand. The dog's tail thumped hard against the floor, and when Connor petted him, he stood up and leaned his entire body against Connor's.

Connor rocked backward into Kira, and she made a low 'oof'.

"Sorry," Connor said.

She squeezed out from behind him. "It's okay. I should have warned you that Tank is a leaner."

The big dog made a chuff of happiness before leaning against Kira. Connor slipped his arm around her waist, holding her steady as she patted the dog's head. Tank was so tall that his nose pressed against Kira's chin when he lifted his head.

He licked her chin, and she wiped the moisture away with a grimace. "Yuck, Tank. Bad dog."

"Dog or horse?" Connor petted Tank's back, and the big dog chuffed again.

"He's a Great Dane," Kira said. "They get... big."

"How much does he weigh?" Connor asked.

"About a buck seventy-five," her brother said. "Who are you, exactly?"

Kira groaned inwardly. Gideon was studying Connor like the dentist might be a mass murderer. Her brother was above and beyond protective of her, had been ever since her parents died, and she'd had this half-hearted idea that she could keep her fake relationship with Connor a secret from Gideon.

It would be bad enough for a real boyfriend to be subjected to Gideon's grilling. Her fake one didn't need to be put through it.

Gideon had brushed past Daniel like he wasn't even there, which was not surprising - there was no love loss between her brother and Daniel – and he was now standing in front of them. Her brother was born with heterochromia, making his right eye a wintry shade of blue and his left eye the pale green of a large jungle cat's eye. The colour difference was particularly noticeable this morning. Of course, it usually was when he was pissed off.

Keeping his arm around her waist, Connor held out his other hand. "Connor MacMillan. I don't think we've ever formally met, Sheriff Walker."

Gideon studied his hand for a second or two before shaking it. "You're the dentist who opened the new practice on Hudson Road with Grant Henderson. That right?"

"Yes. H&M Dental Clinic," Connor said.

"You're from Willington," Gideon said.

"He's lived here like two years now, Gideon," Kira said hurriedly. Her brother wasn't a fanatical Willington hater like most people in Harmony Falls, but the idea of her dating someone from Willington was bound to set him off.

"Why are you in my sister's kitchen this morning, Dr. MacMillan?" Gideon's voice had an edge.

"Gideon, knock it off," Kira said.

"We're dating," Connor replied.

She was surprised by how relaxed Connor looked and sounded. Connor was tall, she guessed he was around six feet and muscular, but at 6'4", her brother was one of the biggest men in Harmony Falls. It wasn't just his height, either. He had a physically intimidating build. His broad shoulders, wide chest and thick thighs made even the most belligerent of drunks think twice about crossing him. That Connor didn't seem intimidated by her brother was a surprise.

The muscle ticking at Gideon's temple was the only sign that he heard Connor.

"Kira," he said, "can I speak to you in private, please?"

"I have to go to work," she said. "I'll text you later. Why are you here anyway?"

Gideon lifted the travel coffee mug he held in one large hand. "I'm dropping Tank at Guardians for the day, and I'm out of coffee. The house is on the way."

"You know where the coffee pods are," she said.

Gideon's nostrils flared, and she gave him a don't-push-me-look that he completely ignored. "I would prefer to speak with you now," he said.

"Well, I'm busy with Connor and -"

"It's fine," Connor said. "I need to get to work as well."

He pulled her close and pressed a kiss against her mouth. It was a brief kiss, but she still felt like flames had seared her lips.

He stepped away from her and gave Tank a final pat. "Nice to meet you, Sheriff. Kira, I'll call you later."

"Right, okay. Bye." Kira gave him a stupid little wave before her eyes widened. Shit, she'd forgotten about Daniel.

She sidestepped around her brother and Tank. "Daniel, I'm sorry, I…"

The kitchen was empty. Daniel was gone. Feeling a little sick to her stomach, she barely noticed when Connor walked out of the kitchen. Was Daniel mad at her? Had he left because she'd ignored him from the moment he walked in, or had he left because of her brother?

She didn't know, and worry gnawed at her stomach. She should text him. She was reaching for her phone when her brother cleared his throat. He was putting a coffee pod into the machine and giving her a pointed look.

"What?" she said.

"Since when did you start dating a dentist from Willington?"

"He's been in Harmony Falls for two years, Gideon."

"When did you start dating?" he repeated.

"A few weeks ago. Why?" The smell of freshly brewed coffee filled the air. Tank, who had stretched out on his side, thumped his tail against the floor when she stepped over him.

"He doesn't seem like your type," Gideon said. "How did you meet him?"

"He's my dentist," Kira said. "Isn't he yours?"

"I see Grant."

"Oh. Well, you should try seeing Connor instead. He's a great dentist. Listen, I have to go, or I'll be late for -"

"What about Daniel?"

She opened the fridge and grabbed her lunch. "What about him?"

"Don't play dumb, Kira. You've been," Gideon gestured vaguely in the air, "smitten with him since you were a kid."

"Yeah, well, maybe I finally grew up. Make sure you lock the door when you leave." She picked up her purse from the table and left the kitchen before Gideon could grill her further.

"CONNOR? THERE'S A MAN HERE TO SEE YOU." KEISHA POPPED her head into the break room.

"Who is it?" he asked.

"He wouldn't tell me his name." The receptionist shrugged before studying her nails.

He returned his lunch bag to the fridge before following Keisha down the hall toward reception. His eyes widened, and a smile broke out across his face.

"Lucas!"

He pushed past the reception desk and grabbed his best friend in a hard hug. Lucas hugged him in return, pounding him on the back before stepping backward and looking him over. "You're looking good for an old man."

Connor laughed. "What are you doing here?'

"I came down for the weekend. Mom's throwing a yard sale and threatened to sell all my childhood stuff if I didn't come down and sort through it. Figured I'd stop in and see you before I went home. You got time for lunch?"

"I do. Give me five minutes."

———

LUCAS TOOK A BITE OF HIS BURGER, CHEWING AND swallowing before saying, "This burger's not half bad for a Falls burger. It's not as good as Ted's, but it'll do."

Connor laughed. "Don't let Nan hear you say that. She'll kick you out so fast your head will spin."

"Shit, do you mean the infamous Nan that Ted's been fighting with for the last thirty years?"

Connor nodded, and Lucas shook his head. "I can't believe you're eating at Ted's mortal enemy's diner. If he finds out, you'll be banned from his diner."

"Nan's food is so good, I'll risk it," Connor said.

"You even go back to Willington anymore?" Lucas asked.

Connor popped a fry into his mouth. "What have you heard?"

Lucas grinned. "The shit I've heard, buddy... you wouldn't believe it."

"Try me," Connor said.

"My favourite one is the rumour that you go back every weekend and sit outside Lisa's place, playing emo music and crying."

Connor groaned, and Lucas laughed. "It's better than the one that circulated a few weeks ago."

"I'm almost afraid to ask."

"You should be. That one had you going crazy at work and yanking out some poor dude's teeth without provocation. You got fired and are now living in your mother's basement in shame."

"You're fucking kidding me." Connor pushed his plate of food away. "What the hell is wrong with people in Willington?"

Lucas ate another fry. "They're bored. Besides, you're the tragedy that keeps giving. You were the town's golden boy, about to become the biggest name in Willington since... ever. And then poof... you blow your knee and lose your baseball career and the girl."

"I didn't lose the girl right away." Connor could hear the edge in his voice. "She stuck around for another few years."

"Yeah, well, she was a right bitch to do that. She should never have dragged it out like that, buddy. She made your life miserable."

"It wasn't like that," Connor said.

"Wasn't it?" Lucas raised an eyebrow at him.

"Fuck, I don't know," Connor said. "But can you blame her? I ruined her life, Lucas. I made one stupid mistake and ruined mine and Lisa's lives forever."

"Bullshit," Lucas said. "Maybe your life didn't turn out as planned, but you didn't ruin it or Lisa's. She couldn't accept that she wouldn't marry a famous baseball player and have everything her greedy little heart wanted, and that isn't your fault. Frankly, it's good that she showed her true colours before you married her, right?"

Connor just shrugged. What Lucas was telling him wasn't

anything he hadn't said before, but like always, it didn't lessen his guilt or convince him that he wasn't a world class screw-up. Nausea bit at the edges of his stomach. Christ, would he ever not feel guilty about what he did?

Lucas leaned forward. "Hey, you okay?"

"Yeah."

"Sorry, I didn't mean to bring up bad memories, but you can't live your life swallowed up by guilt. It's not healthy. You started dating yet?"

Connor hesitated before shaking his head. "No."

Lucas ate another bite of burger. "What's her name?"

"There isn't anyone."

Ketchup dripped onto Lucas's finger, and he licked it off before pointing it at Connor. "I've been your best friend for-fucking-ever, Connor. You think I can't tell when you're lying? Spill it, asshole."

Connor took a sip of his water before glancing around the diner and lowering his voice. "Her name is Kira, and we're not *really* dating."

"LET ME GET THIS STRAIGHT," LUCAS LEANED BACK IN THE booth, "this is all fake, but you keep grinding on her like some horny frat boy whenever you're alone?"

"Keep your voice down," Connor said.

"How was the meal?" Their curvy redheaded server stopped at their table to take their plates.

Lucas gave her a flirty grin, his gaze dropping to the nametag pinned above one ample breast. "Well, Georgia, that burger might just have been the best damn thing I've ever put in my mouth."

Her lips twitched. "You're not putting the right things in your mouth then."

"Is that right?" Lucas said with another flirty grin. "Maybe you have something else I could put in my mouth."

The redhead leaned closer to him, her smile warm. "Oh, sweetheart, you're just a Willington boy. You couldn't handle what I have to give your mouth."

She pinched his cheek and winked at him before turning and walking away. Lucas stared at her ass and swallowed hard. "Fuck, I think I'm in love."

Connor laughed. "You realize you were just shot down, right?"

Lucas was still staring at the redhead's ass. "Hell, I'm starting to rethink my belief that Willington girls are better than the Falls girls. How did she know I was from Willington?"

"No idea," Connor replied.

"Anyway, back to you," Lucas said. "You're really gonna bring a fake girlfriend to Mandy's wedding?"

"Yeah. Kira needs someone to make her crush jealous, and it's the only way to stop my parents and the rest of my family from trying to get me and Lisa back together."

"Yeah, but… this isn't like you," Lucas said. "Maybe you should rethink your decision."

"It's too late. I already told Mom and Mandy I had a girl-friend named Kira, who I was bringing to the wedding."

"What did your mom say?"

"Not a lot," Connor said. "I think she was stunned into silence."

"Yeah, I bet. My mom says that your mom and Lisa still hang out together all the time. All the time, dude."

Connor rubbed at the back of his neck. "I didn't know that, but I'm not surprised."

"It was a real shitty thing for your parents to take Lisa's side."

"They didn't take sides," Connor said. "They just…"

"They took her side," Lucas said. "I know it hurts to hear that, but they did. So, tell me more about this Kira chick. Obviously, she's hot if you can't stop kissing her."

"I told you, I only kissed her because we needed to make sure we had chemistry as a couple."

"Oh yeah?" Lucas said. "So, why do you keep going over there to play kissy-face with her?"

Connor didn't answer, and Lucas frowned. "She's in love with this firefighter, right?"

"Yeah."

"Don't forget that," Lucas said.

"I haven't," Connor said. "I've known her for two days, Lucas. I'm not falling for her. Stop freaking out."

"I just want to make sure you're not setting yourself up for another broken heart," Lucas said.

"I'm not. I'm not ready for a relationship and have no fucking idea when I will be," Connor said.

"Do you still love Lisa?" Lucas asked. "Are you doing this to keep your family off your back or to make Lisa jealous?"

"I'm not in love with her," Connor said. "I still care about her, but I'm not in love with her."

"You sure?" Lucas eyed him.

"Yeah," Connor said. "I'm sure. I'm doing this to stop everyone from pushing Lisa and me back together, nothing else. Which is why it's so perfect that Kira is in love with Daniel. I don't have to worry about *her* developing feelings for *me*.

"Right." Lucas slid out of the booth. "I'm gonna hit the head."

He walked away, and Connor sat back in the booth, feeling like he'd been put through the wringer. He knew his best friend meant well, but if he was being truthful, he was still a little shaken by what had happened this morning.

He shouldn't have even shown up at her place this morning. They had chemistry, and Kira was fine at kissing him now.

Better than fine. You're getting hard just thinking about her kissing you.

He shifted in the booth, trying to relieve some of the pressure in his groin. Last night when she had asked him about practicing, he'd been so damn tempted. He should have said no and told her they didn't need to practice anymore, but he couldn't.

But saying yes last night would have been dangerous. Her bedroom was too close, too tempting. It was all too easy to imagine taking her to her bed, undressing her in the dark and kissing every part of her body until she was moaning and pleading in that soft, sweet voice of hers for him to fuck her.

So, he'd compromised and said this morning, figuring it was easier to resist fucking her if he was on a time limit.

Only, all his good intentions had flown out the damn window, and he couldn't even fool himself into thinking that if she hadn't admitted to being a virgin, he wouldn't have tried to coax her into having a quickie with him this morning. The way she reacted when he touched her, the way she tasted, and the little breathless cries she made had him twisted into a knot that he couldn't seem to loosen.

He wanted Kira Walker. Their relationship might be fake,

but it didn't stop him from getting half a damn stiffy every time he was around her now. Didn't stop him from wondering just how tight her little pussy was.

Very tight. She's a virgin, remember?

He grimaced. She was, and she was saving herself for Daniel Moore. An idiot who didn't deserve it.

He supposed that was unfair of him. He knew nothing about the man. Besides seeing him on the ball field, he didn't travel in the same social circles as Daniel.

You don't travel in any social circles. You're barely a step above social recluse.

He gulped down the rest of his water. He'd found it hard to make friends in Harmony Falls, but whose fault was that? He made no effort. The guys on his ball team had invited him for drinks after games how many times, and he always said no. The idea of belonging to a team again, of thinking that playing ball once a week was for anything more than exercise, made him feel a little anxious.

You'll need to be much more social now that you're with Kira. She sounds like a damn social butterfly.

Not to mention that if they were going to make Daniel jealous, they needed to be seen together around him and other people. Of course, Daniel seemed pretty comfortable just walking into her house. He scowled, a weird part of him a little pissed that Daniel walked into Kira's place like he had the right.

He'd seen Daniel walking up the driveway and immediately returned to Kira. He hadn't needed to kiss her again, but she'd still been sitting on the counter, her mouth swollen and her nipples hard against her bra. He couldn't resist. Besides, it was an effective way to announce their fake relationship to Daniel and start them down the path of making him jealous.

Yeah, except you weren't supposed to do that for a couple of weeks, remember? Kira might have promised to go to the wedding with you, but she's been in love with Daniel for years. She'll back out of your arrangement the minute he goes after her.

He grimaced again. Fuck, he'd screwed up, and he could only hope that Kira kept her word. If she didn't, well... there was always the option of coming down with a bad case of food poisoning right before the wedding.

Lucas returned and sat down again. Before he could grill him anymore about Kira, Connor said, "So, how's work going?"

"Busy," Lucas said. "The company has exploded ever since Shadow Dragons went to number one. We're expanding operations. The boss is looking for a building in Harmony Falls."

"Sorry, what?" Connor blinked at him. "He's starting up a company in Harmony Falls?"

Lucas nodded. "Yeah. I mean, it's the same company, just a second location."

"But why Harmony Falls?"

"Apparently, he had some connection to this place when he was a kid. I dunno. The guy's close-mouthed as shit about his personal life. He wants me to be the head developer at the second location."

Connor's mouth dropped open. "You're moving to Harmony Falls?"

"Thinking about it."

"Seriously? When you moved to New Cassel, you swore you'd never live in a small town again."

"Yeah, I know. But," Lucas traced a finger over the

chipped table top, "big city living isn't all it's cracked up to be. I haven't accepted the position yet, but it is a promotion and a pay raise, so I'd be an idiot not to do it."

Connor grinned at him. "Who knew that all those years of playing video games in your basement would lead to this, huh?"

Lucas rolled his eyes. "Dude, how often do I have to tell you I don't play video games at work? I develop them."

"I know," Connor said. "Listen, for what it's worth, Harmony Falls is a great little town, and I'm full on team 'Lucas moves here.'"

"Thanks, man. Listen, keep this under your hat for now, okay? My boss hasn't found a building yet, and not everyone in the company knows he's expanding."

"Yeah, okay."

"Anyway," Lucas checked his watch, "I'd better get on the road. I told Mom I'd be there by two, and she'll kick my ass if I'm late. If I get the chance, I'll stop in on my way back on Sunday, okay?"

"Sure. Say hi to your mom for me."

"I will."

CHAPTER 5

Kira was sitting on the porch swing when he parked in the driveway. He climbed out of the car and headed toward the steps. Daffodils were poking their way through the dark earth in the flower beds in front of the porch, their bright green leaves unfurled to soak in the early evening rays and their yellow heads nodding in the breeze.

He'd texted Kira just before his final appointment, and once he was finished for the day, he'd gone home, eaten a quick sandwich, and changed his clothes before driving over. He climbed the porch stairs and, after a moment's hesitation, chose the Adirondack chair to the right of her rather than sitting in the swing beside her. Being that close to her was… dangerous.

On the drive over, he'd decided the smart thing to do was to keep his distance from Kira. Yeah, he wanted her, and she was attracted to him, but she'd made it clear that she only wanted to sleep with Daniel. If he kept touching her, kept kissing her, he'd end up trying to seduce her into his bed, and that made him a total dickhead.

"I'm so sorry about this morning." Kira wouldn't look at him. "My brother is a bit... overprotective."

"It's fine," he said.

She traced her fingers over the worn wood of the swing. "Are you hurt?"

"By your brother?" He had no idea what she was talking about.

"No, I mean from Tank barrelling into you this morning. He can be, um, a bit enthusiastic."

"I'm not hurt," he said.

She glanced at him before looking away. "Thank you again for taking the brunt of his greeting. That was really nice of you, and I appreciate it."

"It's what we fake boyfriends do, right? Save our fake girl-friends from being flattened by horses masquerading as dogs." He gave her a teasing grin before mentally berating himself. Was he flirting with her?

"Right," she said.

"Hey, you okay?" She still wasn't looking at him, and he touched her arm. "You seem upset."

"I'm not. Just, uh, a long day." She kept her gaze firmly in her lap.

He shouldn't be prying into her life, but he couldn't resist. She seemed so defeated. "Look at me, Kira."

She sighed and faced him. Her face was pale, and her eyes rimmed with red. Shit, had she been crying? Had he upset her? He'd been a dick to her this morning when he found out she was a virgin.

He cursed inwardly. He wasn't great at emotional stuff. Lisa had referred to him as "emotionally distant" when she was trying to be polite and "cold as ice" when she was pissed with him. He didn't doubt that his refusal to show affection in public and his inability to share his feelings effectively added to her decision to walk away from their relationship.

"Listen, what I said this morning was stupid of me. It's your body and your decision what you want to do with it," he said. "I apologize for making you feel bad about your choices."

She shook her head, and he was a bit horrified when it became apparent that she was close to crying. "No, it has nothing to do with that. I'm fine, really."

"I might be a fake boyfriend, but even I know the 'I'm fine' line is bullshit," he said.

She pressed her lips together before staring at the daffodils. "I'm pretty sure I'm about to lose my job."

"Because you haven't made a sale yet?"

She nodded and quickly swiped away the tear leaking down her cheek. "Yeah. Ray pulled me into his office this morning, and he was, well, he was super nice about it, but he made it clear that if I don't sell a house in the next couple of weeks, they'll have to let me go."

"Dick move," he muttered.

"No," she said immediately. "It isn't. Ray and Rose are the nicest people around, and I owe them a lot. They gave me a chance, and it's not their fault that I suck at selling houses."

"Maybe it's the market," he said. "You can't tell me that there are a lot of places selling in Harmony Falls. It's not that big."

"Maybe," she said, "but they have another agent working for them, and he's sold two houses and one commercial property in the last month."

More tears were falling, and she sniffed loudly before knuckling away the tears. There was awkward silence, and feeling useless, he blurted out, "Are you looking for comfort or a solution?"

Shit. Lisa had hated it when he said that to her. He hadn't learned a damn thing about being a good boyfriend.

Fake boyfriend.

Instead of getting pissed off, a small smile crossed her face as she gave him a considering look.

"Sorry," he mumbled.

"Why? It's a fair question. I like it, actually. It gets straight to the point, right? I'm probably looking for comfort, but since we're practically strangers, I won't make you do that."

She sat up a little straighter and wiped away all the lingering traces of tears from her face. "So, before we get started on learning all there is to know about Dr. Connor MacMillan, I just want to reassure you that even though we had to start our little dating ruse early, I'll still go to your cousin's wedding with you, no matter what.

A little of the tension he'd held all day left his body. "Thank you. I appreciate that. I'm sorry we had to announce it early, but Daniel was already halfway up the porch stairs, so I…"

"No, I get it," she said. "You had to come back and kiss me again so that Daniel would, uh, believe it."

"Yes," he said.

Now, he was the one not looking at her. Just talking about the kissing from this morning was threatening to give him a stiffy. Christ, he needed to get control of himself.

"Okay, well, um, do you want to come inside? I can make us some iced tea, and you can give me details about your life."

He rubbed the back of his neck as fresh anxiety trickled down his spine. "What do you think about going for a walk or something?"

He needed to be away from her house and her bed. Keeping his distance from her hot little body would be much easier if they weren't a few feet from her bedroom.

"Sure," she said.

"We could drive to the Falls and hike one of the easier trails," he said.

"Okay." She stood. "Just let me change my clothes and my shoes. I'll be back in five."

"Sure." He waited a few minutes after she left before he pulled his phone out of his pocket. He stood and paced back and forth on the porch, keeping his eye on the hallway through the screen door as he phoned Lucas.

Lucas answered on the second ring. "Dude. S'up?"

"Hey. Do me a favour?"

"Sure."

"You said your boss will look at commercial properties here, right?"

"Yeah."

"When is he coming to look?"

"I don't know. Maybe this weekend or next?"

"Text him and recommend that he speak with Kira Walker at Rose and Ray Realty."

Lucas didn't ask questions. "Yeah, all right. Rose and Ray Realty."

He could hear Kira walking down the stairs, see her sneaker-clad feet through the screen, and he walked to the far end of the porch and lowered his voice. "Kira Walker, Lucas. Make sure you recommend her specifically."

"Yeah, yeah, got it. Recommend your fake girlfriend. I'll text him."

"Tonight?"

"Jesus, dude, what is up with you?"

"Just do me a favour and text him tonight."

"Fine," Lucas said. There was the muffled sound of cheering, and Lucas muttered a curse. "Are you kidding me? The guy was clearly out. He tagged him like a mile before he stepped on the base."

"Lucas! Tonight, text him tonight."

"I will," Lucas said. "I promise. Later, dickhead."

"Bye, asshole." He hit the end button, shoved his phone into his pocket, and turned around just as Kira stepped onto the porch.

"Ready to go?" she asked.

He smiled at her. "Yes."

"GRACE, YOU ARE A WORLD-CLASS IDIOT." WITH A FRUSTRATED puff of air, Grace blew the hair that had escaped her ponytail away from her face. She held up the map of the Falls and the surrounding park and studied it carefully. "Okay, so according to this map, you entered the trail here. You didn't leave the trail, so you should be back at the park entrance by now…"

Yeah, she should have been. Only she wasn't, and she had no frackin' idea why not. She hadn't taken a foot off the damn path. She pulled her phone out of the pocket of her yoga pants and tried to Google directions out of the park, muttering another curse when she realized she didn't have service.

"Oh, for the love of God," she said before shoving her phone back into her pocket. "I can't seriously be lost in the goddamn park."

She could, and she was.

She should have known better. When Addie had called and cancelled their hike last minute, she should have kicked off her damn shoes, ordered take-out, and binge-watched *Good Girls*. But, oh no, she went to the Falls anyway, even after promising Addie she wouldn't.

Both Addie and Kira were well aware of her challenges with directions. More than once, they had affectionately teased that she wouldn't be able to find her way out of a wet paper bag. Sadly, they were right. It was why they'd made her promise never to go hiking at Harmony Falls Park alone. Not even the easier, shorter trails. The odds of her having to spend the night out here were way higher than she liked to consider.

She glanced around, her unease growing a little. It was only a little after seven, and she still had at least an hour before the sun went down, but what if she didn't find her way back to the park entrance by then? There were plenty of bears in Harmony Falls woods, and she didn't fancy being a snack.

"You idiot," she muttered again. No one knew she was out here. She lived alone, and she told Addie she wouldn't go hiking. No one would even think to look for her until she didn't show up for work tomorrow morning.

More unease, tinged with the slightest amount of fear, made the base of her spine itch. She took a deep breath and marched forward, arms swinging at her sides, the small bell on her backpack to let bears know she was around ringing steadily with every step.

She was fine. She was still on the path, and eventually, she'd come to the park entrance. All the trails, even the difficult ones, were big circular trails that led back to the park entrance. As long as she didn't panic, she'd be fine.

Until it gets dark and you can't see the trail anymore.

She ignored her inner voice. She would get back to the park before it got dark. She had to. She had a small first-aid kit, water, and a few snacks in her backpack, but nothing else. No emergency flares, no bear spray, no matches, no –

Her breath caught in her throat, and the hair on the back of her neck stood up. She turned slowly to her left, staring intently into the bushes that lined the path. They rustled again, and the air wheezed out of her.

"Oh shit," she whispered. Wetting her lips, she backed up, stepping carefully and wishing like hell she'd grabbed the goddamn bear spray.

The bushes rustled again, she caught a glimpse of fawn-coloured fur, and her eyes widened when the dog wiggled out of the bushes and spied her.

Fuck. She'd rather it be a bear. Not that she didn't love the big stupid dog, she was probably a little too attached to him, but where he went, his master went, and she didn't want –

"Shit! Tank, no! No, boy! Sit!" She realized far too late that the dog had made a beeline for her, and, as usual, his enthusiasm was notched up to a thousand. Tank hit her with what felt like the full speed of an out-of-control train. She went ass-over-teakettle, her muscles screaming in protest. Before she could curl into a protective ball, Tank dropped on top of her like a one-hundred-and-seventy-five-pound medicine ball, driving the last of the oxygen from her lungs.

He licked her face repeatedly, chuffing happily before blowing air from his nose like a horse. Spit and – *gross* - dog snot covered her face in a fine spray, and she pushed at the heavy dog.

"Off." Her voice was barely above a croak. "Tank, off... can't breathe."

He chuffed again before licking her face from her chin to her forehead. She decided that the noise she heard was her ribs cracking. She let her body go limp and accepted her fate. Shuffling off this mortal coil by being crushed under the weight of a giant, happy, dumb dog wasn't the worst way to go.

"Tank, off."

His deep voice made her groan inwardly. She closed her eyes as Tank licked her face a final time before he jumped up. His big paw gouged her in the side as he left, and she winced.

"Sorry about that. You okay?"

A shadow covered her face, and mentally preparing herself, she opened her eyes and stared at Gideon.

"Just fine." Ignoring the way every muscle in her body throbbed, she sat up. Gideon made no effort to help her stand, but she hadn't expected him to. He wouldn't touch her. Of course, he wouldn't. He *never* touched her.

He touched you the night of -

Nope. She was noping right the fuck out of that thought, thank you very much.

She struggled to her feet, dusting off her ass and straightening her t-shirt. She could feel dog drool running down her face, and she wiped it off, glaring at Tank, who sat next to Gideon, panting heavily and giving her his big doggie grin.

"Bad dog," she scolded. "Very bad dog."

His ears went down, and he ducked his head before staring at her with soulful dark eyes. She sighed. "You're not a bad dog. You're a good boy."

His big tail thumped against the ground, his grin returning.

"Why are you out here?" Gideon asked.

The irrational hatred that always appeared when he used his 'big brother' tone on her flooded through her instantly, and she glared at him. "It's a public park, Gideon. It's not your private running trails." She ignored the way sweat made his t-shirt stick to his broad chest. "I have as much right to be here as you do."

"I meant, why are you out here alone? You're not allowed to go hiking by yourself," he replied.

"Excuse me? Not allowed? I'm not a helpless little girl. I'm a grown woman who can do whatever the hell I want."

His nostrils flared, and he took a few steps closer until he stood directly in front of her. "We both know that with your sense of direction, hiking alone is dangerous and stupid."

"Oh, so now I'm helpless *and* stupid. That's what you're saying?"

A muscle ticked at his jaw, and his eyebrows drew down. She stared at his odd-coloured eyes, fascinated by the difference even after all these years. She was getting under his skin. After Kira, she knew him better than anyone and a childish glee went through her. He was a constant prickle under her skin. It was nice to turn the tables just once.

"I'm trying to keep you safe." His voice was hard.

"I'm not a child anymore, Gideon. I don't need you to look after me." Her glee was turning to - she hated to admit it - lust. She hadn't been this close to him since his parents' funeral, and the heat of his big body, as well as the good, clean smell of him, made her feel a little dizzy with desire. Fuck, how could he smell so good? He was out running in the middle of the damn forest.

"If that were true, you wouldn't be lost in the middle of the park right now."

"I'm not lost," she lied.

"No?" His voice was silky smooth. "Tell me what trail you're on."

She didn't reply. Her right palm was stinging like a bitch, and she folded her arms under her ample breasts, pressing her palm against her side to try and relieve some of the pain. The motion pushed her breasts together. It gave her a little extra cleavage along the scoop neckline of her shirt and practically invited Gideon to check out her tits. His gaze never wavered from her face, and she swallowed her disappointment.

"What trail are you on, Grace?"

A little shiver of pleasure went down her spine. Gideon rarely said her name. When he did, it never failed to make her the tiniest bit wet.

Her gaze dropped to his mouth, and he immediately stepped back. She flushed with embarrassment and looked away. "I have to go. Bye."

Before she could walk away, Gideon's eyes widened and what almost looked like panic flickered across his face. "You're bleeding."

"What?" She nearly fell over with shock when Gideon grabbed her upper arm. The feel of his rough hand wrapped around her bicep was just about enough to make her swoon. God, she really needed to get laid.

"You're bleeding," he repeated.

She followed his gaze to the splotch of blood that covered her shirt along her ribs. Before she could stop him, he had grabbed the hem of her shirt and was yanking it up.

"Hey!" She tried to twist out of his grasp, and he glared at her.

"Hold still."

"Let go of my shirt," she snapped at him.

He ignored her and pushed her flailing hands away before bending and staring at her pale skin below the band of her sports bra. "There's no wound."

"Because it's not my side." She shoved his hand away and tugged her shirt down, wincing when her palm scraped across the material.

He scowled and wrapped his fingers around her right wrist. He pulled her arm toward him and turned her hand upward. He studied the smears of blood on her palm before muttering a curse under his breath.

His scowl deepened, and he stared at Tank, who was sniffing at a bush a few feet away. "Tank, bad dog."

"It wasn't his fault." She immediately jumped to the dog's defense. "He didn't mean it."

Without replying, Gideon roughly turned her around and unzipped her backpack.

"What are you doing?"

"Hold this." He handed her the water bottle before dipping his hand back into the pack. He rummaged through it and brought out the first aid kit. "Turn around."

She sighed and turned to face him. "Gideon, I don't need -"

"It needs to be cleaned and disinfected," he said before taking the water bottle from her. "Hold out your hand."

She held out her hand, palm up, and he uncapped the bottle and poured water across the bleeding scrape. Water and blood flowed to the ground, and he rinsed it again before leaning over and studying her hand.

"It doesn't look like you'll need stitches."

"It's just a scrape," she said. "Thanks, but I need -"

"It needs to be disinfected." He was already unzipping the first aid kit and pulling out the antiseptic wipes.

He handed her the kit to hold while he ripped open the foil, and she tucked it under her arm before petting Tank, who had wandered over. The big dog leaned against her, but she'd already planted her feet in anticipation and didn't stumble. She patted the dog's side as he pressed his big head against her ribs.

"Tank, sit," she said.

The dog sat obediently, and she winced and pulled her foot free. "Not on my foot, silly boy."

His tail thumped, and he chuffed happily when she scratched under his collar with her left hand. "You're a good boy, yes you are, you're such a… ow!"

She yanked her right hand away, holding it protectively behind her back and glaring at Gideon. He flipped the wipe over to the clean side.

"That hurts," she said.

He rolled his eyes. "It's not that bad. Give me your hand."

"No."

"Grace." He gave her a warning look, and she sighed and held her hand out again. He swiped the wipe across it, not that gently, and she winced as her palm stung and smarted.

"Ouch!" She tried to pull her hand back again, but he was on to her and wrapped his fingers around her wrist, holding her firmly. "Seriously, man, that hurts."

"It's a little sting," he said. "Don't be such a baby."

"You try having antiseptic wiped across your bleeding and raw skin," she said. "Then we'll see who's tough."

Gideon wiped the scrape again, ignoring the way she winced. He snorted and bent his head when she tried to pull her hand away for a third time. She went stock still when he

79

blew on the palm of her hand, every nerve in her body pinging to life and goosebumps erupting across her skin.

Her mind went blank, her nipples went hard, and her pussy went wet.

Gideon blew on the scrape again. "There. Is that better? Or do I need to give you a sucker to make you feel..."

His voice trailed off into a low groan when he glanced at her face. For a moment, the only sound was the rasp of Tank's panting, the soft cry of a bird and the return call of its mate, the low buzz of the insects.

"Grace, don't look at me like that." His voice was dark and rough. She'd only heard it like that once before, and the memory of that night sent more goosebumps to the surface of her skin. Her scalp prickled with awareness, and she stared at his mouth as his thumb swept back and forth over the thudding pulse in her wrist, that soft, simple touch lighting her up like fireworks on the fourth of July.

"Gideon, please," she whispered.

CHAPTER 6

"Okay, so tell me everything there is to know about Connor MacMillan." Kira smiled at him as they walked.

The trail they were on was surprisingly quiet, especially considering the weirdly warm weather, but he took her hand anyway. "Just in case we see someone we know."

She nodded, and he ignored the tingle of pleasure he felt from the softness of her palm. God, his lust for her was bad. He studied her with little sideway glances as they walked. She had to be still upset about potentially losing her job, but she was doing an excellent job hiding it.

"Are you sure you want to do this tonight?" he asked. "We don't have to. I know you're worried about your job."

"No, it's fine." Her smile looked a little fake around the edges. "It's good to take my mind off it, right?"

He didn't reply, and she widened her fake smile. "We need to do this tonight. If I can't answer simple questions about you, the fake relationship crumbles before it even starts."

"Yeah, okay." He skirted around an exposed root in the

path. "My birthday is June thirteenth. I'm an only child. My middle name is Robert, after my dad. My parents' names are Gina and Rob. They own a mom-and-pop store in Willington. Both were born and raised in Willington, and they were high school sweethearts. My dad proposed to my mom the night they graduated high school."

"That's very romantic," she said.

"I had a normal and happy childhood. I played baseball from a young age, just like every other kid in Willington."

She laughed. "Same as Harmony Falls. What position did you play?"

"Short stop."

"Were you good?"

"Average."

He glanced at her, and how she looked at him like she might know he was lying made him nervous. Hell, she probably did know he was lying. Her brother was a cop, after all.

He waited for her to call him on his lie, but instead, she said, "When did you meet Lisa?"

"I first met her when we were kids. We were in the same grade and went to the same school throughout elementary. We started dating in the first year of high school. She was big into cheerleading, and after we graduated, she started up her own cheerleading coaching business."

"Wow, that's impressive," Kira said.

"She always had a lot of drive. I was a little late deciding what to do with my life, so I worked at my parents' store after graduating and then applied for dental school. I earned my bachelor's in biology while attending dental school."

It wasn't a *complete* lie. He had worked at his parents' store once he fucked up and destroyed his dream forever.

"Holy crap," Kira said. "You can do both at the same time?"

"Yeah. It's more work, but I wanted to fast-track my career."

She gave him an admiring look. "Good for you. Why did you decide to open a clinic in Harmony Falls?"

"I met Grant Henderson at a dental convention."

She giggled. "They seriously have dental conventions?"

"Yes."

"Do they hand out free toothpaste and floss?"

He laughed. "Maybe."

She grinned at him, and he studied the way the early evening sun got caught in her blonde locks and how it gave her pale skin a soft, warm glow. His gaze dropped to her mouth. He wanted to kiss her.

Instead, he said, "Grant and I got along well from the start."

"Even though he knew you were a Willington guy?" she teased.

He laughed again. "Even though I knew he was a Harmony Falls guy. Anyway, we kept in touch through email and dinners and at the next convention, we had dinner and drinks one night. Grant told me he was leaving the Harmony Falls Dental Centre and opening his own clinic, and he wanted me to partner with him."

"Wow, you must have made quite the impression on him," Kira said. "You couldn't have been a dentist for very long at that point."

"I hadn't been," he admitted. "But Grant took a chance on me. I accepted his offer and moved to Harmony Falls. It's been two years, and the clinic is doing well."

"I know that Grace has nothing but good things to say

about working with you and Dr. Henderson," Kira said. "She's why I switched to your clinic from the Dental Centre. Hey, do you even remember me as a client?"

He nodded. "Yes. You still have all your wisdom teeth and only one cavity."

"Is that how you remember all your clients? By their teeth?" she asked with another giggle.

"Pretty much," he replied. He couldn't believe he had never even looked twice at Kira. She was gorgeous and sweet, and why had he not seen that when she was in the clinic?

Maybe because, for the last two years, you've been wrapped up in regret and shame over losing Lisa?

He sighed inwardly. He had been pretty obsessed with her for a while there. It was partially the reason he'd accepted the partnership with Grant. If he'd stayed in Willington, his love for Lisa would have continued to burn bright. The distance and long hours as he and Grant worked hard to get the clinic up and running had been a welcoming distraction.

"Connor?"

He had slowed to a stop in the middle of the path, and he stared blankly at Kira. "What?"

"I asked why you and Lisa broke up."

Sweat started to break out on his forehead and between his shoulder blades. He and Kira might be faking this relationship thing, but it didn't mean he wanted her to know what a fuck up he was. Besides, it was the past, and he wanted nothing more than to move on from his mistakes and regrets. "We wanted different things."

"Like what?" she asked.

He started walking again, his voice rough with annoyance. "None of your business, Kira. I'm not discussing my relationship or my break up with Lisa with you. It's off limits."

"Because you're still in love with her?"

"If I was still in love with her, why would I bring a fake girlfriend to my cousin's wedding?" He scowled at her. "I am not talking to you about her. Understood?"

"Understood," she said.

They walked in silence for a few minutes. He was walking fast, his anger and frustration quickening his pace, and Kira was almost jogging to keep up with him. Guilt washing over him, he slowed down and squeezed her hand. "Sorry. I'm being a dick."

"I shouldn't have pried," she said.

"You didn't. I just – it's the past, and I don't want to focus on that."

"Fair enough," she said. "So, what's your favourite meal, vacation spot, and movie."

He was more grateful than he could say she changed the subject. "Popcorn, Hawaii, and *Terminator*."

"Popcorn isn't a meal," she said.

"It is when you're a bachelor who works long hours."

Her look of disapproval was weirdly adorable. "You don't work weekends. Take a Sunday and make a bunch of casseroles and stuff to freeze for the week."

"Is that what you do?"

She nodded. "Yeah. I'm not that great of a cook, to be honest, but I've got some casserole recipes that I don't mess up too much, and my mom taught me how to make her grandmother's lasagne. It's delicious and freezes well. She was going to teach me other recipes, but then she…"

He squeezed her hand again. "You must miss her a lot."

"I do," she said. "But I have Gideon – sorry again for his

behaviour this morning – and I have Grace, Addison, and Harper. Grace stayed with me for weeks after my parents died, just moved into the house and upended her entire routine and life to help me through the grieving process. I don't know what I would have done without her."

She studied her feet briefly as they walked slowly down the trail. "Even with Grace, I was still pretty depressed. Which is why Gideon eventually moved home."

She lapsed into silence, and he waited patiently. He had the feeling that there was more to the story, and he was intensely curious, but he had just chastised her for asking questions about his past.

When it became apparent that she wouldn't say anything else, he said, "Who are Addison and Harper?"

"Addison is Addison Moore. She's Daniel's younger sister and works at Harmony Falls Elementary over on Oak Street. She teaches grade one, and she's engaged to Harrison Frank. He's a lawyer."

"The names are familiar," he said.

She nodded. "Addison goes to your clinic, although I think she sees Dr. Henderson. I'm not sure where Harrison goes, but he plays ball in the same league as you and Daniel, so you've probably seen him at a game."

"Probably," he said.

"Harper is Harper Brandt. Her dad is Warren Brandt."

"Of Brandt Veterinarian?" Connor asked.

"Yes. Do you have a pet?"

"No, but Grant has a dog he takes to Warren, and Warren comes into the clinic."

"Harper moved to New York City last year. She's an artist and got a job at a fancy art gallery. She's hoping to get her work shown at the gallery."

"Is she good?" he asked.

"So good. She works with pencil mostly, and... man, her work is incredible. Anyway, the four of us have been thick as thieves, as my dad says, since we were in grade school, and we miss Harper something awful, but she has to live her dream, right?"

"Yeah, it's important to do what you love."

She glanced up at him. "What's wrong?"

"Nothing," he said. It made him uneasy that Kira could read him so well after only a few days. He was well known for keeping his feelings hidden, and the fact that she already knew when he was upset by nothing more than the tone of his voice was... weird and unexpected.

"You sure?"

He nodded. "So, are you closest to Grace?"

"Yes. Grace is an only kid, and her parents aren't bad parents, but they aren't really there for her. Like, they just kind of did their own thing, you know? Even as a kid, it was like she was always an afterthought. Anyway, she spent a lot of time at our house when we were young, and my parents loved her like she was their kid."

She brushed a lock of hair away from her face. "I mean, we're all close, but Gracie and I are probably closer, and Addie and Harper have their own kind of special thing going on. I know Addie really misses Harper. She's even gone to New York a couple of times to visit her. Harper hasn't returned home since she left, but she's coming home for Addison's wedding."

"When do they get married?"

"September," Kira said. "Grace, Harper, and I are all bridesmaids. Anyway, we're supposed to be talking about you, not me. Do you have a best friend?"

"Yes. His name is Lucas. We grew up together. He lives in New Cassel now and works for a company that develops video games."

"So, he plays video games all day, then?"

He laughed. "Yeah, but when you see him at the wedding, don't say that to him. He's sensitive about it."

"Oh, he'll be at the wedding?"

"Yeah. His family knows Mandy's family."

"Sounds like Willington is a lot like Harmony Falls. Everyone knows everyone."

"Pretty much," he said.

They headed toward a curve in the trail, and she smiled at him. "When I was a kid, I dreamed about moving to New Cassel. I thought I would love to live somewhere I could be anonymous, but now…"

"Now what?" he asked as they rounded the curve.

"I realized that I'm happiest when surrounded by the people I love," she said. "There's something soothing in routine and – Grace? Gideon? What are you doing – Tank, no! Sit!"

Moving on instinct, Connor tugged Kira behind him, protecting her from the Great Dane's now familiar enthusiastic greeting as he ran toward them.

"Tank, sit," he said in a loud voice.

The big dog plopped to his ass, tail sweeping across the dirt trail and his tongue hanging halfway out of his mouth.

"Good boy." Connor petted the dog's head as he stared at Grace and Gideon. The big sheriff stood close to her, his hand wrapped around her wrist. Grace stared up at him, her face flushed and her body noticeably trembling.

"You okay, Grace?" Connor said.

She visibly jumped as the sheriff dropped her wrist and

backed away until there were a few feet of space between him and Grace.

"She's fine. She's with Gideon." Kira stepped out from behind him and grinned at her best friend and brother. "Hey, guys. Did you decide to go on a hike together?"

Considering that Kira was so damn good at reading his body language, he found it remarkable that she was utterly oblivious to the tension radiating between Grace and Gideon.

Gideon shook his head as Grace said, "No, um, we just ran into each other on the trail."

Kira frowned. "Are you hiking alone, Gracie?"

She nodded, and for some reason, Kira gave her a look of disapproval. "Grace Larken, you were not! Addie and I strictly forbade you to go hiking alone."

She glanced up at Connor. "Grace doesn't have a very good sense of direction. She's not allowed to go into the park to hike alone. We're afraid she'll get lost and be eaten by bears."

"I'm fine," Grace said. "I'm not lost, Kira." She wiped her palms on her thighs, and when she winced, Kira dropped his hand and hurried forward.

"What's wrong? Is that blood on your shirt? Why is there blood on your shirt?"

"Tank knocked me over, and I scraped my hand. It's fine."

Kira glanced behind her at Tank, who was sitting beside Connor. "Tank! Bad boy!"

The dog made a low whine and pressed his head against Connor's hip. Connor rubbed behind Tank's ears as Kira turned back to Grace and reached for the first aid kit tucked under Grace's arm. "Here, let me clean it."

"Gideon already cleaned it," Grace said. "It's fine, Kira. It's just a scrape."

Kira smiled at Gideon. "Sheriff Gideon to the rescue. Thanks, buddy."

He grunted before whistling for Tank. The big dog loped over to him as Gideon said to Kira, "Can you walk her out of the park?"

"I can walk myself out of the damn park," Grace said. Her voice was icy cold, and the way she looked at Gideon suggested she was about three seconds from trying to murder him.

"Can you, Kira?" Gideon ignored Grace completely.

"Yes," Kira said.

"Thanks." He stuck his earbuds in his ears and jogged away with Tank at his heels.

Kira smiled at Grace. "So, you were lost, weren't you?"

"I wasn't lost!" Grace snapped.

Kira took a step back. "Gracie? What's wrong?"

"Nothing," Grace said. "I'm sorry. I didn't mean to snap at you, and yeah, I was lost."

Kira put her arm around her and kissed her shoulder. "It's okay, honey. C'mon and walk with Conner and me."

Connor joined them. "Hey, Grace."

"Hey, Connor." When he took Kira's hand again, Grace's eyebrows almost disappeared into her hairline. "I thought you guys were waiting a couple of weeks before announcing you were dating."

Kira shrugged. "Connor stopped by this morning to, um, I mean... so we could get to know a few more personal details about each other, and both Daniel and my brother walked in on us. We kind of had to tell them we were dating."

"Right." Grace eyed him closely and he busied himself

with pulling his cell phone out of his pocket and checking for messages.

"Don't bother," Kira said cheerfully. "There's zero service out here."

He stuffed his phone back into his pocket as Kira smiled at Grace. "How was your day, Gracie?"

"So, um, did you want to come in?" Kira gave him a shy smile when he parked in her driveway.

He hesitated, and she clasped her knees nervously. "I mean, I thought maybe we could practice a bit more kissing. You know, just so we can, for sure, fool people."

More than anything, he wanted to say yes, but that was a terrible idea. Kira was saving herself for Daniel. She was attracted to Connor, just like he was attracted to her, and there was no denying they had chemistry, but that didn't mean she'd change her mind about not sleeping with him.

Maybe he'd go in there tonight, and maybe she'd let him make her come. Maybe she'd even be willing to let him bury his face between her soft thighs so he could find out just how sweet that pussy was that he was suddenly obsessed with tasting. Hell, maybe she'd be willing to give him a handjob or – the front of his jeans suddenly got tight – blowjob, but it didn't feel right to him to hope she would be willing to do those things with him.

Or maybe you know it wouldn't be enough. Maybe you know you'd try to talk her into fucking you.

"Connor?"

He made himself smile. "I think we've proven we have

enough chemistry to fool people, and you're fine at kissing now. I don't think we need to keep practicing."

"Oh." She leaned back, the disappointment etched into her face. "Right, okay. Yeah."

"Honestly, I'm not much for PDAs – in fact, I kind of loathe them – so it's not like I'm going to be kissing you in public anyway."

A look of embarrassment crossed her face, and he groaned inwardly. Christ, he was fucking this up so bad.

"It has nothing to do with you," he said. "I'm not into that kind of thing."

"No, I get it," she said. "It's all good."

"We can hold hands, and uh, you know, the occasional quick kiss is fine, but…"

Shut up, you idiot.

For once, he listened to his inner voice and stopped talking.

She was giving him that fake-edged smile again. "Sounds good. I'll limit physical touch to hand holding when we're out in public. Thanks, Connor. I'll talk to you later."

She was out of the car and walking up the porch steps before he could say anything else. Cursing to himself, he waited until she was safely in the house before backing out of the driveway and heading home.

CHAPTER 7

"Morning, Lainey." Kira smiled at the receptionist and stopped at the front desk. "Happy it's Friday?"

"So happy," Lainey replied. "A Mr. Stark is waiting for you in the boardroom."

Kira cocked her head. "Stark? As in *Iron Man?*"

"Do not make that joke," Lainey said. "I did, and let's just say he didn't find it funny. Anyway, he's waiting for you. Oh, and just a reminder – you need to let me know when you have client appointments so I can add them to my calendar."

"I didn't have an appointment. I don't even know who he is," Kira said.

"Seriously? Because he asked for you by name," Lainey said. The phone rang, and she scooped it up. "Rose and Ray Realty, Lainey speaking. How can I help you?"

Kira walked to her cubicle and set her purse under her desk before glancing at the boardroom. She grabbed a pad of paper and a pen and, straightening her skirt, walked to the boardroom. She pasted a smile on her face and stepped into the room.

"Mr. Stark? I'm Kira Walker."

The man, he was tall and broad shouldered with dark-coloured hair and blue eyes, stood and held out his hand. She shook it briefly before sitting across from him.

"It's nice to meet you, Ms. Walker."

"You as well, Mr. Stark." She tried to sound confident and self-assured, but the man standing in front of her was beautiful. GQ beautiful. Had she ever seen anyone so perfect looking in her life? She didn't think so.

Still, there was a coldness to him that made her a bit nervous. He seemed like the type of guy who wouldn't hesitate to destroy you if you crossed him.

A paper cup of coffee from one of their local coffee shops, "Grind My Beans", sat on the table in front of him, and he took a sip before staring at her.

"How can I help you today?" she asked.

"I'm looking for a commercial property. You were recommended to me. So, what have you got for me?"

She blinked at him, a little taken aback. "I was recommended to you?"

"Yes." The slightest hint of impatience crept into his voice. "Talk to me about commercial properties available in Harmony Falls, Ms. Walker, or," he studied her for a few seconds, "should I be finding someone with more experience to help me."

She took a deep breath. This was her chance, probably her only chance, to save her job. She wouldn't let this man's brusque and teensy bit terrifying personality ruin her shot. Smiling at him, she picked up her pen. "I assure you I am more than capable, Mr. Stark. Why don't we start with you giving me the details of what you're looking for?"

"Wait, so you have no idea who this Stark guy is, but you were recommended to him?" Addie asked.

Kira nodded as she followed Addie toward the canteen. Harmony Falls Sports Complex had been completed early last year, just in time for the start of baseball season. The new facility featured four ball diamonds, a playground area, picnic areas, and a full-service canteen. The town council's pride and joy was built in direct competition with Willington's Sports Complex, built two years prior.

"I wonder who recommended you," Addie said.

"I have no idea. I didn't think to ask him, to be honest. He was a little intimidating," Kira replied. "I spent the rest of the day finding some properties for him to look at and setting up appointments for next Friday when he's back in town."

They crossed the parking lot, and Addie slipped between two parked trucks. "That's awesome. Congratulations, honey."

"It is awesome, but don't congratulate me yet. I need to make the sale first if I hope to keep my job."

Addie stopped and took her hand, squeezing it tightly. "You've got this, Kira. I know it."

"Thanks." She smiled at her friend.

"So." Addie glanced around. There were people all over the parking lot headed toward the ball diamonds, and she lowered her voice. "I met Gracie for coffee after work, and she said that you and Connor had to start the ruse early because my brother walked in on you together."

"Yes. Daniel and Gideon both." She scuffed her toe against the asphalt. "Hey, have you, uh, talked to your brother?"

95

"Not since Wednesday. Why?" Addie smoothed her hair when a gust of wind brushed over them.

Compared to Kira, who had changed into skinny jeans and a t-shirt before driving over to the ball diamond, Addie looked positively perfect in a pale green A-line dress that brought out the green highlights in her hazel eyes. She had paired the dress with a soft pink cardigan and pink Converse running shoes that should have looked ridiculous with the dress but didn't.

Kira shrugged, trying not to let her anxiety show as they continued to walk toward the canteen. She had sent Daniel three texts since he'd walked out of the kitchen on Thursday morning and hadn't heard a thing back from him.

Of course, that wasn't that unusual. Daniel was a busy guy and didn't always promptly respond to her texts.

He's good about texting when he wants something.

She ignored her inner voice. She could only hope Daniel was busy and not mad at her for kissing Connor. She wanted him jealous, not pissed off.

"Speak of the devil," Addison said when Daniel pulled into the parking lot. He parked his truck and hopped out as Kira's heart pounded with nerves and happiness. He grabbed his bag from the back of the truck and slung it over one perfect shoulder before walking toward them.

She smiled at him when he stopped in front of her. "Hey, Daniel."

"Hey, doll." He winked at her. "How are you?"

"Uh, good. How are you?"

"Keeping things real." He shifted the bag. "You here to watch me play against your boyfriend?"

"Um, I, uh…"

Shit, was Connor playing tonight? Embarrassed by his

rejection last night, she hadn't texted him today. Not that she needed to – they were just fake dating after all – but now she regretted not confirming his plans for the weekend so she could act the part of the adoring girlfriend.

"She's here to watch her boyfriend play. Whether you're playing or not isn't anything she cares about," Addison said with a roll of her eyes.

Daniel reached out and ruffled Addison's hair. She glared at him and yanked her head back. "Stop it, Daniel."

He laughed teasingly. "You gonna tell Mom on me?"

"You're such a butthead," she said. "C'mon, Kira, I want to get a drink from the canteen before the game starts."

"Can you give me and Daniel a minute?" Kira said.

Addison hesitated but then said, "Sure." She walked off, giving them some privacy, and Daniel grinned at Kira again.

"Hey, you're not mad at me, are you?" Kira asked.

"Nope. How could I ever be mad at you, doll?"

"I just – you left Thursday morning without saying goodbye."

He grinned at her. "You seemed pretty busy with your new man."

"Right," she said.

"Good for you. I'm glad you found someone," Daniel said.

"Thanks." She fought to hide her bitter disappointment that he wasn't the least bit jealous.

"So, is it serious?"

His tone was weirdly casual, and the hope that had deflated inside her puffed back to life.

She smiled at him. "He's a good guy. I like him a lot."

"Like him or love him?"

Before she could answer, his phone buzzed, and he pulled

it from the pocket of his track pants. He glanced at the screen. "I gotta take this, doll. See you at the diamond."

He walked away, and she studied his ass. God, he had an amazing ass.

So does Connor. And the way he kisses is sexy as hell. Am I right?

She flushed and looked away from Daniel's butt. She needed to be more careful. If anyone caught her ogling Daniel like she usually did, her fake relationship with Connor would be over before it started.

She hurried to catch up to Addison, but Addie had stopped only a few feet away. She stared at the motorcycle before her, studying how the chrome gleamed in the early evening sunlight.

Kira joined her, but Addison continued to stare at the bike. One hand worried at the string of pearls around her neck as the other slowly reached to touch the soft leather of the seat. A big hand, a skull tattooed into the webbing between the thumb and forefinger, clamped around her wrist.

Addison gasped and stared wordlessly at the man standing beside her.

"No touching the bike, sweetheart," he said.

He looked her up and down from her auburn coloured hair to her pink Converse sneakers, his gaze lingering on her breasts for a moment longer than appropriate before he studied her now red face.

He dropped Addison's wrist and reached out to give Kira's ponytail a light tug. "Hey."

"Hello, Preacher. How are you?"

"Good. Just finished watching your brother play. Heard you were dating a dentist."

She sighed. Preacher was Gideon's best friend. Of course her brother had told him about Kira and Connor. "I am."

"You let me know if he isn't good to you. All right?"

"He's a good guy," she said.

Great. Not only did she have to worry about Gideon, but she also had to worry about Preacher.

Preacher had moved to their small town about a year after Gideon returned home. He and Gideon had met in New Cassel, and while she had no idea how they had become friends, neither would talk about it, they were as close as she and Grace were.

The sheriff and the tattoo artist were the unlikeliest of friends, and their friendship had been the subject of town gossip for months.

Preacher didn't talk much, and although she'd spent plenty of time with him and Gideon, Kira still really didn't have a clue about him other than that he was the only man in town bigger than her brother, tattoos covered him, he ran a successful tattoo and piercing shop, and he'd pretty much adopted her like she was his kid sister. She didn't even know his real name.

"Yeah, well, just give me the word if you need me to fuck him up."

"Preacher, let's go. I'm bored." A bleach blonde, her slender body clad in skin-tight jeans and a shirt that hugged her, Kira suspected, surgery-enhanced breasts, gave him a pouty look. Kira didn't know who she was, but she knew for certain she wasn't from their small town. Preacher didn't date anyone from Harmony Falls.

Addison backed away as Preacher swung one jean-clad leg over his bike and sat on the seat. The woman climbed on behind him and slung her arms around his waist. Preacher gave Addison one final look, this time his gaze lingering first on the pearls around her throat before moving to her mouth.

Addison turned scarlet and backed up again until she stood beside Kira. She took Kira's hand, squeezing it compulsively as Preacher's bike started with a low roar.

"See you around, Kira," Preacher said before, with one big hand resting on the blonde's thigh, he drove out of the parking lot.

Beside her, Addison let out a shuddering breath, and Kira said, "Hey? You okay?"

"Fine." Addie swallowed hard. "Preacher is, um… he's a little scary looking."

Kira grinned. "Yeah, I know, but he's not that scary."

"Of course he isn't. The giant tattooed biker isn't at all dangerous or scary."

This time Kira laughed. "You can't judge a book by its cover, Addie. He's got a good heart and maybe doesn't talk much, but he's sweet in his own way."

"Oh yes, offering to 'fuck up' your boyfriend for you is very sweet."

Kira's mouth dropped open. "Oh my God, Addie. I think that might be the first time I've ever heard you use the f-word."

"Harrison says a man doesn't like it when a woman cusses. It makes her look and sound coarse."

Kira rolled her eyes. "Whatever. Harrison won't be happy until you're a damn Stepford wife."

Addison gave her a hurt look, and Kira sighed. "Sorry, that was a stupid thing to say. But Harrison has no right to tell you how to act or talk. He's your fiancé, not your friggin' owner."

"He doesn't," Addison said. "He gives me suggestions,

that's all. And I think it's sweet that he wants me to be the best I can be. He loves me, Kira, and I love him."

"I know," Kira said. "Come on, let's hit the canteen and head back."

———

WHEN THEY RETURNED TO THE BALL DIAMOND, DRINKS IN hand, the teams were starting to warm up, and sure enough, Connor was on the field. He wore a pair of gray track pants, and across the back of his white t-shirt was the number eight and the words "Harmony Falls Healers" in blue lettering. Feeling a little self-conscious, she waved at him.

He nodded and continued to stretch as she walked to the bleachers. Grace sat about halfway up the bleachers, but Addie grabbed her arm before Kira could join her. "Kira, you should sit on the Healers side."

Kira looked at her blankly, and Addie jerked her head toward the other bleachers. "This side is for the Flames. The Healers fans are sitting in the other bleachers."

"Oh, right," Kira said. Feeling a little stupid, she handed Grace's bottle of water to Addie. "Give this to Gracie. I'll, um, see you after the game. Okay?"

Addie nodded, and Kira walked to the other bleachers. The Healers didn't have nearly as many fans as the firefighter team, and she climbed about halfway up to an empty bleacher before sitting down.

She opened her bottle of water and took a sip, watching Connor do a few more stretches before grabbing his glove and partnering up with another guy on his team. They threw the ball back and forth, and she admired Connor's lean length as he stretched to catch a ball. He really did have a fantastic body. She'd always thought that Daniel's thick and powerful looking body was what she liked best, but there was something about the graceful motion of Connor's body that made her tingle.

"Move over, Kira Bear." Grace was climbing the bleachers, and Kira smiled gratefully at her as she slid down the bleacher. Addison was right behind Grace, and the two women sat down on either side of her.

"You guys don't have to sit with me."

"We want to," Grace said. "Besides, as your best friends, we should cheer for your boyfriend's team."

"Yeah, but Daniel is Addison's brother," Kira said.

Addison grinned at her. "You know I love you more than Daniel. You don't try to boss me around or treat me like I'm six years old."

"Where's Harrison?" Grace asked.

"Working late," Addison said.

"Again?" Kira said.

"I know, right? He's been working late so much the last month or so. A few cases at work are a bit more involved," Addison replied. "Which is terrible timing because we need to make final decisions for the wedding."

The game was starting, and as Connor jogged out to the shortstop position, Addison nudged her. "Connor has a pretty great body. I had no idea that a dentist could be so… in shape."

Kira grinned, and Addison leaned forward to stare at Grace. "How come you never told us that Connor had such a smoking hot body, Gracie?"

Grace didn't reply, and Kira followed her gaze. Gideon was walking toward them, the equipment bag thrown over one beefy shoulder. He wore track pants and a t-shirt, just like Connor, only his t-shirt was blue, and the white lettering across the back said, "Harmony Falls Blues".

"Hey, Gideon. How was your game?" She smiled at him as he stopped at the edge of the bleachers and stared up at them.

"We won. Why are you sitting on this side?" He glanced at the Flames side, his upper lip curling just a little when he saw Daniel sitting on the bench.

"Connor's playing," she said.

"Right. Your new boyfriend. We still need to talk about that."

"What's there to talk about?" Grace's face was red. "You're her brother, not her boss. She doesn't need your permission to date anyone."

Gideon's jaw tightened. "That's right – I'm her brother, and it's my job to keep her safe."

"She's an adult. She can take care of herself."

"I am aware she's an adult." Gideon kept his gaze on Kira's face.

"Then maybe you should start treating her like one instead of like a little kid who can't make her own decisions," Grace said.

He finally looked at Grace, the muscle in his jaw ticking hard and fast. "Maybe if she started making the right, *smart* decisions, I wouldn't have to -"

Grace folded her arms across her chest. "Maybe the right, *smart* decisions aren't necessarily what *you* think they are."

"I know what's best for her." Gideon's voice was flat.

"No, she knows what's best for her. I repeat, she is an adult who is perfectly capable of making her own decisions. Maybe those decisions would be a mistake, or maybe they'd be the best thing that ever happened to her." Grace's entire body was stiff, and Kira could see her hands clenching and unclenching into fists. "But it's hard for her to know when you won't allow her to make her own decision."

Gideon's hand tightened around the equipment bag strap until his knuckles went white. "Maybe if she didn't have a history of making bad choices when it came to men, I wouldn't have to -"

"Hey! I don't make bad choices or decisions," Kira said. "Stop talking about me like I do. Both of you chill out. God."

Gideon and Grace continued to glare at each other. After a moment, Grace turned her gaze to the field.

"I have to go. Kira, we'll talk later." Gideon stormed away.

Kira turned to Grace. Grace's cheeks were bright red, and her pupils were so large Kira could only see a thin circle of green around them. She touched Grace's thigh. "Gracie, why are you so angry?"

"I'm not."

"You are." Kira glanced at Addison, who shrugged. "You and Gideon used to be close, and now it's like you're always fighting. Why?"

"We aren't always fighting," Grace said.

"You kind of are," Addie said. She checked her cell phone and missed the glare that Grace threw her way.

"He bosses you around, Kira," Grace said.

"He's my brother, he's supposed to. Daniel does the same thing to Addie, and I don't see you freaking out about it," Kira replied. "Besides, Gideon bosses you around too – he has since we were kids. It's just what big brothers do."

She put her arm around Grace and squeezed her. "It never used to bother you. You liked that Gideon treated you like his sister when we were kids. You said it made you feel like a part of our family. Remember?"

"Yeah," Grace muttered. "I remember."

Kira squeezed her again. "Taking care of us is what Gideon does. He can't help it. Hell, he likes helping everyone. It's why he became a cop."

"There's a difference between caring for someone and controlling them," Grace said.

"Listen, I'm not denying that Gideon is a control freak – we all know he is – but he's not *controlling*," Kira said. "Just talk to him, okay? You guys used to be close, and I hate that you're always fighting and angry with each other now. You need to be honest and tell Gideon how you feel, and he'll back off, I promise."

Grace didn't reply, and Kira gave her one last squeeze. "He loves us and just wants what's best for us. Okay, Gracie?"

"Sure." Grace smiled, although the smile looked a little fake to Kira. "I love you, Kira."

"I love you too, Gracie-Lou."

CHAPTER 8

"Holy smokes, I know I've been saying this all game, but Connor is a great baseball player," Addison said.

Kira nodded, her eyes glued to Connor as he stepped up to bat. It was the bottom of the ninth, and with two men out and the game tied, he was their team's only chance to win.

"Did you know he was this good?" Addison asked.

"No," Kira replied. "Oh God, what if he strikes out?"

"He won't," Grace said. "He hasn't struck out all game, and Daniel's getting tired. You can tell."

Kira studied Daniel. The firefighter didn't look tired to her. He stretched and cracked his neck before bending to retie his shoe. She wanted to admire the muscles in his back, but her gaze kept being drawn back to Connor.

He was swinging the bat idly as he waited for Daniel. Warmth crept into her belly when he bent and gently massaged his right knee, and his pants tightened across his admittedly fantastic ass.

"Does he have a sore knee?" Addison asked. "He rubs it a lot."

"He does the same thing at work sometimes. Usually near the end of the day," Grace said. "I overheard one of the other hygienists asking him about it once, and he kind of blew her off. Has he mentioned it to you, Kira?"

"No, but," Kira lowered her voice, "we've only had one 'get to know you' session."

"Well, when you find out, let us know," Addison said. "I'm curious to find out what -"

"Shh," Kira said. "He's up."

She watched, her hands clasped together, her stomach a tight knot of tension, as Connor stood in the batter's box, his knees slightly bent, the bat held high over one shoulder. He stared unblinkingly at Daniel, and Kira winced when Daniel threw the ball, and the umpire called a strike.

"Oh God," she muttered when the second strike was called, "he's going to strike out."

Normally, she would have been thrilled if Daniel struck out a batter. But despite her relationship with Connor being fake, she desperately wanted him to hit the damn ball.

"C'mon," she whispered. Darkness had fallen, but she could see the gleam of sweat on Daniel's forehead reflecting under the diamond lights. He stared steadily at Connor, and her breath caught in her throat when he threw the ball.

There was a loud CRACK, and she was on her feet, her heart in her throat and her mouth bone dry, as the players and the fans in the bleachers all watched the ball's arc. The center outfielder ran backward, his arm up and his glove-covered hand stretched out.

It wasn't even close. The ball sailed over the fence and disappeared, and Kira screamed excitedly, clapping her hands and pounding her feet as the other people on the bleacher erupted into loud cheers and catcalls.

"He did it!" Kira hugged Grace and then Addison before clapping again. She watched as Connor jogged around the bases, and when he stepped on home plate, he glanced up at her. She waved at him, knowing she had a giant stupid grin but not caring.

He returned her smile, that adorable dimple appearing on his cheek, before slapping the hands of his fellow players. She sank back to her butt on the seat, watching as Connor returned to the bench. He was limping the slightest bit, and her smile faded a little. She'd ask him about his knee after the game, she decided.

"WE'RE GOING FOR DRINKS, YOU IN?"

Connor shook his head as he packed up his bag. "Nah, I don't think so. But thanks for the invite, Jack."

The tall, lean doctor clapped him on the back. "You kicked that smug fire boy's ass tonight. Good job."

Connor laughed. "Yeah, thanks."

"Noticed that Sheriff Walker's sister cheered pretty loud for you," Jack said.

Connor glanced over at the bleachers. Kira was standing in front of them, talking to Grace and another woman. "Yeah, we're dating."

"Oh," Jack said. "Well, good for you. See you at practice on Sunday."

"Yep. Night, Jack."

"Night."

Connor hesitated and then walked toward Kira. Now that he'd told Jack they were dating, it would look weird if he didn't go over to her. He'd barely taken two steps toward her when Daniel joined her. The firefighter put his arm around her shoulders, and irrational jealousy flamed to life in Connor's stomach when Kira gave him an adoring grin.

Ignoring the way his knee throbbed, he quickened his pace. He reached out, took Kira's arm, and pulled her against his body. Without stopping to think about it, he cupped the back of her skull and pressed his mouth against hers.

He swallowed her startled squeak and pushed his tongue past her slightly parted lips to slide against hers for a few seconds before lifting his head. "Hey."

"Uh, hi there." She stared at him, the confusion apparent in her gaze.

Keeping one arm anchored firmly around her slim waist, he held out his other hand to the auburn-haired woman. "Hi, I'm Connor MacMillan. We haven't met yet."

She shook his hand. "Addison Moore. It's nice to meet you."

"You as well." Connor smiled at her before squeezing Kira's waist. "Thanks for coming to watch me play, honey."

"Right, of course," Kira said. "I wouldn't have missed it."

She took a quick peek at Daniel, and Connor tamped down his irritation. The firefighter was studying Kira with an amused look, and Connor stiffened when Daniel reached out and tugged on Kira's ponytail. "Addie isn't going to the Beaver. You need a ride over, doll?"

"She's riding with me," Connor replied.

Daniel gave him a dismissive glance. "You never go for drinks after a game, doc."

"Tonight I am."

"I guess I'll see you guys there then. Unless," Daniel gave Kira a wink, "you want to ride with me?"

Kira hesitated, and Connor squeezed her hip, probably harder than necessary.

"Thanks," Kira said, "but I'll ride with Connor."

"Sounds good, doll." Daniel gave Connor a final glance. "Good job tonight, doc. I'll get you next time, yeah?"

Connor didn't reply, and Daniel ruffled Addison's hair. "See you later, brat."

"Bye, loser." Addison smoothed her hair down as Daniel sauntered away. She glanced at her phone when it buzzed. "Finally."

She smiled at Grace and Kira. "Harrison's home. I'm going to head over to his place for a bit. Gracie, are you going to the Beaver as well? I gave Kira a ride, so I want to make sure she has a ride home."

"I'll give her a ride home." Connor knew he sounded exasperated, but did they think he'd leave Kira stranded at the pub?

"Oh yes, of course," Addison gave him an apologetic look. "Okay, well, nice to meet you, Connor. Kira, I'll see you tomorrow at spin class."

"Yep. Bye, Addie."

"HEY, KIRA?" GRACE LEANED AGAINST THE BATHROOM counter of the Thirsty Beaver.

"Yeah?" Kira tightened her ponytail and smoothed her t-shirt.

"I thought you said Connor wasn't into PDAs."

Kira stared at her in the mirror. "Okay, so it's not just me then... he's being weirdly handsy with me, right? I mean, I know he's not shoving his tongue down my throat or

111

anything, but he specifically said that in public, we could hold hands and a quick kiss now and then, and that was it. But he's had his arm around me or his hand on my thigh the whole time we've been here."

Grace grinned at her. "Maybe you're just too hard for him to resist."

Kira shook her head and glanced under the stalls before lowering her voice. "He doesn't even want to practice kissing anymore."

"Oh." Grace studied her. "Does that upset you?"

"Of course not. Why would you ask that?"

"Because you look upset."

"Well, I'm not," Kira said. "I love Daniel."

"But you liked kissing Connor."

"It was all right," Kira said. "But, honestly, now that we're not doing it anymore, I don't even miss it. I was just a little infatuated with him because he is an incredible kisser, that's all. It's Daniel I want."

"All right," Grace said. "Well, maybe because Daniel is here, Connor's just really throwing himself into the role of loving boyfriend tonight."

"Maybe," Kira said. "Do you think it's working? Does Daniel look jealous to you?"

"Maybe?" Grace said.

Kira frowned. "You don't sound like you believe that."

"I haven't been paying that much attention. I've had to fend off Jesse all night."

Jesse was Jesse Jones, a firefighter and, as far as Kira was concerned, a real cutie-pie. He had dark hair and eyes, and his body rivaled Daniel's muscles. He was on the quiet side but sweet and polite, and he'd been crushing on Grace for months now.

"Why don't you go out with him?" Kira asked. "Jesse's a sweetheart, and he obviously likes you."

"He's not my type," Grace said dismissively.

The door opened, and a group of giggling women walked in. They headed for the stalls, and Grace grabbed her purse off the counter. "C'mon, we've been here so long, the guys will think we've ditched them."

They left the bathroom and headed back to their table. The Thirsty Beaver Pub was the biggest pub in Harmony Falls, and its laid-back atmosphere and casual décor drew in a variety of people, from college students to seniors.

Kira sat down next to Connor. While she was gone, he'd pulled her empty chair over until it almost touched his. Her thigh brushed against his, but before she could shift over, his hand dropped on the back of her neck, anchoring her in place. He was listening to Jesse and Ethan, another firefighter, arguing good-naturedly about some brand of beer, but his fingers kneaded her neck muscles with slow deliberateness.

She hesitated and rested her hand on his thigh, wondering if he would move his leg away from her touch. He turned to her and gave her a lazy grin. He leaned forward and brushed his mouth against hers in a light caress that made her nipples peak.

"Hey," he said.

"Uh, hi," she said.

"Did you want another beer?" His fingers found a tense spot and massaged a little harder.

She bit back her moan of pleasure. "Um, no, I'm good. I don't drink that much."

"So, doll, how did you and the doc start dating anyway?" Daniel was sitting across from them, and he leaned forward, resting his beefy arms on the table. "He's not exactly your type."

"How would you know?" Grace said. She was sitting on the other side of Kira and gave Daniel a stiff smile. "You don't know anything about Connor."

Daniel grinned at her. "Good point, Gracie-Lou."

"Don't call me that," she said.

"Why don't you tell us about your new... boyfriend, Kira?" Daniel said.

"I can tell my own life story, thanks," Connor said.

His body was tensing, and Kira rubbed his thigh. "I told you, Connor is my dentist. I met him at the office."

"And no," Connor said before Daniel could say anything, "it isn't illegal to date my patients."

"Right." Daniel gave Jesse a nudge. "And here I thought being a firefighter would get us the ladies. Turns out dentistry is the way to go."

He turned to Connor. "I guess the ladies just like having you in their mouth, huh?"

"Don't be a pig, Daniel," Grace said.

"Kira loves it when I talk dirty. Isn't that right, doll?"

"Uh..." Kira had no idea what to say. Daniel flirted with her occasionally, but he never talked dirty to her.

Connor's hand tightened on the back of her neck before releasing. "It's getting late. Are you ready to go, Kira?"

Kira nodded. The palpable tension radiating from Grace and Connor made her tense. "Gracie, are you leaving too?"

"Yes," Grace said.

"I'll just pay our tab and meet you outside, all right?" Connor said.

"Sure." She managed not to look too surprised when

Connor pressed another kiss against her mouth before standing and heading toward the bar.

She smiled at the three firefighters and grabbed her purse under the table. "Bye, guys."

"Bye, Kira. Grace, it was good to see you again." Jesse gave the curvy brunette a sweet smile.

"You too, Jesse," Grace replied. "Bye, Ethan."

Ethan waved at them as he watched the game on the big screen TV on the far wall.

"See ya later, doll." Daniel's grin widened. "Thanks for watching me play tonight."

Kira just nodded. "Bye, Daniel."

She followed Grace outside, taking a deep breath of the cool air as Grace gave her an irritated look. "Oh my God, Daniel was being such an ass tonight."

"He was just teasing," Kira said. "You know how he is."

"Yeah," Grace replied. "He's a real charmer."

"Stop it, Grace," Kira said as they walked toward Connor's car. "Besides, I'm hoping he's acting weird because he's jealous. I mean, it's not that far-fetched to think that maybe he does secretly -"

"Kira! Hey, Kira!"

She turned, her heart beating faster when she saw Daniel jogging toward them. "You got a second to talk, doll?" He glanced at Grace. "In private?"

"Sure," Kira said. "I'll just be a minute, Grace."

"Yeah, I'm gonna go. Night, Kira." Grace kissed her cheek and gave Daniel another stiff smile before heading toward her car.

Kira followed Daniel a few feet away, her heart thrumming like a live wire. He smiled down at her before reaching out and taking her hand. "You know you're special to me, right?"

Oh my God. This was it. Daniel was jealous and about to tell her how he felt. Holy shit, Grace was right. Why the hell hadn't she thought of doing this sooner? She could have been dating Daniel years ago.

"You're special to me too," she whispered.

He smiled and brushed back a stray strand of hair from her face. "Good. Are you busy tomorrow afternoon?"

"Um, I... no, I don't think so," she said.

She reminded herself to say no when he asked her out. She had to. She'd promised Connor that she would go to his cousin's wedding with him.

"Cool. Would you be okay with me and the guys coming by tomorrow to watch the game at your place?"

"That's so sweet of you, but I can't...wait, what?" Kira said.

"The game." Daniel squeezed her hand before rubbing his thumb across her palm. "Would you mind if we watched it at your place? The game's a lot better on your sixty-inch screen."

"Right." Disappointment swept through her, and she stared dully at their clasped hands. "Yeah, okay."

Daniel gave her hand a little squeeze before cupping her shoulder. "You sure, doll?"

She made herself smile at him. "Of course, I'm sure."

"Great!" His smile widened, showing off his perfect white teeth. "We'll be by around two then. Do you think you could pick up some snacks for us?"

Before she could reply, she heard footsteps behind her, and she knew instinctively it was Connor. Feeling weirdly guilty, she snatched her hand from Daniel's and shrugged off his other hand before turning.

"Hi there." Her voice was loud and a little screechy.

Connor studied her silently for a moment before holding out his hand. "Ready to go?"

"Yes. Yeah, I sure am. Let's go. Bye, Daniel." Without looking at Daniel, she took Connor's hand and followed him to his car.

Why did she feel so damn guilty?

Connor walked her to the passenger door, and when he didn't open it, she glanced at him. The expression on his face was flat, and she gave him a timid smile. "Connor, are you -"

His arm hooked around her waist, and he drew her up against his body, one hand cupping the back of her skull as his mouth crashed down on hers. She made a startled squeak into his mouth, her lips parting when he pushed his tongue against the seam of them.

He kissed her hard, his usual coaxing and teasing style of kissing gone completely under a rough and demanding type of urgency that took her breath away.

She forgot they were in public.

She forgot this was fake.

She forgot about Daniel.

Until now, she hadn't realized how much she'd missed kissing Connor. Without any shame, she put her arms around him and clung to him, kissing him back with unabashed eagerness.

One big hand reached down and cupped her ass. He squeezed it with casual familiarity before pressing her against the growing hardness below his waist. She moaned into his mouth and rubbed her breasts against him.

His hand squeezed her ass again, and he made a possessive growl against her mouth before pushing her up against the car. He nipped at her bottom lip and then licked her upper lip. She moaned again, and he pulled back, staring down at her red and swollen mouth.

"Connor?" she whispered. "Are you okay?"

His voice was brisk. "Fine."

He pulled her away from the car and opened the passenger door. "Get in, Kira."

She touched her mouth before climbing into the car. As Connor walked to the driver's side, she saw Daniel still standing in the parking lot. He studied Connor, but it was too dark and too far away for Kira to tell if it was jealousy on his face.

Connor climbed in, a flash of pain crossing his face when he bent his right knee and slammed the door shut. Without speaking, he started the car and drove out of the parking lot.

She didn't speak on the way home. Her heart was pounding, lust was flooding through her entire nervous system, and she was desperately trying not to reach across the car and press her hand against Connor's crotch. Was he still hard for her? Was he going to come into the house with her, take her upstairs, undress her and give her exactly what she needed? What she wanted?

Kira! What is wrong with you? One hot kiss from Connor, and you'll give up your V-card to him?

It was a *really* great kiss…

Her inner voice didn't reply, and she kept her hands in her lap and her gaze locked out the window. Okay, things were getting a little weird in her brain, but that was probably just the lust. If the previous two guys she'd kissed had kissed like Connor, she would have been tempted to sleep with them, too.

Her reaction was perfectly normal. Connor was a fantastic kisser, and a woman would have to be completely dead inside not to be affected by it. She was normal, her reaction was normal. Everything was normal.

Perfectly normal.

"Kira?"

She jumped at the sound of Connor's voice. "Uh, yeah?"

"We're here."

She stared blankly out the windshield at her house before turning to Connor. "Thank you for the ride home. Good night."

Was that disappointment that crossed his face? Did he want her to ask him to come inside?

"Good night." His voice was terse.

She opened the door, feeling weird and uncertain and… goddammit, horny as hell. She squeezed the door handle before blurting, "Why did you do that?"

"Do what?"

"Kiss me in the parking lot."

"We're dating. People who date kiss."

"You specifically said that you were against PDAs. You basically made me swear that I wouldn't do anything more than hold your hand in public, and then you… you had your tongue shoved down my throat in the parking lot of the Thirsty Beaver. That's one hell of a PDA, Connor."

His nostrils flared. "Why were you alone in the parking lot with Daniel?"

"What?" She blinked at him.

"You were alone with Daniel."

"I… he wanted to talk to me."

He didn't reply, and she licked her still swollen lips. "Why did you kiss me like that?"

"Because we're trying to make Daniel jealous, remember?"

"Yes, but…"

"But what?" He gave her an impatient look, his hands gripping the steering wheel. "You've asked me to help you make Daniel jealous. I'm doing what you asked me, Kira. Is there a problem with that?"

"No," she said. "Stop being a jerk about it."

He sighed and rubbed his temples. "I apologize. It's been a long day, and I'm tired."

He stared out the windshield, and she climbed out of the car when he didn't say anything else. "Good night, Connor."

"Good night, Kira."

She climbed the porch steps. Her knees shook, and she was weirdly disappointed that she was alone. She glanced behind her as she opened the door. Connor was still parked in the driveway, and she gave him an awkward wave before stepping inside. She closed the door and leaned against it, staring at the ceiling.

She couldn't stop thinking about that kiss in the parking lot. Had Connor really only kissed her to make Daniel jealous? And if so, why did that bother her so much?

CHAPTER 9

Connor studied his cell phone before hitting Kira's number. His knee was throbbing again. It had felt better when he got up and, stupidly, he'd gone for a run. He should have known better. He rubbed it absently as he sat in the kitchen chair.

He'd been a real dick last night, and he'd spent most of today feeling guilty for how he'd treated Kira. But when he left the pub last night and saw Kira alone with Daniel, that weird jealousy immediately reappeared. He hadn't thought about his actions. He'd been driven by a primal need to show Daniel that Kira belonged to him. His stance against PDAs had disappeared into thin air, which both perplexed him and worried him a little if he was being honest.

He'd always been a bit standoffish with his parents, with Lisa… hell, with everyone in his life. He didn't think he was cold or distant, like Lisa sometimes pointed out. He just liked his personal space. Only that seemed to go out the window whenever he was near Kira. The urge to touch her and feel her soft skin was almost impossible to resist.

He gulped down the rest of his water as the phone rang in his ear. He was being affectionate and touchy-feely with Kira because he was playing a part, that was all. He was getting all tied up in knots about nothing. He would apologize again and ask her if she wanted to hang out. He really should learn more about her if he wanted to be an effective fake boyfriend.

Oh yeah? So, you're telling me you're not planning on asking her if she wants to practice kissing again?

No, he wasn't. If she brought it up again while they were hanging out, then yeah, maybe he'd be up for some practice sessions, but he wasn't calling *specifically* for that. He was calling because –

"Hello?" Kira's voice spoke into his ear.

"Hey, uh, it's me."

"Oh, hi."

There was a moment of awkward silence, and he cleared his throat. "How are you?"

"I'm good. You?"

"Fine."

"That's good," she said.

He rubbed his knee and said, "Listen, I wanted to apologize for -"

"Hey, Kira? You got any chips in the cupboard? We're all out."

The voice was muffled, but he knew exactly who it was, and anger flared through him, making his knee pulse and his face hot. "What is Daniel doing at your house?"

"Top left, above the sink," Kira said.

He waited impatiently as he listened to the muffled sounds of Daniel grabbing the chips. After a few seconds, Kira said, "We're watching the game."

"You're watching the game alone with Daniel at your house?" More heat crept up the back of his neck.

"Not alone," she said quickly. "Jesse and Brad are here too."

"That doesn't make it better," he snapped.

She was silent for a moment before saying, "Nothing's happening. We're just watching the game."

"I'm on my way over." He ended the call before she could reply.

Ignoring how his knee throbbed and burned, he grabbed his jacket and keys and limped out of the house.

THE LOOK ON CONNOR'S FACE WHEN SHE OPENED THE DOOR suggested he was this close to putting her over his knee and spanking her. Kira ignored the weird excitement that thought brought on and said, "Nothing's happening, Connor. We're just watching the game. We've done this tons of times before."

He stepped inside, hanging his jacket on the hook before following her into the kitchen. "You should have called me."

"Why? It's not like it's just Daniel and me alone in the house."

He stepped close and cupped her face. Her stomach dipped and dived, her mouth parting in anticipation of his kiss.

Instead, he said in a low voice, "Anytime Daniel or his friends are here, I'm here. Is that clear?"

She nodded, feeling like maybe she should be put out by his actions but oddly turned on instead. He studied her mouth, and she made a soft sound of encouragement in the back of her throat.

His thumb stroked along her bottom lip, and she moaned quietly. "Connor, please."

God, just the heat of his body made her horny.

"Please, what, little Kira?"

"Kiss me," she whispered.

Before he could kiss her, Daniel stepped into the kitchen. "Kira, can I steal some of that beer you have... oh, hey, doc. What are you doing here?"

Connor stepped back, and she controlled the urge to give Daniel an angry look. He was always friggin' interrupting her chance to be kissed.

"I'm her boyfriend," Connor said.

"Yeah, so you keep saying." Daniel lifted his shirt and scratched at his washboard abs. "Doll, you mind if we take some of your beer, too?"

"No, it's fine." Her gaze drifted back to Connor. Usually, the firefighter lifting his shirt would guarantee to have her gaze glued to his stomach. But today? Today, she couldn't seem to stop staring at Connor's mouth.

"Thanks." Daniel grabbed the beer from the fridge. "You stickin' around to watch the game, doc?"

"Yes. Is that a problem?"

"Nope. The more the merrier." Daniel tossed a beer at him.

Connor caught it and set it on the counter. "Thanks."

"Seventh inning stretch is almost over," Daniel said with a wink at Kira. "You guys comin' or what?"

Kira took Connor's hand when he held it out to her. They followed Daniel into the living room. The room was big with an old but large and comfortable sectional, two recliners, and a wooden coffee table. Snacks and empty beer cans covered the coffee table. Jesse was sitting at one end of the sectional, and Brad lounged in a recliner. Daniel sat in the empty recliner beside him before cracking open a beer. "Brad, meet the doc. Doc, meet Brad."

The redhead didn't look away from the TV. "Nice to meetcha.'"

"You as well."

"Hey, Connor." Jesse grinned at him before holding out a bag of chips. "Want some?"

"I'm good, thanks." Limping slightly, Connor led her to the empty end of the sectional. He sat down at the end, and she sat beside him, making sure to keep some space between them. Connor frowned and put his arm around her shoulders, tugging on her until she slid over and her thigh pressed against his.

She leaned against him, and he stroked her hair before running his fingers over her shoulder. She was wearing a tank top, and the warmth of his fingers as he brushed them along her bare shoulder seared into her skin. She shifted a little, and he pressed a kiss against her temple before staring at the screen. Little shivers running up and down her spine, Kira tried to concentrate on the game as well.

IT WAS THE TOP OF THE NINTH, AND SHE WAS TENSE AND squirmy, and her nerves were on the brink of being entirely shot.

Not from the game. She didn't give a shit about the game

at this point. Not when she'd spent the last hour or so being touched continuously by Connor. As if he was reading her mind, his fingers traced across her shoulder again before – oh dear God in heaven – swooping across to trail along her collarbone.

He hadn't stopped touching her since they sat down. Just light grazes of his fingertips across her exposed skin. She held her breath as his index finger dipped into the hollow of her throat before he retraced her collarbone. When his fingers slipped a little further down, running along the neckline of her tank top, she arched her back.

She couldn't help it.

Her hands clenched into tight fists, and her breathing turned shallow when one finger slipped under the neckline.

Oh, please, she silently begged. *Please, oh please, oh please.*

Kira! You are not going to let him touch your tits in front of Daniel and the others.

If he did, she wouldn't object. The others were glued to the screen. They wouldn't even notice if Connor put his hand on her breast. What was the big deal? Her breasts felt heavy and achy, and her nipples were throbbing. She wanted to know what it would feel like to have those warm fingers rubbing against her nipples, wanted to know if…

Her breathing stopped when Connor's finger traced the edge of her bra cup. She arched her back again and bit back her moan when Connor retreated. He pressed his mouth to her ear, his warm breath sending goosebumps popping up on her arms. "Behave, little Kira."

"I am," she whispered indignantly.

"No," he pressed a kiss against her earlobe, "you're not. Arching your back to show off your hard nipples is not behaving."

She glanced down at herself, her face going red with mortification. Her nipples *were* rock hard and pressing against the thin fabric of her bra and top. They were extremely noticeable, and she snatched her cardigan off the back of the sofa and quickly put it on.

Connor tugged her back against him, his fingers rubbing the exposed skin of her chest as he put his mouth close to her ear again. "I've never had a woman's nipples go so hard without me even touching them, sweet Kira."

His fingers touched the neckline of her tank top again. "I'm curious to see what will happen when I touch them," his fingers pulled on her shirt, "or pull on them."

Oh my God. Connor was talking dirty to her. For the first time in her life, she had a man talking dirty to her, and it was… turning her on like a damn faucet.

She squirmed on the couch, trying to ease the ache between her thighs as Connor stroked his fingers back and forth over her upper chest. His voice was barely above a whisper in her ear. "Have you had your nipples sucked on before, Kira?"

Her moan was drowned out by the crowd's roar on the TV screen and the groans of dismay from Daniel and the others.

"Have you?" Connor nipped her earlobe.

"You know I haven't," she whispered.

"Would you like me to suck on them?"

"Yes." There wasn't even a hint of shame in her voice. "Yes, I want that."

"Are they aching?" he asked.

"So much," she whispered. "I can't stand it, Connor."

"It's too bad we're not alone," he said. "If we were, you could take off your shirt and your bra and show me your sweet nipples. Maybe I could do something about that ache for you."

He nipped her earlobe again. "If we were alone."

"You guys have to go now." Her voice was low and shaky, and she cleared her throat before trying again. "Hey, it's time for you to leave."

Daniel glanced at her. "What? The game's almost over, Kira."

"You need to go," she said.

Connor squeezed her shoulder before giving her a teasing grin. "They gotta finish watching the game, honey."

"Yeah," Brad said. "Seriously, Kira. You can't kick us out now."

She glared at Connor, who kissed the tip of her nose. "It's the bottom of the ninth."

Feeling achy and unsettled and horny as hell, she settled back against Connor, trying to ignore the touch of his warm fingers against her skin.

She gave the back of Daniel's head a grouchy look. Dammit, she was never letting Daniel or his friends come over to watch the game again.

"Thanks, doll. I appreciate you letting us watch the game over here." Daniel grinned at her.

"Yeah, of course, no problem. I had fun." She could hear the impatience in her voice. Jesse and Brad had already left, but Daniel lingered in the hallway, and she wanted to screech with frustration. She glanced behind her. Connor was in the living room. He was in the living room and waiting for her to come back so he could do what he said he would do.

Her nipples throbbed anew, and she crossed her arms over her chest, pretty sure that, at this point, they were so hard not even her cardigan would help disguise it. "Okay, Daniel, bye."

He gave her a teasing look. "Trying to get rid of me, doll?"

"Connor and I have plans," she said.

Hell, yes, we do. Plans that involve his mouth and your nipples. Get this guy out of here before Connor changes his mind.

"Right." Daniel opened the door. "I'll see you soon, all right?"

"Yeah, sure, okay. See you soon." She glanced behind her again before giving Daniel a distracted smile. "Bye, Daniel."

He leaned in to press a kiss against her cheek. Without thinking about it, she stepped back, pressing her hands up against his chest to stop him. If Connor didn't like that she was alone with Daniel, he sure as hell wouldn't like Daniel kissing her.

Daniel cocked his head at her, and she gave him a faint smile. "Uh, sorry. Just having a big personal space bubble day."

He stepped out onto the porch. "Bye, Kira."

"Bye, Daniel." She shut the door in his face and tried not to run back to the living room. She stopped just inside the living room, giving Connor a look of apprehension. He was sitting on the couch and staring at his phone. What if he had changed his mind? What if he'd decided to leave, and she would be alone with an aching pussy and nipples?

"Connor? They're gone."

He glanced up at her, and her legs went a little shaky at the hunger in his eyes. He studied her mouth and then her tits before saying, "Come here, little Kira."

She stumbled across the living room, sinking onto the

couch beside him. He leaned down and kissed her, a coaxing, teasing kiss that made her moan and press her body up against his.

He stroked her back with his big hands as he teased her lips with tiny nips and licks that set her on fire. She loved Connor's kisses, but she wanted – *needed* – more.

"Connor, please, you promised," she moaned.

"Are you sure this is what you want, Kira?"

She muttered a curse and, worried that he would change his mind, she shrugged out of her cardigan and ripped her tank top over her head before he could stop her. "Yes. I'm positive."

She wore a pale green bra, and her nipples pushed against the thin fabric. He cupped her waist and pressed a kiss against her collarbone before sliding his hands up her ribs. She arched her back before he even cupped her breasts, and he made a low chuckle before licking her throat. "So needy, sweet Kira."

He licked and nipped her throat, his hands still resting against her ribs. She grabbed them and tried to tug them upward, making a noise of frustration when she couldn't move them. "Connor!"

He laughed again, and she cried out when one big hand cupped her right breast. His thumb rubbed over her nipple, and she arched, her hands clutching at his upper arms through his t-shirt.

"Such hard nipples," he said before plucking at one through her bra.

She mashed her mouth down onto his, kissing him with frantic need. He let her suck on his tongue, let her explore every part of his mouth as he continued to knead and cup her breasts through her bra.

"I want more," she demanded.

He smiled at her, unclasped her bra and tugged the straps down her arms. He tossed her bra aside. Any feeling of self-consciousness disappeared at the look of pure hunger on Connor's face when he stared at her naked breasts.

He reached out, and she was surprised to see his hand trembling. He gently cupped her naked breast. His hand covered her breast entirely, and she felt a moment of embarrassment that washed away when he rubbed his thumb over her nipple.

"Oh my God!" She grabbed at his arms again as he cupped both her breasts and teased her nipples with his thumbs.

Holy crap, she knew her nipples were sensitive, but the touch of Connor's fingers sent butterflies careening and crashing about her belly like they were drunk. She could only watch helplessly as, for long moments, Connor teased and tormented her aching nipples with tugs of his fingers and caresses of his thumbs. He pulled on her right one and then gave it a little pinch, leaning forward and kissing her collarbone when she gasped.

"Sorry, honey."

"No," she gasped again, "I, uh, I liked it."

He kissed her neck, his hands kneading her breasts, and she made a low moan. "Connor, you promised you'd suck on my nipples."

He kissed just below her earlobe before sucking on the lobe. "Did I?"

"Yes." She grabbed his shirt and yanked on it. "Take this off."

He pulled it over his head, and she touched the coarse hair on his chest before kissing his collarbone. He groaned, and she gave him a delighted look before licking his throat.

He muttered a curse and pressed one hand between her tits.

"Lie back, Kira."

She fell onto her back on the couch, wiggling over to give him room as he lay beside her. Pain crossed his face, and she paused. "You okay?"

"Fine," he said.

"Are you sure? You look a little… oh God!"

Connor had bent and kissed her nipple, and she forgot about her worry at the touch of his firm lips. He licked the tip of her nipple, and she clutched at his head, her body arching up and her mouth dropping open as she sucked in a gasp of air.

He kissed and licked around her nipples for long moments, never quite giving her what she wanted, as she moaned and squirmed on the couch. He cupped her right breast and pulled at her nipple before licking her left nipple.

"Connor!" She couldn't stand the torment a moment longer.

"Yes, little Kira?"

"Please!"

He smiled up at her before licking her nipple and then blowing lightly on it. "I don't want you alone with Daniel anymore."

"I – what?" She could barely think past the need.

"You're my girlfriend, and I don't think it's appropriate that you're alone with Daniel. Do you agree?" He licked her nipple again before nipping the soft underside of her breast.

"Okay, yeah, sure, I agree."

He kissed her nipple, his mouth hovering over it as he stared up at her. "No more spending time with Daniel alone."

"Connor, please." She tried to push his mouth onto her nipple but couldn't budge his damn head an inch.

"Promise me, little Kira. You won't be alone with Daniel."

"I won't be alone with Daniel," she said. "I promise. I promise I'll never be alone with him. Just *please*, Connor… your mouth, please.

His hot, wet mouth closed around her nipple and sucked. She cried out, her hands fisting in his dark hair as he sucked hard. Each pull of his mouth sent an arrow of pleasure straight to her pussy. When he shifted, and his thigh pushed between her legs, she hooked her legs around it and humped his thigh shamelessly as he moved back and forth between her nipples, sucking and licking on the sensitive tips.

He shifted again, and she could feel his erection poking against her hip. She grabbed his arms and pulled on them, widening her legs and trying to get him to slip between her thighs. Now that they'd had the attention of his mouth, her breasts were no longer aching as bad, but the ache had moved lower and deeper, directly between her legs.

If she'd thought the ache and throb of her tits were bad, it was nothing compared to the throbbing of her pussy. She needed relief and knew precisely how she could get it.

When Connor didn't move, she groaned with frustration and reached down, grabbing his thigh just above his knee and giving it a hard yank to try to move him over. He made a harsh cry of pain, and she let go of him immediately, giving him a horrified look.

He struggled to sit up, his face pale and his body trembling. Kira scrambled back, staring at him as he rubbed his right knee, his lips drawn down with pain and little drops of sweat breaking out on his forehead.

"Connor?" She touched his naked back. "Connor, I'm so sorry. I didn't mean to hurt you."

"It's fine," he gritted out.

He was lying, and she gave him a helpless look. "What should I do?"

"Nothing. Just give me a minute."

Feeling sick, she yanked her tank top over her head before sitting quietly beside him. After a few minutes, he relaxed and took a deep breath.

"I'm so sorry," she said.

"It isn't your fault."

"It is," she said. "I'm very sorry."

"It's okay."

She chewed on her bottom lip. "What happened to your knee?"

"Tweaked it during the game last night," he said.

She frowned. Why was he lying to her?

"Grace said she's seen you limping at the office. Did you injure it when you were a kid?"

He tensed and grabbed his shirt from the floor, shoving it over his head. "It's fine, Kira."

"That isn't what I asked," she said.

He sighed. "Yes, I hurt it when I was younger, and sometimes it acts up."

"Oh. I've got an ice pack in the fridge. I'll grab it."

He shook his head. "Don't bother. I'm fine."

"You're obviously not fine," she said. "What did you do to it when you were a kid?"

"None of your business," he said.

She gave him a hurt look. "We're dating, Connor. This seems like something I should know."

"We're fake dating," he said. "And I'm not talking about my knee injury with you."

He stood up and limped his way to the door. "This was a mistake. I gotta go."

She jumped up and followed him down the hallway. "Are you kidding me? Why do you get to be the one to decide when it's a mistake or not? You were the one who started this with your damn touching and your... your nipple talk during the game!"

He glared at her. "I wouldn't have even been over here if you hadn't invited Daniel to come over."

"I didn't invite him over, he asked, and I said yes because it's something we always do."

"Yeah, well, you have a boyfriend now, remember? Letting him hang out here when I'm not around is a slap in my face."

"It's not real," she said. "We aren't actually dating!"

He glared at her. "He doesn't know that, and no one else does either. If you want Daniel to buy this relationship, you need to think about your actions and act like you and I are dating. It's that simple, Kira."

"Fine," she snapped. "I fucked up. I get it. I'll try to be a better fake girlfriend in the future."

"Good."

There was a tense silence between them, and then Connor took a deep breath before running his hand through his hair. "Fuck. Okay, I'm being a dickhead, and I apologize. I know you want to be with Daniel, and I'll do my best to help you achieve that goal, but you have to use your head about this. He won't be jealous if he thinks this isn't real."

"I said I get it," Kira replied. "No need to elaborate. I'll do better in the future."

He looked like he was going to say something else, and she crossed her arms over her chest, giving him a cool look. "Good night, Connor."

"Good night." He yanked open the door and stepped out onto the porch. He slammed the door behind him, and she gave his retreating back the bird before screeching in frustration and stomping back to the kitchen.

CHAPTER 10

"What's wrong with you tonight?"

"Nothing. What's wrong with you?" Kira said. Gideon patted Tank's head before leaning against the counter. "You're acting weird."

"You're acting weird."

He rolled his eyes and grabbed a tart from the cupboard. "Have you shown that tech guy the properties yet?"

"No, that doesn't happen until Friday." She stared at her hands as Gideon sat down across from her.

"Nervous?"

"Yeah. If I can't find a property he likes and wants to purchase, I'll lose my job."

"Sorry, kid," he said.

She shrugged. "I just need to think and stay positive. There has to be something he likes, right?"

"Yeah. How are things going with your new boyfriend?"

"Don't say it like that." She scowled at him as he shoved the rest of the tart into his mouth.

He chewed and swallowed before saying, "It's Wednesday, and we still haven't discussed it."

"You've been busy at work, and there's nothing to discuss. I'm dating Connor."

"But you're in love with Daniel," Gideon said.

"No, I had a pointless crush on Daniel that I'm now over."

He studied her silently and wilted under his gaze. She hated how her brother could always tell when she was lying.

"I haven't seen Connor's car here since Saturday," he said.

She glared at him. "Are you spying on me?"

He gave her a grin, not the least bit ashamed. "It's not spying when I'm a cop, Kira. It's called doing my job."

"It's called spying, and you need to stop. Besides," she lied, "I've been at his house a couple of times this week."

"Now I know you're lying," he said.

"Shut up."

"Connor lives in an apartment, not a house," he said.

"How do you know that?"

"I'm the sheriff," he said as if that answered everything.

"Well, I just," she waved her hands around, "meant house in general."

"Oh yeah? What's Connor's address?"

"I don't know his exact address, Gideon." Sweat was dripping down her back. "Hey, did you see they have steaks on sale at Safeway? I know you've been itching to barbeque again."

"Stop changing the subject. Where does Connor live? Just give me a general area of town."

She stared at him before sighing. "Fine, I don't know where he lives, all right?"

"You've been dating him for almost three weeks, and you don't know where he lives," Gideon said.

"Don't make a big deal out of it," she said. "He usually comes here."

"Kira, you're hiding something from me," Gideon said. "Why?"

"I'm not. God, Gideon, I'm not a little kid anymore. Stop treating me like one."

Gideon tapped his fingers on the table, and Tank sat up, making a soft 'woof' as he stared toward the front door.

"I realize you're not a kid, but you're my kid sister, and I'm going to worry about you. Especially if you're dating someone who isn't a good guy."

"Connor's a great guy," she said. "You hate Daniel. I thought you'd be happy that I'm dating someone else and finally over him."

Gideon stood and leaned over to kiss her on the forehead. "I would be if I thought you were actually over Daniel. Come by the house tomorrow night at six for dinner. Bring your... boyfriend with you."

"I'll check and see if he has plans," Kira said.

"Love you, kid." Gideon whistled for Tank, and the big dog lumbered to his feet and followed him out of the kitchen.

"I love you too." Kira waited until the door shut before grabbing her phone. She hesitated and then typed Connor a quick message. She hadn't heard a word from him since Saturday, and honestly, she wasn't even sure if they were still fake dating. He'd been super pissed when he left.

Yeah, well, that's not your fault. He was the one who was acting all weird and shit.

It was true, he had been acting weird and shit. She'd had supper with Grace last night and, without telling her what happened on Saturday, asked her what Connor's mood was like.

"Terrible," Grace had sighed. "He's been a real bear all week. Why? Did you two fight?"

She'd brushed off the question, and although she could tell Grace wasn't buying any of her excuses, she didn't question Kira further.

She stared at her message, rereading it quickly.

KIRA

> Hey. My brother wants us to come over for dinner at his place tomorrow night around six. Are you available? Fair warning, he's even more suspicious because I couldn't tell him where you lived.

She hit send and then hesitated before typing some more and sending it.

> Hope your knee is better. Are we even still fake dating?

She didn't have to wait long for a response. Her phone dinged, and she scanned Connor's text a little too eagerly.

CONNOR

> Hi. Yes, we're still fake dating, and yes, I'm available for dinner tomorrow. I'll pick you up at quarter to six.

She slumped in her chair. That was it?

What were you expecting? Her inner voice sounded grumpy.

She didn't know, she supposed. It's not like Connor would tell her he missed her or something. Or that, like her, he'd slept terribly the last four nights with weird sex dreams that left him cranky and sexually frustrated.

She rubbed her forehead before leaving her phone on the table and heading upstairs to take a bath. Maybe the combination of a hot bath and – her cheeks flushed – some dedicated time spent masturbating would help her sleep tonight.

———

WORRIED HIS KNEE WAS STILL BOTHERING HIM, SHE WAS waiting on the porch when he pulled into the driveway the next night. She hurried down the stairs and climbed into the car, giving him a tentative smile. "Hey."

"Hi, Kira."

"Thanks for doing this."

"Of course."

"My brother lives on Wilshire Avenue." She put her seatbelt on as he pulled out of the driveway.

"All right."

There was silence, and hating the awkwardness between them, she said, "Connor, I -"

"Kira, I shouldn't -"

They both stopped, and she smiled at him. "Go ahead."

"I shouldn't have acted the way I did on Saturday. I'm sorry. I was wondering if we could, I don't know, forget the fight and start over? I was in pain and being an idiot."

"Yeah, I'm - I mean, I wasn't exactly acting mature, so I'm sorry too."

"So, truce?" His dimple deepened when he smiled at her, and a healthy dose of lust washed over her.

"Truce." She silently thanked God she'd had the foresight to wear a tank top, t-shirt and a thick sweatshirt to hide her traitorous nipples. She'd discovered over the last few days that just *thinking* about Connor and his perfect mouth made her nipples go hard. Seeing his mouth in person, with that stupidly adorable dimple, proved she didn't stand a chance.

The idea that her brother might realize she was horny was too horrifying to comprehend.

"So, how's work been this week?" she asked.

"Good, busy. How about you?"

"Fine. I have an appointment on Friday to show a client some commercial properties."

"Oh yeah?" He glanced at her. "That sounds promising."

"It is. It's kind of weird, though. He said I was recommended to him, but I don't know who would have done that. I asked Rose and Ray if maybe they had done it, but neither had even heard of the guy before he came into our office."

"Strange," he said as he turned onto Wilshire.

"I thought so," she said. "Gideon's house is third on the right."

He pulled into the driveway and parked before shutting the car off. She smiled at him. "I'm going to apologize in advance for the grilling you're about to get from my brother."

He grinned at her. "It's cool. I can handle some big brother grilling."

She sighed as she climbed out of the car. "See, you think you do, but you haven't been subjected to Gideon yet. I mean, we'll be lucky if he doesn't handcuff you to the chair and, I don't know, waterboard you or something."

He laughed out loud as they met in front of the car. When he held out his hand, she took it and squeaked in surprise when he pulled her in close. "Don't worry about me, little Kira. I promise I won't crack under the pressure."

He studied her mouth before leaning down and pressing

a kiss against it. She returned his kiss, knowing she should keep it chaste but unable to resist skimming her tongue along the seam of his lips. To her surprise, he parted them, and she slipped her tongue into his mouth, moaning quietly when he sucked on the tip.

He pulled back, and she said, "I thought you weren't into PDAs."

He grinned and squeezed her hand. "Just putting on a show for big brother."

Gideon stood on the small front porch, and she waved at him before muttering, "Shit."

"What? Was that the wrong thing to do?" he asked. "I thought it might help with the suspicion."

"No, it's just..." she stared at her boobs. "Can you see my nipples?"

"What?"

"My nipples. Are they visible? I wore layers, but I'm not taking any chances. I am not walking up to my brother with hard nipples."

"No, you can't see them," he said. "But if you don't stop talking about your hard nipples, we're gonna have a bigger problem. Trust me when I say that me sporting a full-on boner in front of your brother will be a much larger issue than your," his gaze dipped to her breasts again, "hard nipples."

A flush of heat went through her, and her giggle was a little high-pitched. "Sorry, I didn't mean to...that is, I'm not...."

He squeezed her hand and gave her an adorable grin. "I know you didn't. C'mon, let's get the interrogation over with."

"So, Connor, you haven't even told Kira where you live. Is that right?" Gideon set the plate of steaks down on the table as Kira brought over the bowl of salad and the grilled mushrooms.

"Knock it off, Gideon." She sat down next to Connor at the table.

To her surprise, Gideon had been perfectly polite to Connor from the moment they walked in. He'd gotten them both a beer, and they'd made small talk on the patio in the backyard as Gideon grilled the steaks.

But now, it seemed like the niceties were over, and her stomach churned as she patted Tank on the butt. "Tank, go to your bed."

The Great Dane had taken a liking to Connor and was standing in front of him, his long tail waving happily as he rested his big head on Connor's shoulder. Connor patted his side as Gideon said, "Tank, to your bed."

The big dog chuffed but left the kitchen. Kira heard him sigh loudly as he flopped down on the bed in the living room.

"Connor, do you want another beer?" she asked.

He shook his head and sipped at his water. "No, thank you. Water is good."

She could almost feel Gideon's silent approval. Not that her brother had anything against drinking beer, but Connor was driving, and the fact that he stopped after one would earn him a point in Gideon's mind.

"This looks delicious," Connor said as Gideon handed him the steaks. He took one and gave the plate to Kira, who took the smallest one. She put some salad on her plate and passed the salad bowl to Connor.

"So, about Kira not knowing where you live," Gideon said again. "Any particular reason for that?"

Connor shook his head, squeezing Kira's thigh under the table when she started to protest. "No, other than my apartment is small and not as nice as Kira's place. We just naturally go to her place, but I'll bring her by my apartment this weekend. Give her the tour."

He cut into his steak and ate a piece. "This is delicious. Thanks."

Gideon nodded and cut into his steak. "You grew up in Willington?"

"I did. Born and raised."

"Why'd you move here?"

"Gideon," Kira said.

"What?" Gideon gave her an innocent look. "I'm making conversation. What's wrong with me getting to know your boyfriend?"

"There's nothing wrong with it, but can you make it less like a police interrogation?" she said.

Connor laughed. "It's fine, Kira. Really. I moved to Harmony Falls because I met Grant Henderson at a dental convention. We got along well, and I said yes when he asked me to open a practice with him here. The chance to be a partner in a dental firm before you're thirty-five is rare, and I didn't want to give up that opportunity. Even if it meant leaving Willington."

Gideon studied him before taking a bite of salad. "How do you like Harmony Falls?"

"It's very clean," Connor said.

Kira snorted laughter, and Connor grinned at her. "What? It is. In all seriousness, I like it here. The people are nice, and the town is quiet. I do a lot of running at the Falls Park, and it's surprisingly peaceful."

"Wait until tourist season starts," Kira said. "By the end of June, this place has swelled to three times its size. Those nice, quiet runs through Falls Park will be a thing of the past. None of the locals even go near the Falls or the park during tourist season. The campgrounds are overflowing with tourists."

"Which is desperately needed by local businesses," Gideon reminded her. "Those tourists bring a lot of money to the town and are why we can do things like build a shiny new sports complex."

"I know," Kira said. "I'm just saying – the town gets a little overrun by tourists."

Connor grinned at her. "I've lived here for two years, remember? I know what it's like."

"Right." She shook her head. "God, sorry. I haven't slept well the last few nights, so I'm not thinking straight."

"Have you dated anyone else since you moved here?" Gideon asked.

"Subject change," Kira said. "I saw on the Harmony Falls Daily website last night that they'll be showing that firebug movie you like so much at the Falls Theatre. Did you see that?"

Gideon's head shot up. "Are you serious?"

"Yes. You didn't see it?"

"Firebug movie?" Connor gave her a confused look.

"She means *Firefly*, and the movie is called *Serenity*, Kira," Gideon said. "How many times do I have to tell you that?"

"Maybe I've blocked it out because you made me watch the show and the movie so many times." Kira turned to Connor. "I was eight when the show premiered. Gideon was babysitting me while Mom and Dad were out, and he made me watch the show with him. I was traumatized."

"Please," Gideon said. "Nothing was traumatizing about the show."

"There was a bloody corpse hanging by its feet, Gideon!" Kira said.

"I would have thought Mal kicking Crow into the Serenity's running engine would have been more traumatizing," Connor said.

Kira stared at him as Gideon said, "Are you a fan?"

Connor grinned. "Does owning the series on DVD, the director's cut of the movie, all the Funko figurines and an autographed photo of Alan Tudyk make me a fan?"

"Holy shit," Gideon said. "When did you meet Alan Tudyk?"

"I went to Granite State Comicon a few years ago. He was one of the guest speakers. He and Nathan Fillion were there, but the lineup for Fillion was huge."

Gideon was staring wide-eyed at Connor. "What was Tudyk like?"

"Really cool guy, actually," Connor said. "I heard that he's going to be back there this year. I'd go again to meet him. I've been obsessed with the series since I was fifteen."

Gideon sat back in the chair. "I swear you're the only person in this town besides me who even has an inkling of an understanding of how fantastic the show was. Kira, when did you say they were showing Serenity?"

"In a couple of weeks, I think," Kira said.

"If you're not busy, we should grab tickets to the show," Gideon told Connor.

Kira's mouth dropped open as Connor nodded. "Yeah, I'd like that."

147

"Good. What's your favourite episode?"

"Well, I love 'Ariel', but I have to go with 'Our Mrs. Reynolds'," Connor said.

Gideon actually grinned like a schoolboy. "Me too! Here's the thing: people don't get just how incredible Christina Hendricks is in that episode. They totally wasted her in the 'Trash' episode, so people forget how good she was in episode six."

"Couldn't agree more," Connor said.

Kira stared in silent shock as Gideon and Connor talked animatedly about the stupid bug show. Holy crap. Gideon and Connor were...bonding.

CHAPTER 11

"Tell me, Ms. Walker, why exactly are you showing me the town's former firehouse station?" Mr. Stark studied the brick building in front of them.

"I know it's unconventional, but if you look inside, you'll see why I believe it'll work for your new office space." Considering she was so nervous she was close to vomiting, Kira was proud of how confident she sounded.

She'd shown Isaac Stark five commercial properties, but none worked. Bringing him to the city's former fire station had been a last-minute decision on her part, and she hoped like hell she could convince her client it would work for him.

He studied the building for a moment before glancing at his watch. Kira crossed her fingers and sent a prayer to every god she could think of as the silence stretched out.

"You have seven minutes to convince me, Ms. Walker."

"I'll only need five."

What almost looked like a smile flickered on his features before he nodded. "Lead the way."

She led him into the building. They were standing in the

vehicle bay area, and Mr. Stark studied the two large overhead doors and the staircase that led to the open upper area.

Kira took a deep breath. "You're looking for an open, airy building that promotes teamwork, right? This place is perfect for that. With a few renovations, you could have this place turned into the perfect open-concept office space."

His look suggested that he wasn't seeing her vision. She hurried on. "The overhead doors leading into the bay area could be replaced with windows, allowing plenty of light in. Along this wall," she pointed to the far left, "three offices could be built. The use of frosted glass would keep that open and airy feeling. The building is equipped with bathroom and shower facilities. You said you'll have fifteen employees working out of this building, correct?"

"To start," he said.

"Right here in the middle of the bay area, you could set up the working stations for your current staff, and there is plenty of room to add more stations as needed."

She walked toward the stairs, resting her hand on the railing. "Upstairs could function as your staff room – there's already a kitchen with a full-size stove and fridge. You mentioned wanting an area for your staff to test out video games, socialize, etc. Upstairs would be perfect. It's sectioned off from the main working area, but with the vault ceilings and the upstairs open to the downstairs, you still get that modern, open-air concept you're looking for."

Mr. Stark was staring at the metal pole that jutted down from the upstairs to the downstairs, and Kira said, "And you have a metal pole as a bonus."

A ghost of a smile crossed his lips. "I'm sure it would get plenty of use from employees."

"With a few renovations, this place could be exactly what you're looking for, Mr. Stark."

"A few renovations? I see your vision, Ms. Walker, but this place was last updated in what – the eighties? The entire interior would need gutting, and the renovations required would cost at least a few hundred grand."

"Yes, but the town has been trying to sell this place for five years. They're highly motivated to sell," Kira said. "I'm confident that we can make an offer to the town that will be well below your purchasing budget, and they'll accept."

He studied her silently, and she gave him a self-assured smile. "I've lived in Harmony Falls my entire life. My father was a contractor who built a good quarter of the homes here. I can set you up with the best and most competent trades-people in this town to do your renovations."

Mr. Stark continued to study her, and she resisted the urge to keep talking. She'd said everything she could to convince him. She'd have to hope it was enough. After what felt like an eternity, he nodded.

"You've convinced me, Ms. Walker. Come, we'll have lunch and discuss the offer you'll send on my behalf."

She wanted to shriek with joy.

She wanted to hug the tall and scary man standing before her.

She wanted to dance like a crazy person.

Instead, she smiled and said, "I know the perfect place for lunch, Mr. Stark."

***

Kira stared at the paperwork in front of her. Isaac Stark's signature was a dark slash, and she traced his name before sitting back in her chair. She'd done it. She'd made her first sale.

"Kira?"

She turned and smiled at the stylish, silver-haired woman in her cubicle. "Hi, Rose."

"Congratulations, honey. I knew you could do it. How do you feel?"

"I... it happened so fast," Kira said. "They accepted our initial offer in, like, half an hour. I did the paperwork, and Mr. Stark signed it and left me a money order for the down payment. I'm taking the paperwork over for the representative from the town to sign, and it's done. It happened so fast."

Rose laughed. "Yes, well, it doesn't always happen that way, so don't get used to it."

She squeezed Kira's shoulder. "I am so proud of you, Kira. I know your mom and dad would be too."

"Thank you, Rose." Kira picked up the papers and put them into an envelope. "I'm going to take these over now. I'll be back in an hour or so."

"Sounds good." Rose walked away, and Kira grabbed her purse and headed to her car. She was nearly vibrating with excitement, and she climbed into the car and shut the door before grabbing her phone. She had to share her news. She couldn't keep it inside a moment longer. She drummed her fingers on the steering wheel with nervous energy as the phone rang in her ear.

"Hey, Kira. What's up?"

"Connor, I did it!" Her voice was shrill with excitement. "I did it! I made my first sale!"

"That's fantastic. Congratulations, I knew you could do it." The warmth in his voice made her tingle all over.

"I can't believe it. I mean, I still need to take the paperwork over to the seller, but my client's offer was accepted right away – which *rarely* happens – and he already signed the paperwork and left me a money order for the down payment. As long as I don't get into an accident on the way to the seller's, it's a done deal."

He laughed. "Okay, let's not get into an accident."

"I won't, I just... I can't believe it. I won't lose my job, and I'll get paid!"

"Congratulations," he said again. "What did your brother and Grace say about your first sale?"

"Oh, um, I haven't told them yet," she said.

"You called me first?"

"Uh, yeah. Sorry, you're at work, and I guess I shouldn't have called. Shit, did I interrupt an appointment?"

"No, it's fine," he said. "I'm in between appointments. I'm glad you called me, Kira."

"I am too," she said.

There was a moment of silence, and then Connor said, "This calls for a celebration. If you're not busy, I'd like to take you for dinner tonight."

"I'd love that," Kira said.

"Perfect. I'll pick you up at seven."

"HOPEFULLY, YOU LIKE THIS PLACE." CONNOR PULLED INTO THE parking lot of the Urban Cuisine and parked the car.

"It's my favourite restaurant," Kira said. "So, good choice."

She climbed out of the car and smoothed her dress as Connor shut his door and locked the car. The Urban Cuisine was one of three casual dining restaurants in Harmony Falls.

It had a modern and eclectic style, and the food was – in a word – delicious.

Connor took her hand, and she realized she was beginning to crave even that simple touch from him. He led her into the restaurant and smiled at the hostess. "We have a reservation under MacMillan."

The pretty blonde studied the screen in front of her before tapping a few buttons. "Of course. Right this way, please."

They followed her through the bar section and into the restaurant area. It was busy, and she held tight to Connor's hand as they weaved their way past the booths and tables toward one of the tables at the back of the restaurant.

Her mouth dropped open when Connor stepped to the side, and she saw the people sitting at the table. Gideon was sitting at one end of the table, with Preacher on his right and Ray and Rose on his left. Addison and Harrison sat beside them, and Grace sat beside Preacher.

"Connor, what… did you do this?"

He grinned boyishly at her and squeezed her hand. "I wanted to make this a real celebration."

"Oh my gosh, this is… this is so nice." Her throat was burning, and her eyes were watering. She stood on her tiptoes and kissed his cheek. "Thank you so much."

He cupped her face and gave her a real kiss, one that made her mouth tingle and her pulse race. "You're welcome, little Kira. But Grace had a big part in helping me organize everything."

For a moment, she was tempted to wave at everyone and then drag Connor back to his car. The urge to have him alone, to ask him to drive them home so he could take her upstairs to her bedroom and do all the delicious things to her she couldn't seem to stop dreaming about, was almost too much to resist.

Before she could act on that madness, her brother stood before them. Connor let go of her hand, and Gideon swept her into a bone-crushing hug.

"Congratulations, Kira. I'm really proud of you." He kissed her cheek before setting her back on her feet.

"Thank you, Gideon." She smiled at him. "I wish Mom and Dad could have been here."

A flicker of sorrow crossed his face. "Me too, kid. Me too."

She squeezed his hand and blinked back the tears before following Connor to the empty seats beside Grace. Gracie stood and hugged her hard. "Good job, honey."

"Thanks, Gracie. And thank you for helping Connor arrange this." Kira kissed Grace's cheek.

She and Connor sat down, and Preacher leaned forward to give her a rare grin. "Congrats, kid."

"Thanks, Preacher. And thanks for coming tonight."

"Wouldn't miss it." He leaned back in his chair and studied Connor. Connor held out his hand, and Preacher shook it.

"I'm Connor MacMillan."

"Preacher."

"Nice to meet you," Connor said.

"You too." Preacher looked like he would say something else, and Kira held her breath. There was no telling what the tattoo artist would say. In some ways, he seemed even more protective of her than her actual brother.

He studied Connor for a few seconds more. "Be good to her."

"I will," Connor said.

"You better." Preacher took a drink of beer before turning away.

Connor leaned down and put his mouth to her ear. "Would you think less of me if I said I was just a tiny bit afraid of the giant tattooed guy?"

She giggled and shook her head, and Connor pressed a kiss against her temple. Addison reached across the table and took her hand. "Congratulations, Kira. Harrison and I are so proud of you. Aren't we, Harrison?"

"Sure are, babe." Harrison, who was tall and on the thin side with blond hair and dark blue eyes, smiled at Kira. "If your client needs a lawyer, you'll give him my name, right?"

"Yeah, of course," Kira said. "But I thought you were already pretty busy at work."

Harrison gave her an easy grin. "A lawyer can never have too many clients, Kira."

The server appeared and poured some wine into her glass and Connor's. "I'll return to take your order in a few minutes."

Addison's phone rang, and she pulled it from her purse. She answered it and said, "Hold on a minute."

She turned the screen toward Kira, and Kira made a soft sound of happiness. "Harper!"

Harper's smiling face filled Addison's phone screen. "Congratulations, honey! I'm so proud of you."

"Thanks, Harper." Kira took the phone from Addison. "How are you?"

"I'm good," Harper replied. "I'm sorry I couldn't be there in person tonight to celebrate with you."

"That's all right," Kira said. "This is mostly acceptable."

Harper laughed and blew a kiss at her. "I am very proud of you, honey."

"Thank you! Oh, I, um, want you to meet my boyfriend, Connor," Kira said.

No doubt Addie had told Harper all about the fake relationship, but it would look rude if Kira didn't introduce them. She tilted the phone so Harper could see Connor. "Harper, this is Connor. Connor, this is my other bestie, Harper."

"Nice to meet you," Connor said.

"You as well." Harper smiled at him. "I hear you're an excellent dentist and an even better ball player."

Connor gave her a modest grin. "I do my best."

Harper laughed, and Kira turned the phone back to face just her. "How's New York?"

"It's good. Listen, I'll call you next week, and we'll get completely caught up, but right now, I'll let you go so you can enjoy your special night. Love you, Kira!"

"Love you too, Harper." Kira made a kissy face at Harper before handing Addie back her phone.

Addie smiled at Harper. "I'll call you later."

She tucked her phone away, and Ray tapped his glass with his knife. "I'd like to make a toast."

As Ray began to speak, Kira smiled up at Connor. He returned her smile before putting his arm around the back of her chair. She leaned against him, warmth and happiness infusing her entire body.

CONNOR MADE HIS WAY THROUGH THE CROWDED BAR SECTION toward the bathrooms. It had been almost three hours, and – he grinned a little – Kira was starting to show the effects of the wine she had drunk with dinner. She wasn't exactly drunk, but she was definitely tipsy, and he'd quickly realized that he found a tipsy Kira incredibly adorable.

She and Addison had left to use the bathroom just shortly before he did, and his entire body stiffened when he realized that not only were Daniel and his friend Brad here at the restaurant, but Kira and Addison were with them.

Trying to keep his cool, he quickly joined them at the bar just as Daniel made a loud shout and picked up Kira. He hugged her hard, and Connor's hot jealousy abated a little when Kira immediately pushed on his shoulders and wiggled out of Daniel's grip. She backed up a few steps, weaving just the littlest bit, as Daniel grinned down at her.

"Congratulations, doll. I'm so proud of you."

"Thanks, Daniel," Kira said.

Connor put his arm around her waist and tugged her back against him. "Hey, honey."

"Hi." She gave him a sweet smile, and he knew he had a smug grin on his face when she leaned against him instead of trying to escape his grip.

"Hey, doc." Daniel picked up a shot and held it out to Kira. "Just in time to help us do celebratory shots."

"Oh, no, thank you," Kira said. "I've already had enough to drink."

"C'mon, you gotta do one. This is your big moment." Daniel held out another shot to Addison. "Addie, you do one too."

"Uh, no way," Addison said. "The last time I did shots with you, I ended up puking all night."

Daniel laughed and held the shot to Connor. "Doc?"

"No, thanks."

Daniel shrugged and handed one shot to Brad before

drinking the other. He winced and clapped Brad on the back. "Damn, man, what was in that?"

"You don't want to know," the redhead mumbled. He was drunk and leaned against the bar before squinting at Addison. "Hey, sexy."

"Shut up, idiot." Daniel punched him in the shoulder. "That's my sister, remember?"

Addison rolled her eyes before taking Kira's hand. "C'mon, let's go back to the table."

"Are you coming, Connor?" Kira asked when he let her go.

"In a minute," he said. "I just need to use the bathroom."

"Okay." She and Addie left, and Connor stared at Daniel.

The firefighter grinned at him. "What's up, doc?"

Before Connor could reply, Daniel said, "I know you and Kira are dating now, but I've known her for a long time. We have a special relationship that a Willington boy like you wouldn't understand."

"You're drunk, Daniel. Go home and sleep it off."

Daniel shrugged again. "All I'm saying is that you don't know Kira the way you think you do. She might be a bit infatuated with you, but when the novelty wears off... she'll come back to what she wants. What she'll always want."

Connor bit back his urge to punch Daniel in the face. The firefighter was drunk off his ass and probably wouldn't even remember the conversation tomorrow.

He gave him a tight grin and started toward the bathroom. "Have a good night, Daniel."

"You too, doc."

CONNOR HELPED KIRA UP THE PORCH STAIRS. SHE WAS ONLY weaving a little, and he probably didn't need to keep his arm around her waist, but she wasn't objecting to his touch, and he liked the feel of her slender body against his.

She giggled and dug her keys out of her purse when they stopped in front of the door. "Oh man, my head is a little foggy."

He laughed and took the keys from her before opening the door. "You need to drink some water and go straight to bed."

She giggled again and draped her arms around his shoulders before – fuck – pressing her soft lips against his throat. "Why don't you come in with me?"

"Not a good idea." His hands cupped her hips when she pressed her pelvis against him.

"I think it's a fine idea," she whispered before nipping at his throat. "Come inside, Connor."

"You don't want to have sex with me," he said. "You're saving yourself for…"

He couldn't bring himself even to say Daniel's name.

She traced one finger over his chest. "Here's the thing… I thought it would be a good idea for me to practice some other stuff, too. I mean, I sucked bad at kissing, right? Which means I probably suck at other sex-related things. You could give me all sorts of lessons that don't end in sex, right?"

"Yeah," he said hoarsely.

"So," she kissed his throat again, "why don't you come in and teach me some… stuff."

"I can't," he said. "You're drunk, Kira."

"I'm not drunk," she said. "I'm a little tipsy."

He grabbed her hands when she tried to slide them under his shirt. "Too tipsy for me to come in."

"You don't want me," she sighed.

"Trust me, I want you. Enough that I'm thinking this crazy idea of lessons is a good one."

Her face lit up, and she gave him a sweet little smile. "It's the best idea ever."

He made a low laugh before catching her wandering hands again. "Tomorrow night, if you still think this is a good idea, I'll come by and give you a lesson. Deal?"

Shit. What was he doing? This was so fucking wrong. But he'd spent the last week masturbating every single night to thoughts of Kira. The idea that she might let him have a taste of her sweet pussy or teach her how to blow him was impossible to resist.

They knew what was happening wasn't real, but did that mean they couldn't have a little fun together? They were attracted to each other and had chemistry, and Kira asked him to help her. It was the gentlemanly thing to do, right?

She gave him a cute little pout. "You could spend the night with me. It's late, and you're probably too tired to drive home. I have a queen-sized bed. There's plenty of space for both of us, and I promise I'll be a good girl."

His cock pressed against his jeans. He had plenty of ideas of how Kira could be a good girl, all involving her naked.

"No, honey, we can't. Not tonight." He lifted her hands to his mouth and kissed her knuckles. "We'll talk tomorrow night, okay."

"Okay," she sighed. "I'll be at your ball game tomorrow."

Happiness flickered through him. "You will?"

"Of course," she said. "Girls go to their fake boyfriend's baseball games. I'm pretty sure that's a rule in the fake relationship handbook. Besides, I saw on the online schedule

161

that you're playing the Harmony Falls Flames again, and I wanna watch you kick Daniel's ass for a second time."

She giggled until she snorted, and he laughed and kissed her forehead. "Go drink some water and go to bed."

"Yes, sir," she said. "See you at the game tomorrow, and then after that's over, you're gonna come back here, and I'm gonna suck on your penis."

He laughed again, and she put one hand on her hip and cocked her head at him. "I'm good at the sexy talk, right?"

"So good." He gave her a gentle push toward the door. "Good night, Kira."

"Night, Connor."

CHAPTER 12

"What are your plans for tonight, ladies?" Grace took a drink from her water bottle before shifting on the bleachers.

"Harrison is working," Addison said. "It's the third Saturday in a row. We were supposed to be finalizing the seating chart for the reception, but Harrison texted me earlier and said he won't be finished until at least eleven."

She picked off some lint from her dark blue pencil skirt. "He said we could do it tomorrow, but I was hoping to finish it tonight."

"Sorry, sweetie," Grace said. "I wish I could help you with it."

"Oh, you and Kira have been super helpful, and I really appreciate it," Addie said.

Grace nudged Kira. "What about you?"

Kira forced herself to stop staring at the way Connor's back muscles moved as he swung the bat in a gentle arc. "Connor's coming by."

"Really?" Grace said.

"Yes. We're dating. It would be weird if we didn't spend Saturday night together."

"Fake dating," Grace said in a low voice.

"Yes, but there's still a lot we need to know about each other if I'm going to be an effective girlfriend at his cousin's wedding," Kira said.

"Does Kira sound like she's being entirely truthful to you, Addie?" Grace asked.

"Nope," Addie said.

"Shh," Kira said. "Connor's about to bat."

She watched as Connor stepped into the batter's box, her mouth watering a little at the way his track pants clung to his ass and thighs. Maybe, if she were really lucky tonight, she'd be seeing that ass naked and in her bed.

She watched as Connor held the bat over his shoulder, digging his cleats into the dirt and eyeing Daniel closely. Daniel threw the ball, and Kira gasped and jumped to her feet when Connor had to drop to the ground to avoid being hit in the head by the baseball.

She wanted to shout in outrage at Daniel but squashed the impulse as Connor climbed to his feet. He dusted off his track pants as the catcher chased down the ball and threw it back to Daniel.

The firefighter gave Connor an easy grin and called, "Sorry about that, doc. Went a little high on that one."

Connor just nodded and raised his bat again. Kira returned to her seat, sudden tension eating at her belly. Daniel wasn't deliberately trying to hit Connor, was he? Was he angry or jealous that Connor was dating her?

Don't be stupid, Kira. You want Daniel to be jealous, but he isn't. It's time to face the facts. He doesn't give a crap that you're dating Connor. He's just pissed that Connor is a better ball player than he is.

She jumped to her feet when Daniel threw another wild ball. This time, Connor wasn't quick enough to avoid it. It slammed into his right knee, and she made a harsh gasp of fear when Connor collapsed. He held his knee, his face the proverbial white as a sheet, as he rolled back and forth on the ground.

She ran down the bleachers, Grace and Addie right behind her, but one of Connor's team members stopped her before she could run past the chain link fence.

"He's my boyfriend!" she snapped at him.

"I know," the man said, "but just give Jack a minute to look at him."

She waited impatiently as Jack crouched beside Connor and spoke quietly to him. She couldn't hear what he said, but Connor nodded and sat up. Jack reached for his knee, and Connor grimaced and shook his head.

A crowd of players from both the Healers team and the Flames team were gathering around home plate, and Kira made a noise of frustration when they blocked Connor from her view.

"Just give him a minute," the man holding her back repeated.

He glanced at Grace and Addie and attempted to explain. "Some guys don't like their woman to see them in that much pain, you know?"

Grace put her arm around Kira's shoulders. "He'll be okay, Kira."

She nodded distractedly. Her gaze fell on Daniel. He and Brad were standing a little apart from the others, and she tore free from Gracie, darted around the Healers player, and marched across the diamond to him.

He smiled at her. "Hey, doll."

"Don't call me that," she said. "I am not a doll."

He blinked at her, and she moved closer until she stood directly before him. "Did you do that on purpose?"

"What?" Daniel said.

"Did you hit Connor with the ball on purpose," she said through gritted teeth.

"Of course not, doll – Kira."

He spoke sincerely, but she had known Daniel a long time and the way his gaze shifted to the left and back made her see red.

"You asshole! You did do it on purpose. Why? Are you upset that Connor is more of a man than you?"

Confusion crossed Daniel's face. "Kira, what is going on with you? I didn't mean to hit your man, all right? It was an accident. It happens sometimes. My arm is a little tired, and –"

"Bullshit," Kira spat. She wanted to slam her palm into Daniel's chest but resisted. "You did it on purpose, Daniel Moore, because Connor is a better ball player than you, and you know it."

"You gonna let her talk to you that way, dude?" Brad said.

"Shut up, Brad," Daniel said. He tried to take Kira's hand, and she yanked it out of his grasp. "Kira, I didn't do it on purpose, okay? It was an accident."

"You're lying," she said.

"No, you're upset and only think I'm lying," Daniel said. "I promise you I didn't."

"Stop it," she said. "Just stop –"

"Kira."

Connor's low voice made her whirl around. He was standing up, being supported on one side by Jack, and she ran over to him, touching his chest and then his face gently.

"Connor, honey, are you okay?"

He nodded even though his face twisted with pain. "I'm all right. Just need to walk it off. Isn't that right, Jack?"

"No, you need to get off it and put some ice on that knee," Jack said. "Immediately."

Kira made a low sound of dismay when Connor, pain lines etched around his mouth, limped his way to the bench.

"Connor, maybe you should go to the hospital," she said.

He shook his head. "Nah, it'll be fine."

"That knee is already sore," she said. "If it was already injured, then -"

"I said it's fine, Kira." He collapsed on the bench before closing his eyes and taking a deep breath. "I'm sorry. I didn't mean to snap. But," he lowered his voice, "it'll be fine. Trust me. The ball didn't hit me that hard, all right? I have a bad knee, and the ball happened to hit it wrong. It'll be back to normal in the morning."

She gave him a doubtful look as Daniel joined them. He held his hand out to Connor. "Man, I'm sorry. I didn't mean to do that."

"Go away, Daniel," Kira said.

"It's all right, Kira." Connor shook Daniel's hand. "Appreciate the apology."

"Kira, can I talk to you for a second?" Daniel said.

"No," Kira replied. "I'm busy. I'll call you later."

Daniel looked like he would reply, but the umpire shouted, "Time's wasting. Let's get back to it."

"Sorry again, doc." Daniel jogged back to the pitcher's mound.

Jack appeared with ice wrapped in a towel and plopped it down on Connor's knee. He winced but gave the man a nod of thanks.

"Put your foot up on the bench," Jack said.

Connor swung his leg up obediently, balancing the ice pack on his knee and smiled at Kira. "I'm good, but I won't be playing. You don't need to stick around and watch the game."

She frowned, but before she could reply, Jack touched her arm. "The game's starting. You need to go back to the bleachers."

She wanted to sit on the bench with Connor and badger him into going to the hospital. Instead, she made herself smile at him and said, "I'm sticking around. I'll see you after the game."

"Yeah, sure." Connor's voice was distracted, and the way he grimaced when he shifted the ice pack suggested he was in more pain than he would admit.

Worry gnawing at her belly, Kira headed back to the bleachers.

Kira stared at Connor, wondering if her hurt was written across her face. "You don't want me to come back to your place and help you?"

She was standing next to him in the parking lot of the sports complex. The game ended almost half an hour ago, and most players were long gone. After it took nearly twenty minutes for Connor to limp his way to his car, Kira was even more determined that, at the very least, she should go back to his apartment and help him somehow.

"No, it's not that. Honestly, I don't need help. My knee is already feeling better," Connor said.

"Is it?" She studied how he stood, barely putting any weight on his right leg. "Because it doesn't look like it is."

"It is," he insisted. "But it is sore, and I'm tired and won't be good company tonight."

"I don't mind," she said. "I can make you something to eat and bring you ice packs. Whatever you need."

"No, really, it's good," he said. "It's Saturday night. You should go and have fun with Grace and Addison."

"I don't want to," she said. "I want to go home with you and make sure you're okay. Just give me your address, and I'll meet you there, all right?"

"I said no," he said.

This time, she was sure he could see the hurt on her face.

He grimaced and squeezed her hand. "I'm sorry. Look, I'm not the most fun guy to be around when I'm in pain. I'll probably take some Tylenol and go to bed early. I appreciate the offer, but I've been through this before, and it'll be fine in the morning. I'll text you tomorrow, okay?"

"Yeah, okay. Bye, Connor." She knew when to admit defeat.

He squeezed her hand again before carefully easing behind the wheel. She watched as he started the car and then waved goodbye. His face was a solid block of pain as he drove away.

"I KNOW YOU'RE ANGRY, BUT I DON'T THINK MY BROTHER DID it intentionally." Addie plopped down on the couch next to

Kira and patted her leg. "Daniel's selfish, but he's not deliberately malicious or cruel."

Kira sighed. "Yeah, I know. I was just pissed at him. I'll text him tomorrow."

"Maybe he really is jealous." Grace was sitting in one of the recliners. "Maybe he didn't mean to do it on purpose per se but ended up taking out that jealousy on Connor in some sort of macho bullshit way."

"That does kinda sound like Daniel," Addie said.

"Yeah, maybe." Kira glanced at her phone again. Maybe she should text Connor, just to make sure he was okay. She'd already texted him once to see if he made it home, and he had replied, but it'd been half an hour. Maybe he was reconsidering his decision to be alone. She could confirm –

"Kira!"

"What?" She stared at Grace.

"I said that you didn't seem that happy about Daniel's potential jealousy," Grace said.

"I'm worried about Connor," Kira replied. "I think he was in more pain than he let on. Besides, if Daniel shows jealousy by trying to hurt Connor, then I don't want him to be jealous. I want him to leave us alone."

She didn't miss the way Gracie glanced at Addie. Kira frowned at her. "What?"

"What were you and Connor going to do tonight if he hadn't gotten hurt?" Addie asked.

Kira blushed. "I told you, get to know each other better."

"Oh yeah? By talking or kissing?" Addie said.

Her face went even hotter. "Does it matter?"

Grace took a swig of beer. "Have you and Connor had sex, Kira?"

"What? Of course, we haven't. You know this isn't real."

"We know it isn't," Grace pointed to herself and Addie, "but we're starting to wonder if you and Connor do."

"What's that supposed to mean?"

"It means," Addie gave her a delicate look, "that you and Connor are acting like a real couple."

"That's the point," Kira said.

"You're a little too good at it, if you know what I mean," Grace said.

"No, I don't think I do," Kira replied.

"Look, you told us that Connor doesn't like PDAs, right?" Grace said.

"He doesn't."

"Then why can't he seem to stop touching you whenever you're in public?" Addie said.

"I – well, because he's trying to help me make Daniel jealous," Kira said. "He's doing what I asked him to do."

"Yeah, well," Grace drank more beer, "then Connor deserves an Oscar for his performance because the possessive way he gets around you is more than convincing."

Kira didn't reply, and Addie touched her leg. "It's not a bad thing if you're sleeping with Connor, honey."

"We're not," Kira said. "We're not, but we..."

"Ooh, girl, no stopping now." Grace swung her legs over the recliner. "Not when it's just starting to get good."

"We've done some... stuff."

"What kind of stuff? Be specific, Kira. Specificity is important." Grace grinned at her.

"He's seen me without my, um, shirt and bra, and he's," Kira made a motion toward her tits, "done stuff to me, here."

"How was it?" Addie asked.

"Amazing," Kira said. "He's not just good at kissing."

"Did he make you come?" Grace asked.

"Grace Louella Larken!"

Grace made a face. "Ugh...Louella. God, my parents hate me."

Addie giggled. "It could be worse. My middle name is Mabel, for God's sake."

Grace grinned at her before wiggling her eyebrows at Kira. "Did he, babe?"

"No, we haven't. I mean... we just kind of fooled around a little."

"But you want to do more," Grace said.

Shit. She hated how well Gracie knew her. "Yes. Okay? Yes. Last night, I asked him to come in and show me some other stuff. He said no because I was tipsy but said he would come over if I were still interested tonight. I've decided I'll have a better chance with Daniel if I know some sex stuff. Like, not necessarily sex, but you know..."

"Handies and blowies?" Grace made the universal wanking off sign in front of her mouth as her tongue pushed against her cheek.

"Gross, Gracie." Kira tried to scowl at her, but a giggle slipped out.

"Is blowie even a sex term for fellatio?" Addison said.

Grace shrugged. "I dunno, but it's better than saying - hey, Connor, will you give me a lesson on fellatio? I would like to learn how to fellate like a fornicating fool."

Kira burst into laughter, and even Addie giggled. "You're nuts, Gracie."

"Yep," Gracie said solemnly. "Okay, let's recap. Kira and Connor are in a fakey-fake relationship. Dr. 'I Don't Like PDAs' Connor puts on an Oscar-worthy perfor-mance as her boyfriend, complete with the most public displays of PDAs I've ever witnessed. Kira is asking him for not-quite-sex lessons to improve her chances with Daniel, even though she suddenly doesn't seem to care all that much that Daniel might be jealous. Are we all caught up?"

"I care," Kira protested. "I love Daniel."

"Do you, though?" Grace said.

"I do," Kira insisted. "I just – I'm attracted to Connor, and he's attracted to me and with as much sex experience as Daniel has -"

"Gross." Addie drained her wine glass.

"I just think it would be the smart idea not to go into this completely naïve to sex. I'm not going to give up my virginity or anything to Connor, but there's no harm in fooling around a bit. We both know what this is."

"Are you sure? Because this sounds like a swift way to complicate things," Grace said.

"It isn't," Kira said. "We're both adults, and why shouldn't I have a little fun with him? I'm not going to have sex with him."

"You thinking what I'm thinking?" Grace said to Addie.

"Me thinks the lady doth protest too much," Addie said.

"Fuckin A, Addie. Fuckin' A." Grace raised her beer bottle to Addie in a salute before taking another swig.

"I'm not having sex with him," Kira repeated. "But, even if I, for some weird reason, decided to have sex with Connor, what's the big deal? You're always telling me that a woman's virginity is nothing special, Gracie."

"And you're always telling me it is," Grace said.

Kira just shrugged. "Maybe I'm changing my mind."

"Which is your right and we will support you no matter who you choose to be your first banging partner," Grace said. "But that said, think carefully about whether this infatuation with Connor is worth giving up something you've held on to for a deliberate reason."

"You don't think having sex with Connor is the right decision?"

"I didn't say that," Gracie replied. "Ultimately, it is your choice who you sleep with for the first time. But remember that Connor isn't interested in a relationship. I don't want you getting hurt, honey."

"I won't," Kira said. "I know this is fake, and besides, my feelings for Connor are just lust. But, like Addie said before, maybe it isn't such a good idea to save yourself for just one person. Why shouldn't I do a little tasting off the menu? Right, Addie?"

"Do as I say and not as I do," Addie said.

"So, you regret that Harrison is the only guy you've slept with?" Kira said.

Addie hesitated. "I don't – I mean, obviously, I love Harrison and want to spend the rest of my life with him, but there might be a little bit of – not regret – but more curiosity about what other guys may or may not be like in bed."

"You ready to share who you have a dirty little crush on yet, Addie-pants?" Grace said with a grin.

Addison pulled at the pearls around her neck. "I already told you, no one in particular."

"Okay, Addie, whatever you say." Grace pointed her beer bottle at Kira. "Honey, we love you and want what's best for you. Just make sure you think long and hard about your decisions regarding Connor, okay?"

"I will," Kira said. "Stop worrying, Gracie. I don't think Connor is falling for me or something like that. He wouldn't even let me help him tonight. The only reason we were going to hang out tonight was because of the sex stuff. He didn't want me anywhere near him once he knew that was off the table. Those aren't the actions of a guy crushing on a girl."

"Maybe," Addison said. "Or maybe he just didn't want you to see him in pain. It's like the guy at the game said. Some guys are super weird about women seeing them in pain. Makes them think they've lost their man card or something."

Addison's phone buzzed, and she checked it before bouncing to her feet. "I have to go. My mom just got a migraine, and Dad is at his woodworking club. If she needs to go to the hospital, I'll need to drive her."

"Your poor mom," Kira said. "Give her our love."

"I will." Addie gave them a distracted smile before leaving. The front door slammed, and Grace gave Kira another shrewd look.

"Now that it's just you and me, is there anything else you want to say?"

"Nope," Kira said. "I don't have feelings for Connor, and he doesn't have feelings for me."

Grace drank the last of her beer. "If you say so, Kira-bear."

CHAPTER 13

S hit. He was in trouble. He knew it even before he was fully awake. Knew it even before he threw the covers back and saw the swollen purple mess that used to be his right knee.

He sat up, groaning loudly when it sent fire radiating from his knee to his toes. He grabbed the pill bottle from his nightstand and muttered a curse. He'd taken the last leftover Percocet last night. It had done a great job of dulling the pain and allowing him to get some sleep, but now the agony had roared back to life, even worse than last night. Hell, had he been in this much pain since the surgery?

Shit. Double fucking shit.

Panic surged through him. What if he'd torn the ligaments again? What if he'd destroyed his knee, and this time, they couldn't put him back together again like Humpty Dumpty? He could forget about even playing baseball recreationally. Hell, he'd be fucking lucky if he didn't have to use a cane for the rest of his life.

The panic made the pain worse - made his knee throb

and pulse until he thought he might puke. He leaned back against the headboard, taking shallow breaths and waiting for the churning in his guts to settle.

Fuck, he really needed to take a piss. Moving slowly and carefully, holding his right leg steady with both hands just below his knee, he swung his legs over the side of the bed. Just bending his knee sent fresh new agony through his leg up to his hip, and he grabbed the pillow and buried his face in it to muffle his scream of pain.

Sweating profusely and groaning under his breath, he lifted his right leg back onto the bed before reaching with a shaking hand for the bottle of Tylenol. He took four, chasing them down with a sip of water. The Tylenol might, if he was lucky, dull the pain enough for him to at least not scream when he bent his knee, but he couldn't walk on it. He knew that without a doubt.

He needed to get his ass to the hospital and find out how much damage that asshole Daniel had done to him.

It wasn't done on purpose.

No, maybe not, but he wasn't exactly feeling charitable this morning. Because of Daniel, the likelihood of him pissing his own damn bed was high.

He grabbed his phone and then hesitated. Who the fuck could he call? If he called his parents, it would take them at least forty minutes to an hour to get here and forgetting his need to take a piss, Connor wasn't sure he could stand the pain for that long. If he didn't get to the hospital soon and get some goddamn pain medication, he'd go insane.

Call Kira.

He took a deep breath and stared at his knee. He was wearing just a pair of boxers, and even the thought of trying to get pants on past his swollen, angry knee made him want to vomit. Which meant that if he called Kira, she'd see his knee and the scars from his surgery. She'd start asking questions and –

Who fucking cares! The alternative is calling your parents and then lying in a pool of pure agony and your own piss while you wait for them to show up. Is that what you want?

Nope. Definitely not. And if Connor was being truthful, he wanted to call Kira. Wanted the comfort of her soft voice and hands. Even if it meant having to tell her about the accident and the surgery.

His fingers trembling, he hit her number. She answered after only one ring, her voice a bit raspy. "Hey, Connor."

"Hey, did I wake you?"

"No, I'm an early riser, even on the weekends. How's your knee?"

"Uh, not great. I can't get out of bed or walk on it. I hate to ask, but do you think you could pop by and…"

"Text me your address. I'll be right over."

"Thanks, Kira."

"Wait, if you can't walk… how will I get into your apartment?" she said.

"Shit. I don't suppose you're good at picking locks, huh?"

"Nope. But do you have a building supervisor or manager in the apartment building? Maybe you could text them and have them open the door for me?"

"You're brilliant." He shifted on the bed, grunting with pain.

"You okay?"

"Yeah. I'll text Arnold and have him meet you downstairs in the lobby. Okay?"

"Text me your address, and I'll be there in about ten," she said.

———

SHE WAS THERE IN THIRTEEN MINUTES. CONNOR HEARD HIS front door open, and he could have wept with relief when Kira said. "Thank you so much, Arnold. It was very nice to meet you."

The door shut, and she called his name. "Connor?"

"Hey," he shouted. "The bedroom is the last door on the left."

The door opened ten seconds later, and Kira and Gideon walked into the room. Kira crossed the room and stared in horror at his knee. "Oh, Connor."

"It's not as bad as it looks," he said.

"I call bullshit on that," Gideon said.

"Hey, Gideon," Connor said.

"I called Gideon and asked him to meet me here because I don't think I'm strong enough to help support you," Kira said. "Is that okay?"

"Yeah, that was a good idea." Shit, she was fucking brilliant. "Not to be rude, but I need to use the bathroom."

"Right, of course." She stepped back. "Gideon, can you help him?"

"Sure." Gideon stepped closer to the bed and studied his knee. "Christ, that looks fucking painful. You going to pass out on me when I get you standing?"

"No," Connor said.

"You sure?"

"Mostly. But I am going to piss the damn bed in about two minutes."

"Well, in that case," Gideon said, "let's get your ass to the bathroom."

"Hey, remember last night when I was crouching over your body and telling you that you needed to go to the hospital? Is this a good time to tell you I told you so?" Jack ducked past the curtain in the emergency room and grinned at Connor.

Connor grimaced. "Please tell me I'm not your patient."

"You bet your sweet dentist ass you are," Jack replied with another grin. He held his hand out to Kira. "We haven't formally met. Jack Reed."

"Kira Walker. I'm Connor's girlfriend." She probably didn't need to say that, but she *liked* saying it. If she hadn't been so freaked out about Connor's knee, she might have stopped to wonder why she liked it so much.

"Nice to meet you, Kira." Jack shook her hand before grabbing the chart from the end of Connor's bed. "We'll do an X-ray first to ensure there isn't a fracture or dislocation, and then we'll go from there."

He eyed Connor's swollen knee. "Talk to me about your knee history."

Connor glanced at Kira, and for a moment, she was sure he would ask her to leave. To her relief, he reached for her hand instead.

"Just before I graduated high school, I was on a quad with friends. I had an accident, and I tore my ACL, MCL and meniscus."

Connor's voice was flat, but she could see how tense his body was, feel that tension leaking out from his hand into hers.

"What grade were the tears?" Jack's voice had lost all of its previous good humour.

"Grade three tears on both the MCL and the meniscus."

"Okay." Jack bent over the bed and studied Connor's knee. "Arthroscopic?"

Connor nodded. "Yeah, all in one shot. They repaired the MCL and meniscus and reconstructed the ACL."

"I'm assuming it was an autograft?" Jack said.

"Yes. The surgeon said it would significantly decrease the risk of re-rupture." Connor's hand squeezed down on hers briefly, and he swallowed hard. "But I know the risk of re-rupture can increase in your thirties."

"Usually closer to thirty-five." Jack was studying his chart again. "Did they use hamstring or patella for the reconstruction?"

"Patella," Connor said.

Kira listened quietly. They could have been talking Greek for all she understood.

"Okay. X-ray today, and we'll book you for an MRI tomorrow or Tuesday. That will tell us if you've re-ruptured the ACL or torn the MCL or PCL."

"Do you think that's what I've done?" Connor's voice was like broken glass on gravel.

"We really won't know without the MRI," Jack said. "Sorry, Connor. In the meantime, you know the drill… keep your knee elevated, ice it, and no weight on it."

"I've got an extraction tomorrow, a root canal and -"

Jack shook his head. "You need to take the week off from work."

"Jack -"

"Nope," Jack said. "No arguing. You don't want to worsen it if you have re-torn or re-ruptured something. Right?"

"Yeah."

"Good. How's your pain level? On a scale of one to ten?"

"Seven," Connor said.

Jack turned to Kira. "You know him better than me. What's his actual pain level?"

"Nine, closer to ten," Kira said.

"Kira." Connor gave her a pointed look.

"He couldn't walk on it this morning," she said. "I had to get my brother to come over and practically carry him to the bathroom and then to the car just to get him here. He was pale and shaking, and I thought he might throw up."

"Okay," Jack said. "We'll send you home with a knee brace to keep it stable while waiting for the MRI. I'll write you a prescription for pain meds and an anti-inflammatory. But we'll also give you a shot here at the hospital that'll significantly reduce your pain level. Are you staying with Kira while you recuperate?"

"Oh, um…"

Connor looked like a deer in the headlights.

"He is," Kira said. "I have a bathroom and a guest room on the main floor, so he won't need to navigate any stairs."

"Perfect," Jack said. "It's slow at the moment, so it shouldn't take long to get you the X-ray. Hopefully, we'll have you doped up and out of here in the next few hours."

He wrote something on Connor's chart before smiling at Kira. "The shot we give him today will last twelve hours, but if you can get the prescription filled today, he can have two pills around eleven tonight, all right?"

Kira nodded. "Yes. I'll stop at Walgreens and get it filled."

"Good." Jack turned to Connor. "The shot's going to make you… loopy. Don't be an idiot, and try to get out of bed on your own. Got it?"

"Yeah," Connor said.

Jack grinned at Kira. "It's well known that doctors make

the worst patients. If he gives you any grief, call me, and I'll come over and talk with him."

Kira smiled at the doctor. He looked to be in his forties and handsome with his dark hair, dark eyes, and tall, lean body. "I appreciate that, Dr. Reed. Thank you."

"Call me Jack," he said. "Connor, I'll see you before you get discharged."

"Thanks, Jack," Connor said.

Jack left, and Kira gave Connor a tentative smile. He studied her without speaking, and she squeezed his hand. "Do you want me to ask them if you can have the shot before the X-ray?"

He shook his head. "No, I took some Tylenol before I called you. It's helped a little."

She gave him a skeptical look that he ignored. He lowered his voice. "I appreciate you telling Jack I could stay with you, but I'm not expecting you to play nursemaid. If you could help me back to my apartment, I'll be fine to -"

"No, you won't be," she said. "You heard what Jack said. You need to keep it up and rest and ice it. You need my help, Connor."

"I don't want to inconvenience you."

"You're not," she said. "I am happy to help. Staying at my place will make it easier for both of us. We'll get you back to my place, and once you're settled, I'll get your prescription filled and grab some clothes and toiletries from your place."

"Thank you, Kira." He gave her a grateful look. "I really appreciate it."

"Of course," she said. "It's not a problem."

His face suggested he didn't quite believe her, but he nodded. "I need to call Grant and tell him what's happening."

"Okay." She handed him his phone. "I'll run out to the waiting room and update Gideon. I'll be back soon."

She stood and leaned over, brushing her mouth against his. "See you in a little bit."

———

"I DON'T THINK HE SHOULD CLIMB THE PORCH STEPS ON THOSE crutches." Kira gave Gideon a worried look as they stood at the bottom of the steps to her house.

Connor was standing to Gideon's right, crutches tucked under his arms, and he made a pfft sound. "I'm fine. I'm a total pro at crutches. See?" He waved one crutch wildly in the air, and Gideon grabbed his arm when he nearly fell on his ass.

"You're also incredibly high," Gideon said. "Kira, take his crutches, and I'll help him up the stairs."

She moved to Connor's other side, but he gave her a stubborn look when she tried to take the crutches. "I can do it."

"You can't," she said. His pupils were blown, and he swayed back and forth like a flower in the breeze. "Gideon's right, you're too high from that shot they gave you."

"They put it in my butt cheek," Connor said to Gideon. "The nurse just jabbed it in, didn't warn me or anything. I didn't cry, though."

"That's good, buddy." Gideon clapped Connor lightly on the back. "Give your crutches to Kira."

"I don't wanna."

Oh my God, if she weren't so worried about him, she'd find Connor ridiculously adorable when he was hopped up on pain meds.

"Don't argue, please," she said. "Give me the crutches."

"Give me a kiss." Connor grinned at her.

Gideon rolled his eyes when Kira hesitated. "Oh, for God's sake, Kira, just kiss him. I don't have all damn day."

She stood on her tiptoes and gave Connor a soft kiss. He licked the seam of her lips, and she quickly pulled back. Playing tonsil tag with Connor in front of her brother wasn't her idea of a good time.

"Crutches." She held out her hands and gave Connor a stern look.

He handed them over as Gideon steadied him with a hand around his arm.

"How you wanna do this, big guy?" Connor asked Gideon. "Are we thinking a half hop, half drag combination or..."

With a loud grunt, Gideon picked him up like a knight rescuing a fair maiden, careful not to touch Connor's right knee encased in a brace. Kira swallowed her immediate spat of giggles as Connor made a high-pitched "Whee!" and slung his arm around Gideon's shoulder.

Gideon staggered up the first step. "Fuck, man, how much do you weigh?"

Connor grinned at Kira over Gideon's shoulder. "I look skinny, but I'm all muscle, baby. The stupid fire boy thinks he's strong, but I could beat him in an arm-wrestling contest."

Gideon grunted his way up another step, and Connor said, "What? I could. I'm way better for your sister than idiotic Daniel Moore."

"You're preaching to the choir, buddy," Gideon puffed as he crested the final step.

Breathing heavily, he set Connor down on the porch.

"Wait, aren't you supposed to carry me over the threshold?" Connor asked.

Kira giggled as Connor leaned against Gideon and batted his eyelashes at him. "It's tradition, big fella."

Gideon laughed. "Kira, give your boyfriend his crutches before he starts trying to make out with me."

"I can't help it if I'm a friendly guy," Connor said as Kira helped him tuck the crutches under his arms. She unlocked and opened the front door.

Moving surprisingly quickly, Connor crutched into the house and down the hallway.

"Guest room is down around the corner." Kira walked behind him, keeping her hands out in case Connor fell over. He was a little wobbly but made it to the bed and collapsed with a soft sigh.

She helped him lift his leg onto the bed, then grabbed some extra pillows from the closet and placed them on the bed.

"Ready?" she asked.

Connor nodded, and bracing one hand under his thigh and the other under his calf, she raised his leg and slowly swung it over until it was resting on the tower of pillows. She tucked another under his head, and he smiled sweetly. "Thank you, honey."

"You're welcome." She took the blanket from the end of the bed and tucked it around him as he yawned hugely. "Get some sleep."

"Nappie-time," he sang before sliding a hand out from under the blanket and grabbing her wrist. "Kiss me."

She pressed a kiss against his mouth, pulling back when he tried to deepen it. "Be good, Connor."

"I am." He traced her collarbone with his fingers. "Get naked and nap with me."

"I'm still in the room," Gideon said.

ELIZABETH KELLY

Connor's eyes widened. In a loud whisper, he said, "Don't panic, but I think your brother heard me tell you to get naked."

"He did," Gideon said.

"I'm about to be arrested, aren't I?" Connor said.

Kira laughed. "No. I'll walk Gideon out and then return with some water for you. Stay in bed, Connor."

"Yes, ma'am." His slow grin and the way his gaze dipped to her chest made her wish she could get naked and nap with him.

Instead, she patted his shoulder and stood.

"Thank you for carrying me up the stairs, Gideon," Connor said. "I'll cherish that moment always."

"Yeah, don't mention it." Gideon glanced at Kira. "You sure you don't need me to stick around for a bit?"

"No, I think we're good. I'll call you if I need anything, though." Kira shut the bedroom door with a soft click.

"What will you do with him tomorrow when you're at work?"

Kira shrugged. "Not sure yet. I guess it will depend on how much pain he's in and how bad the swelling is."

"I can do a few drive-bys and check in on him," Gideon said.

"Thanks, Gideon." Kira followed him down the hallway to the front door. "I appreciate everything you did for him."

"No problem." Gideon paused on the threshold. "Did you tell Connor about your former crush on Daniel?" He accented the word former just a little, but it was enough to make Kira's stomach clench.

"Uh…why do you ask?" she stalled.

"Seems a little weird that he'd be trying to convince me

188

he's better for you than Daniel. Especially since you're already dating him."

She didn't say anything, and Gideon leaned against the jamb. "Listen, I know it's none of my business, but Connor seems like a great guy, even if he is from Willington. Don't give up what you have with Connor for a guy who will never be good enough for you."

Kira made herself smile at him. "Stop worrying about me and my love life. Okay? Maybe I should start worrying about yours for a change. You haven't dated anyone since you moved back. Why not?"

Like she suspected he would, Gideon immediately straightened and stepped onto the porch. "Call me if you need me, kid."

"Bye, Gideon."

———

KIRA STUCK HER HEAD INTO THE GUEST ROOM. SHE'D BEEN upstairs in the tub when she'd heard the thump-thud-thump of Connor's crutches. By the time she'd gotten out of the tub and gone downstairs, Connor was out of the guest bathroom and back in the bedroom.

He eased back onto the bed, and she frowned at him. "You should have called me. I could have helped you."

He just shrugged. "I had it. It's been a while since I've been on crutches, but apparently, it's like riding a bike."

She could hear the bitterness in his voice, and she rushed over to the side of the bed, helping him to prop his leg up on the stack of pillows again. His face was pale and a little sweaty, and after sleeping most of the afternoon away, the high from the drugs was long gone.

"I'm sorry. I know it hurts, but I can't give you any more pain meds until tonight before bed," she said.

"It's fine." He waved off her concern. "The pain is manageable."

"Is it?"

He nodded, and she sat down on the side of the bed as he stared moodily at the ceiling. She waited a beat and said, "I'll bring you an ice pack for your knee, and then I'll start dinner. I've got a lap tray I can bring you to eat dinner on."

"You don't have to wait on me hand and foot," he said. "I can eat dinner at the table."

"Not for a few days," she said. "It's better to keep it raised as much as possible, which means bed rest. You heard Jack. You only get out of bed to use the bathroom."

He grunted irritably and, still looking at the ceiling, said, "I don't want to be a pain in your ass."

"You aren't," she said.

Another bitter laugh. "You didn't sign up for this, and you're not required to help me. Our relationship is fake, so -"

"I want to help," Kira said.

"Or you feel obligated because people in this town think we're dating, and you'll look like a bad girlfriend if you don't."

"I don't care what people think. I'm doing this because I'm a nice person, and my friend is hurt and needs my help." Now, she was the one who sounded irritable.

"Is that what we are? Friends?"

She paused, feeling weirdly hurt. "You don't think we're friends?"

He blew his breath out with a loud puff of air. "Sorry. Yeah, we're friends. And I appreciate what you're doing even if I'm acting like a dick."

She patted his thigh. "It's okay. You're in pain and upset about your knee. I get it. But stop feeling bad about asking me for help because I don't feel obligated and want to help you. All right?"

"Thanks, Kira."

"You're welcome. I'll be right back with the ice pack, and then I'll get started on dinner."

"ARE YOU SURE YOU HAD ENOUGH TO EAT?" KIRA RETURNED from the kitchen and took the lap tray off the bed. Connor stared at her perfect ass in her yoga pants as she bent and tucked the tray between the nightstand and the wall.

"Positive. Thank you again. You're a great cook."

She laughed. "I'm so not, but even I can't screw up chicken and rice."

"I think you're a good cook." He tried not to stare at her tits as she sat down on the side of the bed.

"Only because you think popcorn is an acceptable dinner," Kira said with another laugh.

He studied her face, itching to reach out and snag a strand of that amazingly soft blonde hair between his fingers. His urge to touch her got stronger with every passing day. The part of him that was worried about what that meant was almost buried under the part of him that desperately wanted her soft body tucked under him while he slid his dick into her wet, tight pussy.

Kind of hard to have sex with Kira when your knee is fucked.

He massaged just above the brace on his right knee. There was an ice pack on his knee, and he wasn't even the tiniest bit tempted to lift it and study the swollen mess. He didn't want to see the bruising that would be starting or the way the flesh strained as the swelling worsened. It reminded him too much of what it looked like after the accident.

You know you fucked it again, right? Everything's torn to shit in there, and this time they won't be able to fix it. You'll never walk right again, let alone jog or run or play baseball.

He tried to block out his inner voice, afraid that if he started to listen to it too long, he'd lose his fucking shit. The thought that his knee might be jacked for good sent terror through him. It didn't help that inner Connor wouldn't shut the fuck up about how he was facing a long road of surgery and physical therapy, and what Grant would say when Connor was off work for six goddamn months or more, and —

"Connor?"

Kira's soft voice pulled him out of his spiral. He stared at her, knowing his anxiety was written all over his damn face, but utterly helpless to hide it.

When she took his hand, he linked their fingers, fighting back his urge to ask her to lie on the bed beside him, to wrap her arms around him and tell him everything would be fine.

"Everything will be fine," Kira said.

He jerked, sending the ice pack sliding sideways on his knee. He winced when fresh pain lanced up and down his leg. Shit, was she reading his goddamn mind? Kira reached out with her free hand and shifted the ice pack back onto his knee, her touch infinitely gentle.

"You okay?"

"Yeah." His voice was hoarse, and he was holding her hand too tight. He made himself relax his fingers so he wouldn't crush hers.

"It's going to be just fine," she said. "I did some reading

while you were sleeping this afternoon, and I know I'm not a doctor or anything, but I don't think you've torn your ACL or MCL again. You didn't do a sharp stop and twist or anything like that, and that's usually how they get torn, right? You go one way, and your knee goes the other, and it's," she paused, "rip city."

His smile was more of a grimace, and she rubbed her thumb along the knuckle of his thumb. "I know it's sore and looks awful, but it isn't fractured or dislocated and the odds of it being re-ruptured or re-torn are low. It's probably so swollen and sore because your knee was already trauma-tized. I've seen you limping, and I know it bugs you some-times. It's predisposed to be injured more easily."

"Yeah, maybe," he said.

She squeezed his hand until he looked at her. "It's going to be fine. The swelling will go down after a few days of bed rest and anti-inflammatories. You'll see."

"You really believe that, don't you?" He said.

"I do." Her voice was firm, and the way she refused even to accept any alternative about his knee was, oddly, making him feel better.

"Thanks, Kira," he said.

"You're welcome." She released his hand, and he almost immediately wanted to capture it again. "Now, I'll bring my laptop in here, and we can watch something on Hulu or Netflix. What do you think?"

"I'd like that," he said.

"Great." She stood and smiled at him. "I might even make you some popcorn later."

CHAPTER 14

"Oh no, that poor boy." Rose leaned back in her chair. "I'll keep my fingers crossed that his knee is only bruised. When did you say he was having the MRI?"

"Tuesday morning. Would you be okay with me taking the morning off to drive him to his appointment?" Kira asked.

"Of course, dear," Rose said. "He's such a lovely young man. Ray and I were very impressed with him at dinner the other night. Well-spoken and polite, and it was just the sweetest thing to throw you a congratulatory dinner."

"It was," Kira said. "Connor is a great guy."

A great guy that you want to see naked.

Maybe. But now that he'd hurt his knee, she'd lost her chance to do some not-quite-sex stuff with him. Which she wasn't the least bit pouty about.

Definitely *not* pouty. Her main concern was Connor and his knee and that it wasn't severely damaged. She wasn't at all thinking about how soon he would heal so that he could do all sorts of delicious things to her.

Nope, not at all. Because she was a good person, not a selfish horndog who suddenly couldn't stop thinking about what it would be like to climb naked into the bed with Connor, straddle his good leg and hump her way to an epic orgasm.

Freak.

No, not a freak. Just horny... and selfish. Connor was in pain, a lot of pain, despite the pain meds, and she couldn't stop thinking about her own needs. Which was stupid because even her hope that Connor would ask her to stay in the bed with him in case he needed help during the night hadn't happened.

Still, it hadn't stopped her from coming up with a dirty little fantasy that involved her giving Connor a sponge bath before going down on him. She had masturbated silently but furiously to that fantasy, covering her face with her pillow when she came to muffle her cries of ecstasy.

She'd straight up die of shame if Connor knew she was masturbating to thoughts of blowing him. She was a total pervert and –

"Kira?"

She glanced up to see Rose staring at her. Shit, how long had she drifted off for?

"I'm sorry, what?" She gave Rose an apologetic smile.

"I said, who's staying with Connor while you're at the office?"

"Oh, um, no one. He's pretty good at using crutches, but I'm still worried he'll fall while alone. I made him promise me he'd stay in bed for the morning. I'll go home to check on him at lunch, but I might be a few minutes late getting back with traffic. If that's okay?"

Rose gave her a startled look. "You left him alone? Honey, you get home right now and look after your man."

Kira blinked at the silver-haired woman. "I'm sorry?"

"I said, get your cute behind back home. You can't leave him alone." Rose made a shooing motion with her hands. "Go on now."

"I can't just leave work. I mean…"

"You can and you will," Rose said. "In fact, take the next few days off. We'll survive without you, sweetheart. I promise. Text me Wednesday night, and just let me know if you're coming in on Thursday."

"Rose, I can't, I mean…"

Rose made another shooing motion. "Go on, Kira. Both Ray and I always stress that family is the most important thing. Go and take care of yours. If we need you or something comes up, I'll text you. All right?"

"If you're sure?" Kira said.

"Positive," Rose replied.

Kira stood and moved to the doorway of Rose's office. "Thank you, Rose. Both Connor and I appreciate it."

"Of course, sweetheart. Give Connor our best and tell him we are crossing our fingers it's nothing serious."

"CONNOR?" KIRA STUCK HER HEAD INTO THE GUEST ROOM. Connor was lying on the bed with his leg on the stack of pillows, and he gave her a look of surprise.

"What are you doing at home? I thought you were stopping by at lunch?"

"Rose gave me the next few days off so I could look after you."

197

Worry crossed Connor's face. "I don't want you getting in trouble at work because of me."

"I won't," Kira said. "I didn't ask for the time off, Rose insisted. It's fine, Connor. I promise."

He still looked worried, and she smiled at him. "How do you feel?"

"Maybe a little better?"

She lifted the ice pack and studied his knee. "I think it might be a little less swollen. The bruising is worse, though."

He shifted on the bed before running his hand through his hair. "I wish I'd thought to shower after the game on Saturday night, but my knee was already killing me."

"I can help you shower."

Shit. Did she sound too eager? She sounded too eager.

"I didn't... I mean, I wasn't trying to hint that I wanted you to help," Connor said. "You've already done a lot for me."

"I don't mind," she said. "I'm happy to help you with whatever you need."

He studied his knee as her heart beat fiercely in her chest. The thought of a naked Connor in her shower made her brain go haywire.

She'd have to get naked too, of course. It only made sense, right? Wearing clothes to help bathe Connor in the shower was just silly. Obviously, nakedness was the way to go. How big would Connor's cock be? Would he get hard? She hoped he did. If he had an erection, it would only be polite for her to help him with that, too, right?

"Kira?"

"Sorry, what?" She wondered just how red her face was.

"I said I think I can do this myself," he said.

"How?"

"Well, it's a walk-in shower in the guest room, so I don't

have to step into it, and I can put a stool in there to sit on," Connor said. "I didn't check the shower nozzle, though. Is it a hand-held one?"

"Yes," she said.

"Great, I won't need your help at all," he said.

Could he see the disappointment on her face? She schooled her features into something that said, 'brilliant idea' rather than 'what do you mean I don't get to see you naked?' and forced a smile. "All right. I'll grab some towels and the stool and take them and your toiletries to the shower."

"Thank you, Kira. I appreciate this."

Connor's look of gratitude made guilt roll through her. God, she was so selfish. With a small smile, she hurried out of the room.

———

"Shit!"

"Connor?" She knocked lightly on the bathroom door. "Everything okay?"

Was it weird that she'd been hovering outside the bathroom since Connor climbed into the shower?

Maybe a little weird.

"Yeah. I just dropped the soap behind me and can't reach it," he said.

"Do you want me to grab it for you?" She raised her voice to be heard over the sound of the shower, hoping like hell he couldn't hear the excitement in it. Seeing Connor naked was an almost frantic need inside of her.

He paused. "I'm naked."

"Most people are when they're in the shower. If you don't want me to come in, I get it. But I'm not going to, like, ogle you or anything. I'll just get the soap for you and leave," she said.

Liar.

She flushed. She wasn't lying. She might want to see Connor naked, but she wasn't going to do anything that would make him uncomfortable, either.

"Hold on a minute," he called.

She waited nearly two minutes before he said, "Okay, come in."

She opened the door and stepped into the steamy bathroom. She shut the door to keep cool air from coming in. She could only see a hint of Connor through the foggy shower door, but excitement and lust already crowded her belly.

"I'm opening the shower door, okay?" she said.

"Okay."

Do not look at his penis, Kira. Do not look at his penis.

She slid open the door and looked at his penis.

For the second time that day, thick disappointment washed over her. Connor had placed a hand towel over his crotch, and she could see... nothing. Absolutely nothing.

A damn towel had thwarted her chance to see her first penis in real life.

Connor cleared his throat, and blushing furiously, she said, "Let me get the soap for you."

"Thanks. Sorry, I was trying to wash my back, and the soap slipped from my hand."

"It's fine," she said. "I'm happy to help."

"I could have maybe stood and turned around, but..."

"No, absolutely not. You don't want to risk slipping and falling by standing up. It's no problem at all."

She was talking too high and too fast, but damn, a mostly naked Connor was a dream come true. She might not have gotten to see exactly what she wanted, but watching the water run down over Connor's bare chest and abdomen was making her pussy plenty wet enough.

She had a hot dentist naked in her shower, and it was the best damn moment of her life.

He held the shower nozzle in one hand and pointed it downward so she wouldn't get sprayed as she leaned into the shower. He shifted forward on the stool, and her breath caught in her throat as she stared at the top of his ass.

Her desire to bend over and give his right ass cheek a little nibble was probably inappropriate, right?

"Kira?"

"Sorry," she mumbled. She leaned down, ignoring the fact that Connor's delectable ass was right near her face, and snagged the soap from the bottom of the shower. She straightened and stared at the back of Connor's head. His dark hair was wet and clinging to his scalp, and she could see shampoo suds on the bottom half.

"You missed rinsing some shampoo out of your hair," she said.

His hand twisted behind him to touch the back of his neck. "Dammit."

"Give me the shower nozzle." She held her hand out. "I'll rinse it out and give your back a quick wash for you."

"Thanks." He took the soap from her and handed over the showerhead.

She carefully rinsed the shampoo from his hair before returning it to him. "Now the soap."

He passed her the soap without speaking, and she lathered up her hands before setting it in the soap dish. Her heart pounding and her pussy throbbing, she ran her hands across his broad back in long, slow strokes. She washed his upper back in small circles, taking more care and time than necessary, but Connor's smooth skin and firm muscles were an aphrodisiac she couldn't resist.

She smoothed her hands over the muscles in his back, rubbing lightly before moving to his lower back and stroking and massaging. His low groan sent heat straight between her thighs.

"Okay?" Her voice was shamefully needy.

"Yeah."

She could barely hear him over the sound of the shower. She moved her hands lower, just above his ass, and he groaned again.

"Connor, are you -"

Her breath caught in her throat. The towel over his dick was tented. Connor had an erection. She was touching him, and it made him hard. Her body moved of its own accord, squirming in behind him, not caring that her leggings and shirt were soaking up the water and soap from his skin as she pressed her body against the lean length of his back.

He drew in a harsh breath when she slid her hands around his trim waist and rubbed his flat abdomen. The muscles trembled beneath her touch, and he used his free hand to trap her hands against him when she slid them upwards.

"What are you doing, little Kira?" he rasped.

"Helping you shower," she said. "You missed a spot."

"Is that right?" His voice was a mixture of lust and amusement.

"Yes." She kissed the top of his shoulder. "Let me help you."

"I'm getting you wet," he said.

"So wet," she whispered into his ear.

He made another harsh groan, dropping his hand and tilting his head back as she drew her hands up his body. The soap on her hands was long gone, but she rubbed small circles across his chest, delighted at the feel of the coarse hair beneath her palms. When she brushed her fingers across his flat nipples, his back arched, and the back of his head dropped onto her shoulder.

She stared at the towel that covered his crotch. His right hand, still holding tightly to the shower nozzle, was resting on his thigh, the water cascading down his leg.

"Almost finished." She traced her fingertips across his collarbone. "There's one more spot you seemed to have missed."

"Oh yeah?" He turned his head and nipped at her earlobe. "You want to help me with that?"

"It would be very nice of me to help," she said.

"So nice," he breathed into her ear before sucking on her lobe. "Touch me, little Kira."

She wet her lips, the steam and the heat from the shower making her cheeks flush, before reaching for the towel. She plucked the towel off his lap and dropped it to the bottom of the shower.

She stared unabashedly at his cock, a tremor of excitement tinged with worry rising in her belly. He seemed very long and thick to her, and she studied the head of his cock as her fingers trembled just above it.

His free hand caught hers and squeezed lightly. "Okay, honey?"

"I've never, I mean, I haven't…" She swallowed hard. "I've never touched one before."

He pressed a kiss against her jawline. "You don't have to if you don't want to."

"I want to," she said immediately. "I really want to. I'm just worried I won't do it right."

He lifted her hand to his mouth and pressed a kiss against the palm before guiding it to his dick. "Wrap your fingers around me."

She did what he asked, sliding her hand around his width and holding him loosely. His cock quivered in her hand, and he groaned loudly into her ear.

"Is this wrong?" she asked.

"No," he said. "No, it's good. Your hand is so fucking soft. Stroke me back and forth."

She rubbed back and forth, fascinated by how velvety soft his skin was. That velvet skin covered what felt like hard steel, and she rubbed a little harder, tightening and loosening her grip as she stroked.

"Fuck, oh fuck, that's good, honey." Connor panted into her ear, his hips rocking to meet her rhythm.

She squeezed her thighs together, trying to ease the ache in her pussy, as Connor moaned in her ear. "Touch the head, little Kira."

She ran her thumb over the head, and he made his loudest moan yet, his hips rocking forward. His free hand reached behind and gripped her thigh through her pants, squeezing hard as she continued to stroke him.

"Harder," he rasped.

"I don't want to hurt you," she said.

"You won't," he said. "Jack me harder and faster, honey. Do it."

She did what he asked, watching in fascination as his cock seemed to swell in her hand. His entire body was rocking back and forth, his head moving restlessly against her shoulder as his hand kneaded her thigh.

He sucked in a harsh breath and dropped the nozzle to the shower floor before wrapping his big hand around hers. He forced her hand to move even faster, guiding Kira in the rhythm he wanted as the head of his cock leaked precum.

"Good, honey, good," he moaned. "I'm so close to coming, I'm so close…"

His hand squeezed almost brutally around hers, forcing it to a stop as his back arched, and he made a hoarse shout. Cum poured out of his dick, and he shouted again, the back of his skull digging into her shoulder, his big body shaking against hers as he came and came again.

He released her hand, sagging against her as she kissed his temple. "You okay?"

"Better than okay," he mumbled.

She kept one hand on his back to steady him as she leaned down and grabbed the shower nozzle. She rinsed his back and upper chest before rinsing his cock. He moaned and twitched at the feel of the warm water. She kissed his shoulder and reached past him to turn off the shower.

She stepped out of the shower, her shirt and leggings sticking to her body, and reached for the towel as Connor braced his hands on the shower wall and door and heaved himself to his feet. He balanced on his left foot, and she handed him the crutch leaning on the wall just outside the door. He propped it under his right armpit and carefully maneuvered out of the shower until he stood before her.

"Okay?" she said.

He nodded, and she handed him the other crutch before drying him off. He twitched when she touched his dick, and she gave him an apologetic look. "I'm sorry."

"No, it's fine," he said. "I'm still a little sensitive."

"Can you turn around?"

He turned around. She was again amazed at his dexterity with the crutches, and she dried his back and ass before crouching and drying his legs. She stood and wrapped the towel around his waist, tucking it tight before opening the bathroom door. "C'mon, back to the bedroom before you catch a chill."

He crutched his way down the hallway and into the bedroom. She almost ran into him when he turned around instead of sitting on the bed and dropped one crutch. He slid his arm around her waist and pulled her up against him, balancing on his good leg as he stared down at her.

"Connor, what -"

He dropped his mouth onto hers, sliding his tongue between her lips as she moaned and threw her arms around his shoulders. She wanted to rub her entire body against him like a cat. Fuck, had she ever been this horny?

She sucked at his tongue, nibbling at his lips and making small sounds of need as his big hand rubbed circles on her lower back. Her breasts felt heavy, and her damp bra was rubbing and chafing her suddenly hard nipples.

"Your turn," he whispered against her mouth. "Take off these wet clothes, honey."

"Yes," she breathed. "That's a great idea."

She kissed him again, her hands reaching for the hem of her shirt. She pulled away and started tugging it up, freezing in place when her brother entered the bedroom.

"Connor? How's the leg today? Any – what the hell?"

Her face bright red, she yanked her shirt down, giving Connor a mortified look. His erection was extremely notice-able against the towel wrapped around him – Was that normal? Did guys get hard again that quickly? – and she kept her body in front of him as she spun around to face her brother.

"Gideon? What are you doing here?"

He gave her a look of confusion. "What am I doing here? What are you doing here? You're supposed to be at work, remember? You asked me to stop in and check on him."

He was wearing his sheriff's vest, and when the dispatcher's voice crackled over the radio attached to it, he turned it down before eyeing Kira's wet clothing. "Why are you home?"

"Rose gave me a few days off so I could help Connor. I just, uh, helped him shower," she said.

"Oh." Gideon cleared his throat. "I guess I don't need to stop by then."

"Thanks for stopping, Gideon," Connor said from behind her. "I appreciate it."

"Yeah, don't mention it." Gideon hesitated. "Kira, can I talk to you for a minute in the kitchen?"

"Just let me help Connor get settled, and I'll be right there."

Gideon left, and she sucked in a gulp of oxygen before turning to stare at Connor. He wore an amused look, and she glared at him. "This isn't funny. Gideon almost saw us about to…"

She stopped and took a deep breath before moving around him and pulling back the covers. "Get into bed. I'll bring you some lunch after I've talked to Gideon."

She jumped when his big hand caressed her ass. "Have I ever told you how incredible your ass is?"

"My brother is in the kitchen," she said pointedly. "Get into bed."

He gave her a boyish grin, that dimple making her thighs loosen, and dropped the towel before sitting on the side of the bed. His cock was semi-hard, and she stared at it, licking her lips as a new tremor of lust wormed its way into her belly.

Connor reached out and traced her erect nipple through her shirt. She moaned and pulled away, giving him a look of disbelief. "Behave, Connor."

His grin widened, and she pushed his hand away when he brushed her nipple again. "Get into bed, now."

She helped him swing his right leg into the bed and prop it against the pillows before pulling the covers up to his waist. He caught her wrist with one hand, his thumb rubbing against her pulse point.

She trembled helplessly in his grip, staring at his mouth as he said, "Hurry back, little Kira."

She nodded, her mouth too dry to speak, and backed away when he released her wrist. She left the room and hurried upstairs to her room, whipping off her wet clothes and putting on dry ones before returning downstairs to the kitchen.

Gideon was filling his travel mug with coffee, and she grabbed the milk from the fridge and handed it to him.

"Thanks."

He added milk and stuck it in the fridge as Kira sat at the table. He leaned against the counter and sipped the coffee, staring silently at her.

She fidgeted in the chair, tugging nervously at the hem of her shirt. "How's work going?"

"Fine," he said.

She stared at the Harmony Falls Sheriff's Department logo on the front of his vest as he took another sip of coffee. "Not to be super weird and awkward, but Connor is injured, and with what you told me about his knee history, he probably shouldn't be ..."

She jumped up. "This is beyond super weird and awkward, Gideon."

He grimaced and headed for the door. "Yeah, it is. Text me if you need me."

She waited until she heard the front door shut before taking a deep breath and returning to the bedroom. She peeked inside, and guilt swept through her. Connor was lying on the bed with his eyes closed. He had put the brace back on and rubbed the top of his thigh just above his swollen right knee. Even from the doorway, she could see the paleness of his skin and the little pain lines etched around his mouth and eyes.

What the hell was she thinking? She wasn't. She was horny and needy, and she hadn't even given one thought to Connor's injury. He needed rest, not to be groped in the shower.

She stepped into the room, cupping her elbows. "Connor?"

His eyes popped open, and he moved his hand away from his leg and gave her a flirty smile. "Your brother gone?"

"Yes."

"Good." His gaze dropped to her breasts. "Take off your clothes and climb into bed, little Kira."

She took a few steps forward, hugging herself a little tighter. "Connor, I can't."

"Yes, you can." He patted the mattress next to him. "Come here, honey."

She shook her head. "You need rest."

"No, what I need is to watch you come on my fingers."

Her face turned scarlet at his bluntness, and he grinned again. "You want and need that too."

Oh God, did she ever.

She made herself shake her head no again. "We really can't. I shouldn't have done that to you in the shower."

His body stiffened. "Do you regret what happened?"

"No, of course not," she said. "But you're injured, and I groped you like some horny housewife, and it was inappropriate."

"I didn't mind," he said with a laugh. "Now it's my turn to return the favour."

"We can't," she repeated. "Your knee has to heal and -"

"I don't need my knee for what I'm about to do to you." A hint of impatience crept into his voice. "Let me show you."

"It's better if we don't," she said. "I don't want to risk hurting you again."

"You won't," he said. "Kira, get in the bed. There's no way in hell that I'm having an orgasm, and you're not."

"It's no big deal," she said. "Really."

"It's a big deal to me," he replied. "Get into bed."

"I'm going to make you some lunch and bring you your pain meds, and then you're going to have a nap." She backed toward the doorway. "I'll be back in a little bit."

"Kira, I'm *fine*." He gave her a look of exasperation.

"You're not," she said. "You're in pain and tired and need to rest. The conversation is over, Connor."

She stepped into the hallway as Connor muttered, "Like hell it is, Kira Walker."

CHAPTER 15

Connor sat on the edge of the bed, staring fixedly at his phone. It was just after eleven, and Kira had gone to bed almost two hours ago, saying she was tired and had a bit of a headache. She'd blamed it on a long day, and while he knew it'd been stressful to help him get to the MRI appointment and back, he also knew she was lying.

She'd gone to bed early because she couldn't stand the tension between them. He studied his knee, rubbing absently at the top of his thigh. Not anger. They'd been perfectly pleasant to each other since Monday afternoon when she returned with his lunch and pain meds.

He'd napped, eaten, and stayed in bed just like he was supposed to. Kira had even sat in the room with him last night and tonight and binge-watched some shows on Netflix. But she'd been meticulous not to touch him, and their conversations hadn't gone beyond anything other than talk about the shows they were watching.

No, the tension wasn't anger. It was sexual, and both of them were going crazy because of it.

He sighed and rubbed his thigh again. His knee was feeling better today, despite being manipulated for the MRI, and there was a small part of him that felt a semblance of hope that maybe he hadn't completely fucked it up.

Of course, he hadn't even cared about his knee in the last twenty-four hours. All he could think about was Kira and getting her naked. Sucking on her nipples and touching her wet pussy until she came all over his fingers.

Would she cry his name when she came? Fuck, he hoped so. Wanted her to. Needed her to.

He took a deep breath and rechecked the time. What he was about to do was a dick move, but if he didn't do something, if he didn't convince her to let him make her come, they'd both lose their fucking minds.

It didn't have to go any further than that. She was saving herself for that douchebag firefighter, but she'd said herself that she wanted to experiment with Connor. She learned how to give a handjob, and now she'd find out what it was like to come from someone other than her own hand. It was... valuable information for her.

Whatever, asshole. You just want to make her come so that when she finally does start dating Daniel, you can at least know that you were the first man to make her come. You're pathetic, you know that?

He ignored his inner voice. The thought of Daniel getting Kira's virginity made him feel, well... a little stabby if he was being honest.

Since when did you start thinking of a woman's virginity as being a prize?

He didn't. But Kira thought it was special, and the idea that she would be giving it to Daniel pissed him off. It shouldn't, and he had no right to be angry, but he couldn't deny that at some point in the last week or so, he wanted to be the guy that Kira gave her virginity to.

It was ridiculous. Ridiculous and completely irrational and something he wanted desperately. Daniel didn't deserve it. Hell, he didn't deserve Kira. She was sweet and thoughtful, and he was a selfish dick who only used her. Kira thinking that Daniel was more worthy of her virginity than Connor, was a hard pill to swallow.

Yeah, well, it is what it is. Are we doing this or not?

He was. Maybe it made him pathetic to be so determined to be the first guy to make Kira come, but he could live with that if it meant hearing Kira's soft cries as she climaxed. Hell, if he were really lucky, he'd convince her at some point to sit on his face so he could taste her and make her come on his mouth, too.

She didn't want you touching her yesterday afternoon. Why do you think tonight will be any different? You're down a strike, buddy. Two more, and you're out of the game.

Maybe, but he was willing to take the chance. She wanted him, that was more than apparent, and he wanted to give her what she needed. Seducing her while she was only half-awake would be a dick move, but he was shamefully desperate.

He drank the rest of his water and set it back on the nightstand before texting Kira. He listened intently, his heart speeding up when he heard her climb out of bed and the thud of her footsteps as she crossed her room. She stood in his room in less than two minutes, squinting at him in the moonlight.

"Connor? What's wrong? Are you in pain?"

"No, I'm okay."

She wore a long and faded Harmony Falls High Badgers

213

t-shirt with their mascot – a snarling badger wrapped around the letters H and F – displayed prominently on the front. She was braless, and his cock swelled against his boxers.

"Are you sure?" She sat on his left side, her pale thigh pressing against his. She brushed her tangled hair back from her face and gave him a look of concern.

"Positive. I didn't mean to wake you, but I couldn't sleep."

"You didn't wake me." Her skin smelled like vanilla. She'd had a bath before bed, he'd heard her running the water, and it had taken everything in him not to masturbate to the thought of her naked and wet in the tub.

"Can't sleep either, huh?" he said.

She shook her head. His idea to seduce her while she was sleepy was being tossed out the window, but he didn't care. Just having her sitting next to him, her slender body touching his, made him feel better.

"Thank you for everything you've done," he said. "You've gone way above and beyond the fake girlfriend duties."

"I don't mind," she said. "I like helping you."

His gaze dropped to her mouth, and she visibly trembled. "Connor, I…"

"Please, Kira," he said. He didn't care that he was begging. "I want you so much."

"I want you too," she whispered. "But you need rest, and I don't want to make your knee worse…"

"You won't," he said. "I promise, honey."

He rested one big hand on her slender thigh, stroking the satin skin. "All I want is to make you come, little Kira. Will you let me?"

"We shouldn't," she whispered.

"We should. Neither of us is going to get any sleep until

you've come on my fingers." He loved the way she blushed whenever he said anything remotely dirty.

He leaned forward and pressed a kiss against her throat. "Have you touched yourself since you helped me in the shower?"

She shook her head. "No. I was going to, but I..."

"You what?"

"I was afraid you'd hear me and think I was a pervert."

He grinned and pressed another kiss against her soft skin. "Honey, you go right ahead anytime you want to touch yourself. My only request is you join me in my bed so I can watch you touch that sweet little clit."

"Connor, I can't, I mean... you want to watch me touch myself?" Her voice was thin with shock and maybe a little excitement. He stroked her leg, closer to the juncture of her thighs and sucked on her earlobe.

"Yes. Just the thought of you lying in bed, your legs spread wide while you rub your pussy, makes me hard, little Kira."

He reached for her hand and pressed it against his dick, inhaling sharply when she immediately rubbed him. "See?"

"I want to give you a blowjob," she said abruptly. "Can I?"

Precum leaked from his dick, wetting the front of his boxers as he fought the urge to free his dick and shove Kira's mouth down over it.

This isn't what she's here for, he reminded himself. *She's here so you can make her come.*

He cupped her breast through her shirt, teasing her nipple with his thumb. "Not tonight, honey."

"Why?" She scowled at him. "I want to taste you."

Fuck. She was going to kill him.

"You let me make you come tonight, and I'll let you give me a blowjob tomorrow night. Deal?"

215

It was only supposed to be tonight. He would make Kira come, and then he'd keep his distance. There was no future for them. Only the idea of her mouth on his dick was too intoxicating to give up.

She chewed on her bottom lip. "Deal."

He immediately leaned in closer, cupping her breast as he took her mouth in a hard and demanding kiss. She returned his kiss, making those soft, sweet sounds that drove him mad with desire.

He loved kissing her. Her original awkwardness was long gone, and her shyness at kissing him was no longer an issue. Would she kiss Daniel as easily now? Would she make those same sweet sounds when he kissed and touched her?

He pulled away, and she gave him a confused look, her mouth swollen and red from his kisses. "What's wrong?"

"Nothing." He tugged on the hem of her shirt. "Take this off."

She slipped it off and tossed it on the floor. She was wearing just a pair of panties, and he stared at her naked breasts, his cock twitching with excitement. He leaned down and kissed between her breasts before licking a path to one taut nipple. Her cries of pleasure heightened his own need as he sucked hard on her nipple. Her hands clenched in his hair, and her back arched.

He teased both nipples with his teeth and his tongue. Her nipples were incredibly sensitive, and her reaction to having them touched drove his need higher.

"Connor, please!" she cried hoarsely.

He rested a heavy hand on her thigh and tugged as he traced her collarbone with his tongue. Her legs tensed, and he kissed his way up her throat and licked the curve of her ear. "Open your legs, little Kira."

"I've never let anyone…"

"I know," he said. This was when he was supposed to tell her they could stop. Tell her he wouldn't do anything she didn't want him to do. Instead, he said, "Open your legs for me, honey."

She spread her legs, and he caressed her inner thigh as he kissed her throat. She was trembling, and he pressed a kiss against her mouth. "It's all right, little Kira."

She kissed him again, slipping her tongue into his mouth. He sucked on it as he slid his hand up and cupped her pussy through her panties. The crotch was soaking wet, and he pulled his head back, smiling down at her. "Your panties are soaked."

Red tinged her cheeks, and he sucked on her bottom lip as he rubbed her through the wet material. Her back arched, and he used his left hand to cup the back of her neck, holding her still for his kisses. When she was moaning and twisting against his hand, he released her mouth and studied her.

"Please," she panted before grabbing his wrist. "Connor, please."

He smiled and moved his hand to the waistband of her panties. He slipped his hand inside them. She spread her legs even wider, and he swept his fingers over the soft curls at the top of her sex.

"Connor," she begged, "touch me."

"I am touching you, little Kira."

"Not there." She moved restlessly against his hand before pushing on his wrist, trying to force his hand further down.

"Where?" he teased.

"You know where." She gave him a look of frustration, and he slid his hand down and cupped her wet pussy lips.

He could feel the swollen bud of her clit pressing against

his fingers, and he kept them perfectly still. When Kira rubbed her pussy against his fingers, he squeezed the back of her neck and gave her a sharp nip to her throat.

"Connor!"

He grinned and gave in to her pleading. He used the pad of his fingers to brush repeatedly against her clit, watching her face as she cried out with pleasure. She rocked against his hand, making those small moans that drove him crazy. Still watching her face, he pressed one finger against her tight opening. She immediately tensed, and he placed a soothing kiss on her mouth.

"Relax, sweet Kira. I want to feel your tight little pussy squeeze around me when I make you come."

He kissed her again until she was relaxed and clinging to him before sliding his finger inside of her. She cried out against his mouth, her back arched, and he rubbed her clit with his thumb as she pressed his second finger to her warmth. "Just one more finger, honey. All right?"

She nodded, and he brushed away a strand of hair sticking to her cheek. She clung to his arm, panting slightly, and her cheeks flushed bright red as he slid a second finger into her warmth. She was so fucking tight it made his balls ache with the need to be buried inside of her.

He ignored the urge. She didn't want him to fuck her, and he couldn't forget that. His knee was starting to throb, and he rubbed her clit with his thumb again. He needed to make her come before she realized he was in pain and put a stop to the whole thing. She would stop him, even if it meant she went without her orgasm because she was the sweetest woman he'd ever met.

He threaded his hand in her hair, holding tight when she tried to bury her face in his throat. "No," he said as he flicked her clit with his thumb. "I want to see your face when you come on my fingers, little Kira."

She moaned, and he smiled with satisfaction when she rocked her pelvis against his fingers, taking them deeper inside of her. He continued to rub her clit, and when her body tensed, he pressed harder and faster.

"Connor!" His name leaving her lips as she came was every bit as sweet as he thought.

He held her upright through her climax, watching as her slender body trembled from the sweet pleasure and her wet pussy squeezed impossibly tight around his fingers. Fuck, he wanted to feel her squeezing around his cock like that.

She slumped against him, and with a tinge of regret, he slid his fingers out from her pussy and her panties. He wanted to taste the liquid that covered them but knew it would embarrass her. Instead, he wiped his hand on the sheet and pressed a kiss against her head as she trembled against his body.

"Oh my God," she whispered. "That was incredible."

He kissed her head again. "I'm glad you enjoyed it."

"More than enjoyed it." She reached out in the dark, and he flinched when her hand brushed against his right knee.

"Oh shit!" She sat up straight, pulling away from him and giving him a worried look. "I'm sorry. I didn't mean to touch your knee. I was reaching for your co – I mean, I'm sorry. Oh God, how bad does it hurt?"

"It's fine," he said. "It's just a little sore because I've been sitting with it down for a while."

"Shit," she repeated. "God, I'm an idiot."

She jumped up and grabbed her shirt from the floor, struggling into it before giving him a look of shame. "I shouldn't have let you do that. You're in pain."

"I wanted to do it," he said.

"That doesn't mean I should have *let* you do it," she scolded.

He grinned and reached for her hand, squeezing it hard. "I'm glad you did."

She hesitated and gave him a shy smile. "Me too."

"Good."

He wanted to kiss her again, but she was already moving away to restack the pillows on the bed. "Here, lie back, and we'll get your leg up, and I'll grab a fresh ice pack."

He got comfortable on the bed, lifting his leg onto the stack of pillows as she hurried from the room. She returned a few minutes later with a bottle of water and an ice pack, and she set it on his knee gently before opening the water and handing it to him.

"Ladies first," he said.

She drank nearly half of it before giving him the bottle. He finished it and set it on the nightstand as she cleared her throat. "Okay, well, um, I should return to my room now."

"Stay," he said.

She gave him a look of surprise. Truthfully, he was more than a little surprised himself. Where the hell did that come from?

"What?" she said.

Now was the time to thank her and let her return to her room. Instead, he said, "Stay with me in the bed."

Her gaze dropped to his crotch. He still had a semi, and he shook his head immediately, hating that she thought that was all he wanted from her.

Since when did it become more?

He ignored his inner voice.

"Not for that. I just thought it might be easier on both of

us if you stayed in the bed with me. If I need something in the night, I can nudge you instead of texting you."

Holy fuck. He sounded like a moron.

To his shock, she said, "Sure. Yeah, that makes sense."

She walked around to the other side of the bed and climbed in, lying on her side with her back to him. She wasn't touching him, but he could feel the heat of her body, and it weirdly made him feel more content to have her soft warmth in the bed beside him.

"Good night, Connor. Thank you again for, um, you know," she said.

"It was my pleasure, little Kira. Good night."

He stared at the ceiling, listening to Kira's soft and rhythmic breathing and feeling a peace he hadn't felt in a long time.

CHAPTER 16

"Connor?" Kira shut the front door. "Everything still okay?"

"Just fine. How's Grace?"

She kicked off her shoes, set the bags of food in the kitchen on the table, and walked into the living room. Connor was where she'd left him two hours ago, on the sectional with his leg propped up on the end section and the TV remote in one hand. He muted the television as she sat next to him on the couch.

"Did you get Grace's car towed?" he asked.

She nodded. "Yeah, Wade showed up just as I got there. He thinks it might be her starter, but he towed her car back to his shop and will look at it in the morning. I dropped her off at home and will pick her up in the morning to give her a ride to work. She said she could take the bus, but she'd have to leave at a ridiculous hour in the morning, and Gracie is not a morning person."

He laughed. "Yeah, I've noticed."

She smiled at him. "Grace said to say hi. She really likes

working for you, Connor. Says you're the best boss she's ever had."

"She's a great employee," he said. "Hiring her was one of my better decisions. Do you not have to go back to work tomorrow?"

"No. I texted Rose, and she told me to go ahead and take the week off."

He gave her a worried look. "Can you afford to take the week off?"

"It's all good. My commission from the Stark sale has staved off the wolves for now." She grinned at him, but the worry stayed firmly on his face. "Honestly, Connor. It's fine. Anyway, I picked up some food from Nan's Diner on my way home. The special was her chicken stew and biscuits. I hope you like her stew."

"Love it," he said. "Thanks, Kira."

"You're welcome." She stood and headed toward the kitchen. "We'll eat in here tonight if that works for you?"

"Sure," he said.

She glanced behind her, blushing a little when she realized he was staring at her ass. He didn't look the least bit ashamed to be caught staring at her butt. In fact, he gave her that flirty grin that showed off his dimple. "We'll have a bite to eat and watch a little Netflix. What do you think?"

Her pussy clenched when his gaze flickered to her crotch for the briefest of moments. God, she hoped by Netflix he meant, 'You can suck on my cock'. Her cheeks heated, and she turned away before he could see. "Yeah, that sounds great."

She hurried into the kitchen, her pussy still doing that slow and maddening throb it had been doing all damn day. All she had to do was think about Connor, and she got wet.

She was going insane. She'd spent most of the day alternating between feeling guilty about how much she wanted Connor and daydreaming about stripping him naked and spending the day in his bed exploring every part of his body with her mouth.

Grace could tell immediately something was up, but Kira couldn't talk to her about it. Not yet, anyway. Not when the memory of how absolutely perfect it felt to have Connor touching her was so fresh in her mind.

She grabbed a couple of bowls from the cupboard and spooned the stew into them before grabbing water from the fridge and silverware from the drawer. She set the biscuits on two small plates and put everything on a large wooden tray.

Connor had said she could give him a blowjob tonight, and she was pathetically hopeful that he still meant it. She wanted to taste him. She wanted to hear his harsh moans as she sucked on that surprisingly big dick. She wanted to have sex with him.

She stopped in the middle of lifting the tray, her biceps bulging, and set it back on the table.

"Crap," she whispered. She wanted to have sex with Connor.

No, you don't. You're just on some weird sexual high. It's a normal reaction, okay? Connor gave you the best orgasm of your life. It's no surprise that you want to bang him. The feeling will pass. Don't give up on something you've wanted since you were a teenager just because Connor knows how to make you come.

She stared blankly out the kitchen window. Her head was saying everything it was supposed to say, but she didn't believe a word of it. She wanted to have sex with Connor.

"Hey, Kira?" Connor called from the living room.

"Yeah?"

"Can I trouble you for some water as well?"

"Already got it," she said.

She picked up the tray and took a deep breath. Everything was fine. So, she wanted to give her virginity to Connor. No big deal, right? It was just a stupid piece of skin, nothing special about it, more of an embarrassment than anything. Being a virgin at twenty-five was stupid.

Why shouldn't she sleep with him? He wanted her, and she wanted him, and it was no big deal. In a few more days, after his knee had healed some more and they got the results back from the MRI, she would ask him to have sex with her. Easy as pie.

KIRA WAS RESTLESS. SHE'D BEEN SHIFTING AND SQUIRMING ON the couch next to him for the last half hour. It was entirely his fault, and he couldn't deny that a part of him loved that he affected her this way.

He smoothed his fingers across her upper arm again, smiling blankly at the TV when she trembled against him. He'd casually put his arm around her about an hour into watching TV. She hadn't objected. She'd snuggled in against him, tucking her legs under her and resting the back of her skull on his shoulder.

He'd lost all interest in the TV show they were watching and had deliberately set out to seduce her. Any shame he might have felt about it was buried by thoughts of her mouth on his dick. Not that she'd brought up blowing him since last night, but that didn't mean she wasn't still interested, right?

God, he hoped she still wanted to blow him.

It was all he could think about today, and he'd found himself staring intently at her mouth more than once. Thankfully, she hadn't seemed to notice.

He traced small circles on her skin with the tips of his fingers before bending his head to the top of her skull and inhaling deeply. She always smelled so good.

"Did you just sniff me?" Kira looked up at him.

He grinned at her. "Maybe."

"Thank God I showered today," she said.

He laughed. "You always smell nice."

"Thank you." She shifted against him again before pausing the television. "Did you want to finish the show or…"

"Or?" He studied her mouth and watched the heat rise in her cheeks.

"Um…"

He loved teasing her, loved how she got flustered around him when he flirted. He moved his hand to her upper chest and trailed his fingers just above her small breasts. She made a low moan, and his grin widened. "Why don't we go to my bedroom?"

"How's your knee?" Kira studied his leg.

"Fine," he said. "Not as sore as it was."

She gave him a pensive look, and he bent his head and pressed a kiss against her soft lips. "It's good, little Kira."

"Are you sure?" she asked.

"Yes." He studied her sweet face. "But if you don't want to do this, that's fine. We can keep watching TV."

"No," she said. "No, I want to give you a blowjob. If, uh, you still want that?"

He rubbed his thumb across her lower lip. "Trust me when I say it's all I've thought about all day."

"That might be slightly more pressure than I can handle," she said with a small smile.

He cupped the back of her neck and dropped his mouth onto hers, kissing her with small nips and licks at her lips until she was moaning and her hands fisted his shirt. He would never tire of her reaction to his touch.

"Believe me," he said against her lips, "whatever you do will be amazing. Come to the bedroom with me, honey."

She nodded and shut off the TV as he carefully stood and grabbed his crutches. He crutched down the hall to the bedroom, Kira behind him. He stood beside the bed and leaned his crutches against the wall before smiling at her. "You're so beautiful, Kira."

"Thank you." She stood in front of him and tugged his shirt over his head, dropping it on the floor. She ran her hands over his chest and leaned in to press a kiss just above his right nipple. "You're beautiful too."

He cupped the back of her skull as she kissed across his chest. When her tongue flicked across his nipple, he made a hoarse moan of need. She sucked experimentally as her fingers traced the waistband of his shorts, and he gasped in air before tugging her head away. "Fuck, you're going to make me come before I even feel your hot little mouth around my cock."

She smiled shyly at him before tugging his shorts and briefs down his thighs. His cock sprang free, precum already coating the tip of it, and she stroked him a few times as he groaned with pleasure.

"Lie in the middle of the bed, honey," she said.

He sat down, and she pulled off his shorts and briefs for him. He carefully lifted his right leg onto the bed, then the left, and slid to the middle before lying on his back with his upper body propped up on the pillows.

Before she could lie down next to him, he said, "Naked. I want you naked while your mouth is on my dick."

She blushed furiously, but her hands were already stripping off her shirt and bra. She tugged her leggings and panties off, her face a soft red in the lamp's glow on the nightstand. He studied her pale, naked body, his cock swelling and his balls throbbing for relief.

"So beautiful," he said. "Come here."

She sat down next to his hip, her fingers stroking across his abdomen as she stared at his cock. When her fingers curled around his throbbing length, he groaned and arched his back a little, encouraging her to rub harder and faster.

She curved her fingers over the top, collecting some of his precum on the tip of her index finger. He made a low moan of need when she licked it away.

"It's good." She gave him a shy look. "I was a little worried about, um, taste. I've heard it can taste awful and… oh God, I mean, you don't taste bad, you taste good. I've just heard that other men can taste bad, but I wasn't expecting you to taste bad or anything. I wasn't saying that. I was saying -"

"Kira." He could hear the amusement in his voice.

"I sound like an idiot," she said.

"No, just nervous. It's all good, sweetheart. Whatever you do will feel good, I promise."

"Any tips?" She rubbed his cock with long, firm strokes.

"No teeth and gentle with the balls," he said.

She giggled. "Yeah, I figured that."

He grinned at her and traced his fingers between her small breasts. "Just remember that enthusiasm always wins over experience."

She made another soft giggle before leaning over him and pressing a kiss above his belly button. "In that case, you're about to have the best damn blowjob of your life."

He would have replied, only he was suddenly and incredibly distracted by the feel of Kira's tongue circling his navel. He threaded his hands in her silky, blonde hair, holding tightly as she traced his abs and nipped at his hipbone.

"Fuck," he breathed when her soft fingers caressed his inner thighs. He wanted to grip her hair hard and force her mouth to his dick. Instead, he watched with growing lust as she kissed across his pubic bone and nibbled at his other hipbone.

"Honey, please," he said when she kissed her way up his ribs. "I need your mouth."

"Patience, Connor," she said with a low laugh. "I want to taste all of you."

"You're killing me," he moaned.

"I doubt that." She licked his nipple, and he groaned and arched into her mouth, his hands tightening in her hair.

He tugged on her hair, trying to guide her back down his body. "Kira, please, sweetheart."

She kissed her way down his body, licking and tasting and exploring his skin as he tried not to shove her head down to his crotch.

When her mouth was finally hovering over his dick, she hesitated, and he made a low groan of need. "Honey, your mouth."

Without speaking, she stuck her sweet, wet, perfect tongue out and licked across the head of his dick. He cried out, his hips arching up until his cock brushed across her mouth.

"Fuck," he muttered, and she gave him a smug little grin before sliding her hot mouth down over his cock.

He immediately smoothed her hair back from her face, holding it in a ponytail at the back of her head with one hand so he could watch as she sucked his dick. She gripped the base of his cock with one small hand and sucked at his cock like it was a lollipop, her soft tongue bathing his flesh with stroke after stroke.

"That's so good, honey," he praised before reaching with his other hand to toy with her right nipple. She cried out, the sound muffled around his dick, and another deep surge of lust went through him. Had he ever seen anything as beautiful as Kira with her mouth full of his cock?

She sucked hard, dragging her mouth back and forth over his aching length as one soft hand cupped his balls. She was infinitely gentle, and he moaned encouragingly when she stroked the bottom of his cock with her other hand as she sucked.

"Good, just like that," he said. "Keep sucking, honey."

She lifted her head, dragged in a breath and then sucked his cock with renewed enthusiasm. She braced one hand on his left thigh and rubbed the other up and down his cock as she sucked on just the tip. His pelvis was rising and falling with the motion of her mouth, and he was already close. The feel of her mouth, the way she circled her tongue around the tip every few seconds, drove him mad.

She lifted her head and stared at him before he could warn her that he was close. Her mouth was swollen and red, and she licked her lips. "I want you to come in my mouth, Connor."

"Honey, are you sure?" he moaned.

"Yes," she said and bent back over him. Her warm mouth

surrounded him again, and he gave in to the sensation, pumping his dick between her lips over and over as he held her head still. She made an encouraging little moan, and the vibration of her lips against his cock sent him spiraling closer and closer.

"So close, honey," he moaned. "So close. Be a good girl and swallow all of my cum. Be my good girl, Kira, be my good... fuck!"

He arched his back, sliding himself deep into her mouth as he came hard. She made another muffled sound of surprise before swallowing eagerly. He gasped and moaned, pumping his hips rapidly as he came again and again. She swallowed repeatedly, only sliding her mouth from his dick when he slumped back against the bed.

She wiped her mouth and smiled at him as he gasped in air. "Okay?"

"Amazingly okay," he said. His knee should have been killing him, he'd been twisting around on the bed at the end like a damn puppet, but the endorphins from the best orgasm of his life had effectively muted any pain from his knee.

Kira had sat up next to his hip again, giving him a tentative look. "So, I wasn't terrible on my first try?"

"God, no," he said. "It was amazing, Kira. I swear. You were incredible."

"Thank you," she said with an adorable smug smile. "I liked it a lot."

"Good, I'm glad," he said. He reached out and cupped her breast, rubbing his thumb over the hard nipple. "Now it's your turn."

Kira gave Connor a nervous look. "What do you mean, my turn?"

He grinned at her, the dimple deepening in his cheek. "Pussy eating, little Kira. I'm going to eat your pussy."

Embarrassment flooded through her, but beneath that embarrassment was a healthy dose of lust that was incredibly difficult to ignore.

"I – you don't have to do that," she said. "I didn't give you a blowjob because I expected something in return."

"I realize that," he said. "I want to do this."

"I appreciate that, but I'm not sure it's a good idea with your knee. I don't want to hurt you or -"

"You won't. Sit on my face."

Her eyes widened. "Are you kidding me? No, no way, Connor."

"It's fine, honey," he said. "I can't lie on my stomach with my knee, so you need to kneel over my head and -"

"No, I am not doing that." She started to scoot off the bed, and his big hand clamped around her calf.

"Where are you going?"

"I can't sit on your face," she said as more embarrassment coated her entire body. "I – that's way too intimate for me, and I'm sorry, but I can't."

She glanced at his face, positive he would be angry with her, but he smiled at her and nodded. "All right. That's fine, little Kira. We'll do it a different way."

"We can't," she said. "Your knee is too sore."

He was already sliding down to the bottom of the bed, and she watched as he turned diagonal on the mattress before lying on his left side. "Hand me that pillow."

Biting her lip, she handed him the pillow, and he wedged

233

it between his knees, resting the right brace-covered one on top of the pillow.

"There," he said. "Now, get that sweet pussy in front of my face."

She blushed and chewed some more at her bottom lip. "Connor, I don't think I can."

"You can." He stroked her back. "You're beautiful and sexy, and I want to taste you so much, honey. I know you're feeling shy and a little embarrassed, but there's nothing to be embarrassed about. Your pussy is beautiful, and I can't wait to taste it."

He reached out and traced his fingers over her inner thighs. "Please, honey," he coaxed. "Let me be the first to taste your pussy. It's important to me."

A little shiver went down her spine, and the last of her embarrassment faded away. She also wanted Connor to be the first, she realized. She wanted it very much. Without hesitating, she manoeuvred her body on the bed until she was lying on her back, her right thigh next to Connor's head and her left leg draped over his ribs. Her pussy was directly in front of his face, but his delighted look erased her embarrassment.

"Good," he said, rubbing her left leg with one strong hand. "Shift a little closer, honey."

She wiggled down a little further and moaned when she felt his warm breath on her pussy lips. He kissed her inner thigh and slid one hand under her ass to cup her cheek. "Your pussy is so pretty, little Kira. So pretty and so wet."

She grabbed the sheets in both hands, her back arching when he licked across her lips. His tongue was warm and wet and so soft. She immediately wanted more.

"Please," she said. "Do that again."

She expected him to tease and torment her like he was so fond of doing. To her surprise, he bent his head immediately and licked her pussy again before using his thumb and finger to spread her pussy lips apart.

"Look at your pretty little clit," he said.

She cried out, her hips thrusting off the bed when he licked her clit. He licked it again before brushing his lips across it in a feather-light touch that made her shiver.

"Oh God," she said, "that feels so good."

"This will feel better," he replied.

Her eyes widened, and she made a soft scream of pleasure when he sucked on her clit. She'd never felt anything so good in her life. As his finger slid deep into her pussy, he sucked and laved at her clit with firm strokes of his tongue.

There was no teasing. Connor was a man determined to make her come, and holy fucking hell, she was one hundred percent good with that. She reached down and slid her fingers into his hair, holding tight as she rubbed her pussy shamelessly against his face. The rough stubble on his jaw rubbed against her pussy lips, sending more shivers of delight up and down her spine. He sucked on her clit again, and his finger – no fingers, he'd added another one – slid deeper into her, and she clenched around that thickness, needing, wanting, more.

He didn't seem to care that she was practically shoving her pussy into his face. The pace of his fingers pumping in and out of her increased, and he sucked even harder on her clit. The tip of his tongue flickered across it as he sucked, and that was all it took.

She screamed, her back arching, her fingers digging into his scalp, and came with explosive intensity all over his face. Her pussy clamped down around his fingers, squeezing compulsively as wave after wave of pleasure washed over her. She rocked against his face, her left foot drumming against his back, her right foot slamming into the mattress as her orgasm went on and on, her body rigid with pure ecstasy.

Finally, she slumped against the bed, releasing his head and letting her legs fall open. He raised his head, his face was dripping wet, and then kissed her inner thigh before carefully lifting her leg off of him. She rolled to her side, panting harshly for air as he slid his way up the bed.

He spooned her, his big hand cupping her breast as he wiped his mouth on the sheet and then kissed her back.

"Okay?" he mimicked her from earlier.

"Can't talk," she croaked. "Orgasm-induced heart attack."

He laughed and kissed her back again before resting his head on the pillow behind hers. "Should I be calling 9-1-1?"

"God no," she gasped. "Knowing my luck, my brother would show up."

"Good point," he said. "I do not want to have to explain to him that your heart attack was because I ate your pussy."

"My preference would be for you just to let me die."

He laughed again. "Noted."

She turned to face him, studying his eyes in the dim light. "You're really good at that."

"Thank you," he said.

"Really good. I've never come that hard in my life. I had no idea an orgasm could be that strong. I mean, I know I don't have any experience with it, but Gracie says that it's a lot harder for a woman to come from being eaten out or touched by a guy than most women think. She says it's not like a romance novel where the guy just looks at a woman, and she practically has an orgasm right then and there. She says most women end up faking because they're too shy to tell their partner exactly what they want, or their partner isn't open to watching and learning what she likes."

She slid her arm around his waist and squeezed him briefly. "I wasn't expecting to come from oral sex even though you made me come last night with your hand. I can't believe I did. I can't wait to tell Gracie that I..."

Her eyes widened. "I mean... not that I'm a gossip about my sexual habits. Of course, I won't tell Gracie or anyone else about this. I know it's private and -"

She'd never been so happy when Connor stopped her babbling with a kiss.

He pulled back and grinned at her. "One – Grace is not sleeping with the right guys, and two - do you always talk non-stop after an orgasm?"

"I think we established that I've never had an orgasm like that before."

"You're welcome," he said with an adorable grin.

She returned his smile, cupping his face and staring at him as he studied her. When he shifted a little, she glanced down at his knee. "Are you okay? Do you need to move positions?"

"Nope, I'm good." He put his arm around her and pulled her close until her breasts pressed against his chest, and their lower bodies touched.

"Are you sure? We don't have to cuddle or anything," she said, even though she absolutely wanted to cuddle.

He scowled a little. "Just because I'm not into PDAs doesn't mean I don't like to," he paused, "*cuddle* in private. I'm not completely cold."

Yikes, she'd hit a nerve.

"I know you're not," she said. "I just don't want to make you uncomfortable."

"You're not," he bit out. He closed his eyes and took a deep breath. "Sorry. I shouldn't have snapped."

"It's fine," she said.

He took another deep breath. "I've been called cold and distant in the past, and I'm a little sensitive about it."

She cupped his face. "I don't think you're cold or distant."

"No?" He studied her closely. "You're not just saying that?"

She shook her head, suddenly certain that whatever she said next would be very important to him. "No, I don't. You're sometimes a little...guarded, but that was mostly when I first met you. You're not cold, Connor. I don't even think you're distant. And," she gave him a teasing grin, "you're not nearly as anti-PDA as you think you are."

A small smile played on his lips. "I think that's a relatively new thing. Before you, I didn't do any PDAs."

"Why am I different?" she asked.

"I'm actively trying to make someone jealous for you, remember?" he said.

Stupidly, hurt flooded through her. Of course, Connor was only affectionate because he was playing a part. She shouldn't be upset by that. It's what she asked him to do.

So why was she hurt? Why did she wish he was affectionate because he wanted to be? Because he liked touching her and holding her?

He squeezed her waist. "Sorry, I'm not being completely honest."

"You're not?"

"No. I like touching you, Kira. I like it a lot."

"I like it too," she whispered.

He brushed her hair back from her face and pressed a kiss against her mouth. "Good."

She wanted to have sex with him. She knew that now. She just needed to tell him.

Butterflies danced in her stomach. Should she tell him? What if he said no? What if he thought it was a ridiculous idea? He was attracted to her, that was obvious, but what if he wasn't interested in banging a virgin? Maybe he secretly liked women with experience and she could barely kiss when she first met him.

Stop. You won't know for sure unless you ask. If he rejects you, so what? It's worth the risk. Take a deep breath and tell him.

She took a deep breath and told him. "I want to have sex with you, Connor."

CONNOR STARED WIDE-EYED AT KIRA, SURE HE'D MISHEARD her. "What?"

"I want to have sex with you," she repeated.

"Kira, you were clear that you're saving yourself for... someone else."

Did he really think it would bother him less if he didn't say Daniel's name?

"I've changed my mind," Kira said. "I think it's a better idea to have as much experience as possible. That means actual sex."

"You want to sleep with me for the experience," he said.

"Yes. I mean... no?" She studied him in the dim light. "Connor? Why are you upset?"

239

"I'm not."

"You're lying," she said. "I can tell."

"You said it was special to you," he said.

"I've changed my mind."

"Just like that," he said.

"Yes." She waited a beat and then said, "If you don't want to have sex with me, just say so."

"Obviously, I want to have sex with you," he said.

"Great. Let's have sex." She smiled at him and kissed his chest before licking the hollow of his throat. "I'm sure there's lots you can teach me, right?"

He pulled back. "Kira, don't."

She stared at him in confusion. "Don't what? You just said you want to have sex. So, let's have sex."

"It's more complicated than that."

"No, it isn't." She traced her fingers over his back. "Is it because of all that stuff I said about my virginity being special? Because I was wrong and just being silly. It isn't special. It's just a thing that I need to get rid of, that's all. It doesn't matter who I give it to, or -"

"It does matter!" His voice was too loud. "It matters, and it is special, and I want to be your first, Kira. I want that a lot. But not if you're only giving it to me because you're trying to get it over with, okay? I want to be your first because…"

"Because why?" she whispered.

His heart thudding in his chest, feeling vulnerable and naked in a way he'd never felt before, he said, "Because I like you. You're sweet and kind, and even after being dealt some shitty cards in life, you're still so damn positive and upbeat. I've never met anyone like you before, and when I'm with you, I…

He blew his breath out in a harsh rush. "You can say whatever you want, but I know your virginity is special to you. That makes it special to me. I know what it means to you, and I hate that you think it's okay to give it to me because you want more experience."

He stared at the wall over her head. "We have a lot of chemistry and connection, and I understand the desire to go further. But, if we do this now, if we have sex just so you can get it over with and gain some experience, you will regret giving it to me."

He swallowed hard. "I want to be your first, very much. But I would rather have you give your virginity to Daniel than give it to me and regret it later."

Weariness and disappointment sunk deep into his bones when she didn't reply. Kira was in love with Daniel. Her desire to have sex with him was a spur of the moment thing. She'd been hopped up on pheromones and an orgasm high, and he'd gone and told her exactly how he felt. Now, it was awkward as hell, and why didn't he just keep his damn mouth shut?

Without looking at her, he turned to his other side, flinching when his right knee banged against his left.

"Connor? Is your knee okay?"

"It's a little sore." Stung by her blatant rejection, he said, "I'm exhausted, Kira. I didn't sleep well last night with you in the bed. Would you mind sleeping in your bed tonight?"

"Oh, of course. I'm so sorry. I didn't mean, that is…"

Now, he could hear the rejection and the hurt in her voice. Guilt made him turn to face her. "Kira, wait, I'm being an ass."

"A bit, but I appreciate your honesty." She slid out of the

bed and grabbed her clothes from the floor. "Good night, Connor. Just text me if you need help in the night."

She was gone before he could say anything else. He groaned and fell onto his back, massaging just above his right knee as he stared at the ceiling. Fuck, what did he just do?

CHAPTER 17

Kira stared blankly out the kitchen window. The water was running in the sink, and after a moment, she reached out and turned it off before studying her hands. What had she been doing?

Her brain churned dully before she grasped it. Right. Making iced tea. She grabbed the jug from the counter and filled it with water before setting it down. A squirrel chittered away on a branch of the tree outside the window, and she watched it for a while before making the iced tea.

She put the jug in the fridge, sat at the table and stared in the direction of the living room. Today had been awful. Connor had spent all morning in his bedroom and barely eaten any lunch. He avoided looking at her and gave one-word answers to her questions. When he'd gone to shower, she hadn't offered to help. She knew what his answer would be.

About half an hour ago, he had crutched into the living room. She'd stuck her head into the room, tentatively asking him if he wanted anything. He shook his head, and her plan

243

to talk to him about last night dissolved under a wave of her own cowardice and the weariness on his face.

Her stomach was churning, and she rubbed at it as she listened to the faint sound of the TV. She'd barely slept last night, her mind turning over and over what Connor had said to her. She grabbed her phone off the table. She needed to talk to Grace and Addison. She would text them and see if they could meet her after work.

The doorbell rang, and she shoved her phone into her pocket before walking down the hallway. She opened the door and stared blankly at the man on the front porch.

"Can I help you?" she asked.

"You must be Kira," he said.

She studied him. He was tall with short, light brown hair and hazel coloured eyes. He was lean like Connor, and he wore jeans and a t-shirt with a blue hoodie over top.

"Do I know you?" she said.

"Not exactly," he said with a grin. He stuck his hand out. "I'm Lucas Wright. I'm Connor's best friend."

"Connor's best friend," she repeated as she shook his hand. "You're from Willington?"

His grin widened. "Yes, but don't hold that against me. I live in New Cassel now."

She continued to stare at him, and he cleared his throat. "Uh, is Connor here? He said he was staying with you while he recuperated."

"Yes, of course." She gave him an embarrassed smile. "Sorry, come in, please."

"Thanks." He followed her into the house and shut the door.

"Connor's just in the living room. It's this way." Feeling

extraordinarily stupid, she led him to the living room. "Connor, you have a visitor."

Connor glanced up from his phone. A huge smile broke out across his face, and her breath caught in her throat. God, he was so handsome.

"Lucas! What are you doing here?"

Lucas dropped onto the couch beside him and stretched out his long legs. "I had the afternoon off and figured what better way to spend a Thursday afternoon than driving a couple hours to visit my wounded little bird."

Connor laughed. "Shut up. I can't believe you came."

"Did you not wonder why I texted you for Kira's address?" Lucas said.

"I figured you were sending me flowers," Connor said with a grin.

Lucas snorted laughter. "If I were gonna send anything, it would have been a stripper-gram."

"Shocking," Connor replied.

Lucas studied his knee. "That looks like shit."

"It was a lot worse," Kira said. "It's looking much better than it was."

Both Lucas and Connor glanced at her, and she blushed. Obviously, they had forgotten she was in the room and feeling like an intruder, she backed toward the doorway. "Sorry, I'll leave and give you some privacy."

Connor frowned. "You don't have to leave your own house."

"It's fine. I have some errands to run this afternoon anyway. Lucas, it was nice to meet you. Connor, um, text me if you need anything."

She hurried out of the living room, grabbed her phone and purse from the kitchen and left the house. She climbed into the car and rubbed her forehead. Shit, she probably should have kissed Connor goodbye or something. It's what a girlfriend was supposed to do.

If you think Lucas doesn't know this is fake, you're fooling yourself. He's Connor's best friend. He knows.

Yeah, probably. Connor would have told him the truth, so not kissing him was fine. Perfectly fine.

Except you want to kiss Connor. Hell, you want to be his real girlfriend. Admit it, Kira.

No, she loved Daniel. She'd always love Daniel. He was perfect for her, and they were meant to be together.

Bullshit.

She groaned with frustration and started the car. She backed out of the driveway and drove down the street. She would walk at the Falls while waiting for Gracie and Addie to finish work. It would help clear her mind.

"SAY SOMETHING, YOU GUYS," KIRA SAID.

Addison glanced at Grace before saying, "I don't think we know what to say. You want to give Connor your virginity after saving it for years for my brother. You were in love with Daniel, and now, suddenly, you're not."

"I am still in love with Daniel," Kira said.

"Are you though?" Grace said.

"Shit. I don't know anymore," Kira said.

They were sitting in the small living room of Grace's townhouse. Addison leaned forward and grabbed another pizza slice from the box sitting on the coffee table. She took a bite and chewed slowly. "It's okay if your feelings change, Kira."

"I don't know what my feelings are," Kira said. "I thought I loved Daniel, but now…"

"It sounds like Connor really likes you," Grace said. "Why not give that a chance?"

"Just because he wants to be my first and thinks it's special doesn't mean he likes me," Kira replied.

Grace arched one eyebrow at her. "Uh, that's exactly what it means. Besides, you just told us that he told you he liked you. Remember?"

"Oh my God," Kira leaned back on the couch and stared at the ceiling, "this is so messed up."

"What you need to decide," Addison said, "is whether you want to have sex with Connor because you want some experience or because you want him to be your first rather than my brother."

"My unsolicited opinion?" Grace said. "You should sleep with Connor. You might not want to admit this, but you like him, Kira-bear. You like him a lot. Besides, I'm pretty sure Daniel will be a terrible lover. He's a good guy, but he is on the selfish side, and it's been my experience that selfish guys don't make good sex partners. Do you want that for your first time?"

"Ugh," Addison set down her piece of pizza, "all of this sex talk about my brother makes me lose my appetite."

"Sorry, Addie," Kira said.

"It's okay," she replied. "I know you're struggling, and I want to be a supportive best friend. But if I run out of the room and you hear vomiting, ignore it."

Kira smiled briefly before running her fingers restlessly through her hair. "I like Connor, but I've spent how many years in love with Daniel? Is it normal for a person's feelings to turn off and on like a faucet? Because that doesn't feel normal to me."

"Honey," Grace leaned over and squeezed her knee, "you're completely normal. Loving someone who doesn't love you back isn't the same as being in a committed relationship with someone."

Kira winced, and Grace squeezed her knee again. "I'm sorry. I know that sucks to hear, but it's time for some painful truths. You've been doing this fake relationship with Connor for almost three weeks and Daniel hasn't made a move on you. There have been no signs of jealousy, has there?"

"No," Kira said.

"Which doesn't bother you," Grace said.

"It does," Kira protested.

Grace just stared at her, and Kira looked down at her hands. "At first, I wanted it to bother me, but now…"

"Connor is a good guy," Grace said. "I think you should give him a chance."

"It's too late," Kira said. "I was so surprised and confused by what he said that I didn't say anything, which upset him. He's completely closed down and would barely talk to me today."

"Well, the good news is that he's kind of trapped in your house, and with that knee the way it is, he can't run from you," Addison said with a small smile. "Just take away his crutches and start talking."

Kira huffed out a laugh. "If only it were that easy."

"It is that easy," Grace said.

Kira picked at her nail. "This feels weird. I've been in love with Daniel for so long that to think I'm not in love with him... it's freaking me out. I'm not sure who I am if I'm not in love with him."

"Your crush on Daniel does not define who you are," Grace said. "There's so much more to you than that, Kira-bear."

"Is there?" Kira said. "It doesn't feel like there is."

"Let's see," Addison said. "You're a great sister, an amazing friend, a kick-ass real estate agent, and an excellent fake girlfriend."

Kira stared at her and Grace. "What if being a fake girlfriend is all Connor wants now?"

"There's only one way to find out," Grace said. "Talk to him, honey."

"I will," Kira said. "But not right now. He gets the results of his MRI tomorrow, and I know he's worried about it. I don't want to add to his stress by pushing him for a relationship. Especially when I'm still not certain that's what I want."

She leaned over and rested her head on Grace's shoulder. "Thank you so much, you guys. I don't know what I'd do without you."

Grace kissed her forehead as Addison smiled at her. "We'll always be here for you, honey. Always."

KIRA SLAMMED THE CAR DOOR SHUT AND STARED apprehensively at the house. She was nervous about going in, which was stupid. The place was dark, and she knew Connor was already in bed. He'd texted her over an hour ago to say he was going to bed and ask if she was still available to drive him to his doctor's appointment tomorrow.

Addison had gone home earlier, but Kira deliberately

stayed a little longer at Grace's, too chicken to go home before Connor fell asleep. She needed to talk to him but was tired and confused and needed more time.

"Hey, Kira."

She whirled around, her pulse thumping and coppery fear in her mouth. "Daniel? You scared the hell out of me."

"Sorry, doll – I mean, Kira. I didn't mean to scare you." He leaned against her car, his hands in his pockets and a sheepish smile on his face.

"What are you doing here? It's late."

"It's not that late," he said. "I've been waiting for you to get home."

She glanced around him at his truck parked on the street. "Seriously?"

"You won't answer my calls or text with me anymore."

She sighed. "That's not true. I texted you this morning."

"Not the way you used to," he said. "Listen, I didn't mean to hurt the doc, okay? It was an accident."

"Was it?" she said.

"I'm not a bad guy, Kira."

"I know you're not." She glanced at the house. She had promised Connor she wouldn't be alone with Daniel and felt uneasy about breaking that promise. "I should go. It's chilly, and I'm not wearing a jacket."

"Can I come in for a while?"

She chewed at her bottom lip. "That's not a good idea. Connor's staying with me while he recuperates."

"What? Your boyfriend won't let you have other guys in the house now? Is that why you've been ignoring me? Why you wouldn't let me stop by and watch the game with you earlier this week?"

"That isn't it," she said.

Daniel frowned at her. "If he's stopping you from seeing your friends, that's a shitty thing for him to do. Do you want him to control your life like this, Kira? I know everyone thinks the doc is a good guy, but I'm not sure he is. He's got a coldness to him that -"

"He isn't cold," Kira said. "You don't know him at all, so stop making assumptions. He isn't keeping me from my friends. I was with Gracie and Addison for most of the day."

"So, it's just me he's keeping you away from," Daniel said. "Look, I get that he's jealous of our relationship, but again, do you want someone that insecure? It's pretty immature of him not to allow you to have guy friends."

"Stop it," she said. Her confusion ebbed away as anger replaced it. "Stop talking about Connor like you know him. You don't, Daniel. You don't know him at all."

"I'm just worried about you, doll. You're sweet and trusting, and a guy like that? He doesn't understand our relationship."

"Our relationship?" Kira said. "What exactly is our relationship, Daniel?"

"Special," he said.

She rolled her eyes. "Are you kidding me right now?"

Daniel reached for her, and she pulled away. He gave her a hurt look. "Now I can't touch you? You used to let me hug you."

"It's different now," she said.

"Only because Connor's made it different," Daniel said. "I miss you, Kira. I miss us. I get that Connor is important to you, but you've only been dating him for less than a month. Don't let him make you do something you'll regret, like giving up on us."

"Us," she said.

"Yes," he replied. "Like I said, I miss us."

"What exactly do you miss about *us*, Daniel? Be specific," Kira said.

"You know, I miss how we were together. You coming to watch me play ball and cheering me on, bringing me special little treats at the station, helping me with shit, me coming by to watch the game with you. I care about you a lot, and I hate that we no longer spend time together."

She stared silently at him and shook her head when he tried to put his arm around her. "Don't."

She was an idiot. Daniel would never be jealous of her relationship with Connor. The only thing that bothered him about her dating Connor was that she wasn't around anymore to cater to his every whim, to worship him, and to make him feel good that she pined after him like a fool.

"Are you seriously going to tell me you don't miss me?" he said.

"What would I miss?" she asked, that unexpected anger still bubbling inside her. "You and I aren't friends, Daniel. I thought we were, I really did, and I believed we could have more for a long time, but that isn't true, is it?"

He gave her an uncomfortable look and shoved his hands back into his pockets. "Doll, I don't -"

"Do not call me doll. I am not a doll or a toy for you to play with at your whim. I am a real person with thoughts and feelings, and I know you've been using my affection for you since we were kids. I know that, Daniel. And I was okay with it because I loved you and wanted to be with you so bad that I was willing to take whatever scrap of attention you doled out to me."

"Kira, I didn't -"

"But not anymore," she went on relentlessly. "My eyes are

finally open, and I see you for who you are. A selfish guy who used a girl's crush on him to get what he wanted."

"That isn't true," Daniel said. "I care about you, Kira. I'm sorry I'm not in love with you the way you want me to be, but I still care about you as a friend."

"Oh yeah? When's my birthday, Daniel?"

He hesitated, and she made a small bitter laugh. "What's my favourite colour? When did I learn to drive? How long was I depressed after my parents died?"

He didn't reply, and she sighed and gave him a look of sorrow and regret. "You don't know because you didn't come around much during that time, did you? I couldn't be the attentive, everything is about Daniel, Kira that you were used to, so you just disappeared. You walked away when I needed support the most."

She wiped away the tears streaming down her face. "The pathetic part is I forgave you for it. I loved you so much I told myself it didn't matter that you abandoned me during the worst time of my life. I told myself that not everyone was good with death and with grieving, and it didn't matter because I had Gideon and Grace to take care of me."

"I'm sorry, Kira." Daniel's voice was low, the look on his face one of genuine regret.

"I know you are," she said. "But it's too late. I don't love you anymore, and right now? I don't want to be your friend either. I can't keep giving and giving and not receiving anything in return. That isn't how a friendship works. I deserve better than you, Daniel Moore."

She turned and walked away. Halfway up the porch steps, Daniel called her name. She turned around and studied him in the glow of the street lights.

"I'm sorry, Kira. I really am," Daniel said.

"I'll see you around, Daniel."

CHAPTER 18

"It's twenty minutes after your appointment," Kira glanced at her watch. "I'm going to ask the nurse where he is."

"It's fine," Connor said. "Orthopedic specialists are always running late."

She chewed at her bottom lip, and without thinking, he reached out and caught her hand, linking their fingers together. "He'll be here soon."

She smiled at him before staring at their clasped hands. "I'm sorry. I'm supposed to be supporting you in this moment."

"You are supporting me," he said.

"Yeah, my skyrocketing anxiety must be super helpful for you," she said.

He smiled and squeezed her hand. "I'm glad you're here with me."

"Me too." She studied his mouth and then looked away, the telltale flush of embarrassment rising in her cheeks.

"I'm sorry about yesterday," he said. "I ignored you all day, which was really immature of me."

"It's okay," she said. "I upset you."

"But that's no excuse," he said. "I hate when people call me cold, but that's what I was to you, and it wasn't right. I'm sorry."

"You're not cold," she said. "But apology accepted. Also, I'm sorry for upsetting you Wednesday night. I didn't mean to."

"It isn't your fault that I'm jealous of Daniel. Some fake boyfriend I turned out to be, huh?"

"You don't have to be jealous of Daniel. I'm not -"

"Dr. MacMillan?" The door opened, and a short and stocky man with thinning hair and a goatee bustled into the room. He shook Connor's and Kira's hands before sitting behind the desk. "Sorry, I'm late. I'll get right to your results."

Connor tensed and was grateful when Kira immediately scooted her chair closer and linked her arm around his. He held his breath as the doctor sat back in his chair.

"Good news. Nothing is torn. The MCL and ACL are looking good, as is your meniscus."

Connor blinked at him. "I – what?"

"Everything's good. Well, other than the bruising and swelling but," the doctor stood and moved around the desk to crouch in front of Connor, "even that is looking better. He probed a bit at Connor's knee. The swelling has gone down significantly, I see."

"Nothing is torn," Connor said.

The doctor nodded, and the weight that had sat in his stomach for a week dropped away. He took a deep breath before staring at Kira. "Nothing is torn."

"That's such good news," she said.

She squeaked in shock when he leaned closer, cupped her face, and planted a kiss on her mouth. He pulled back as the doctor stood and returned to his chair.

"I'm going to recommend you wear the brace for at least another few weeks, just to be on the safe side. Keep icing it, and on Monday, try switching to a cane and see how that works for you. Sound good?"

"Yes," Connor said. "Can I return to work on Monday?"

"Depends on whether you can sit while you're filling a cavity or doing a root canal," the doctor said with a grin.

"I'll make it work," Connor said.

"Maybe start with half-days," the doctor said.

"Yeah, sure, okay." He sounded giddy, but hell, he *was* giddy. His knee wasn't wrecked.

He glanced at Kira again. Her face radiated happiness, and she gave him a genuinely excited smile. She was nearly as happy as he was about his knee. He studied her face for a moment. God, she was fucking gorgeous, and he'd screwed up royally with her. Once his cousin's wedding was done, she'd walk away, and he'd never get to touch her again.

His hand tightened on hers, and worry flickered across her face when she looked at him. "You okay?"

"I'm good," he said.

"You sure?"

He nodded, and she smiled at him. "Let's get out of here and celebrate."

"THIS DOESN'T FEEL LIKE MUCH OF A CELEBRATION." KIRA took the empty plates to the dishwasher and loaded them in as Connor collected the empty food containers into a shopping bag and crutched his way to the garbage can. "Is your knee hurting? Is that why we ordered to go instead of eating in the restaurant?"

She gave him an anxious look as Connor joined her by the sink, propping his crutches against the counter and leaning his hip on the counter to support his weight. He shook his head. "No, it feels fine. This is the best it's felt all week."

"That's good," she said.

Connor was standing so close to her that his body heat made her feel too warm and too aware of the sudden achiness in her lower body. She wanted him so much.

"I'm thrilled that your knee is only bruised," she said.

"Me too." He studied her face, and she stepped back to avoid standing on her tiptoes and planting a kiss on his mouth.

Disappointment flashed in his eyes, as well as regret, and she blurted out the truth. "I'm sorry, I just – I want you a lot, and it's hard to be this close to you without throwing myself at you."

"I want you too," he said in a low voice. "It's all I can think about."

"Me too," she whispered.

She shuffled closer, and he slid his arm around her waist before bending his head and resting his forehead against hers. He inhaled deeply, his warm hand cupping her hip. "I want to sleep with you, I do, but I -"

"I saw Daniel last night," she said.

He tensed against her, raising his head to study her. "Where?"

"He was waiting outside when I got home last night."

Was it wrong that she got a little thrill from the jealousy that crossed Connor's face?

"So, he's stalking you now?"

She shook her head. "No, he just wanted to talk. He was upset because we weren't hanging out as much."

His body was now so stiff it was like hugging a board. "Well, I guess that's good, right? You want him to be jealous."

"He was only jealous because I'm not fawning over him anymore," she said.

He didn't reply, and she rubbed her hand over his chest. "What I said on Wednesday night about only sleeping with you to gain experience? It wasn't true."

"No?" His voice was guarded, unwilling to accept what she was saying yet.

"No, it wasn't," she said. "I do think my virginity is special, and maybe that's silly, but it's how I feel. It's important to me, and I want to give it to someone who knows that. I want to give it to you because you understand what it means to me and because it's special to you, too."

"What about Daniel?" he said.

"I don't want Daniel to have it anymore. In fact, I don't want Daniel at all."

"Since when?" he said.

"Since I realized that I want and need someone who is interested in me for more than just what I can do for them. Someone who wants to get to know me better, looks out for me, makes me laugh, and accepts me for who I am. Someone like you, Connor."

"Kira, I'm not... I'm not always great at being in a relationship. I can be moody sometimes and closed off."

She shrugged. "I've never even been in a serious relationship before. I might suck at it too. I'm a little needy occasion-

ELIZABETH KELLY

ally, and I'm still struggling with my parents' deaths. I take medication for depression, and I have twice monthly therapy appointments, but some days are harder than others. I have no idea if I'll be a good girlfriend."

He pulled her up tight against him and pressed a kiss against her forehead. "You're a great girlfriend. You can't expect yourself to be perfect in a relationship, honey."

She smiled a little. "Neither can you."

He paused. "I walked right into that, didn't I?"

"Yep."

He laughed and kissed her forehead again. "Did we just decide to try dating for real?"

"I think we did," she said.

The dimple in his cheek made an appearance. "Best day ever."

"Actually," she said, "I could think of one more thing that would make it the best day ever."

"Oh yeah?" The heat in his eyes made her nipples harden. "What's that?"

"You and me banging like bunnies," she said.

He burst into laughter. "So romantic."

"To quote Gracie – that's me, romantic as fuck," Kira said. She took a deep breath. "In all seriousness, I want you to be my first, Connor. If you still want that?"

Connor smoothed her hair back from her face. "I want that so much, little Kira."

"Then take me to your bed."

SHE SHOULD HAVE BEEN NERVOUS, RIGHT? SHE WAS ABOUT TO have sex for the first time with the hottest man in

Harmony Falls, and that should have her filled with anxiety.

Except she wasn't. Not one bit. Nope, she wasn't feeling anything but a raging horniness and an almost frantic need to get Connor on the bed and inside of her.

They were standing next to the guest bed, and she pulled Connor's shirt off so roughly that he almost fell on the bed. She grabbed him around the waist. "Sorry, you okay?"

He grinned at her. "Fine. You can slow down, you know. We have all night."

"Easy for you to say, you've had sex before," she said. "I want to get to the good stuff."

He laughed and tugged her shirt over her head, dropping it on the floor. "Fair enough. Are you okay with being on top for your first time?"

"Perfectly fine with it." She pulled his shorts down his legs and then his briefs, making a small sound of excitement when she saw his cock. "Your dick is my new favourite thing."

He unhooked her bra, and she wiggled out of it, tossing it aside before unbuttoning her jeans and shoving them and her panties down her legs. She stepped out of them and kicked them aside. "Lie down on the bed, Connor."

"Honey, we have plenty of time." He pulled her close, and she rubbed her abdomen against his erection, smiling when he inhaled sharply.

"I want you," she said.

"I want you too. But I'm not rushing this," he said.

She pouted at him, and he kissed the tip of her nose. "You're adorable when you pout. Still not rushing it."

She kissed his chest, and he cupped the back of her head, moaning quietly when she sucked on his flat nipple.

"You sure about that?" she said with a small grin.

He reached down and squeezed her ass. "Positive. Do you have any condoms?"

Horror rushed through her, and she froze against him. "Shit! Dammit, I don't have any condoms, and I'm not on the pill. Fuck."

He kissed her into silence before pointing at his wallet on the nightstand. "I have a couple in my wallet."

"Oh, thank God," she said.

She wiggled out of his grip and grabbed his wallet, pulling a condom out and setting it on the nightstand as Connor carefully eased onto the bed. He was wearing the brace on his knee and carefully moved until he was lying on his side facing her. He patted the bed. "Come here, little Kira."

She eagerly climbed onto the bed, lying on her back beside Connor and staring up at him as he cupped one small breast. She arched her back when he teased her nipple with his thumb, her lower body moving restlessly.

"You're so beautiful, honey," he said. He dipped his head, and she weaved her fingers into his hair as he licked around her nipple before sucking lightly on it. She closed her eyes, relishing in the feel of his warm mouth and tongue as he tasted and teased both her nipples.

Already, she was soaking wet. She could feel liquid dripping down her thighs, and she widened her legs, silently urging Connor to touch her. Instead of touching her, he lifted his head and rested one heavy hand on her flat stomach, studying her face as she gave him a pleading look.

"Connor, I can't wait. I really can't."

"I want you to come first," he said before leaning down and pressing his mouth against hers.

As he slipped his tongue into her mouth, he ran his

fingers down her stomach and between her legs. He rubbed at her clit as he sucked on her tongue, and she clutched at his broad shoulders, frantically returning his kiss.

She was so wet that she couldn't get the friction she needed against her clit. She made a harsh sound of frustration as Connor lifted his head. "Shh, little Kira."

She didn't even feel a flicker of embarrassment when Connor used the sheet to wipe away some of her wetness before rubbing his fingers against her clit again. She moaned happily, sparks of pleasure igniting in her belly as Connor touched her with firm circles.

She clutched at his forearm, panting hard and rocking her pelvis against his fingers. He pushed two fingers inside of her, thrusting lightly as he continued to caress her clit with his thumb. He bent his head and sucked hard on her nipple.

She cried out and arched her back, staring sightlessly at the ceiling as the pleasure of her orgasm overtook her in slow, sweet waves. Connor touched her lightly, rubbing the wet lips of her pussy and avoiding her oversensitive clit as she turned her head and buried her face in his throat.

She pressed a kiss against his skin, and he stroked her inner thighs. "That sounded like a good one."

"Hmmm." She reached out blindly for his cock, smiling when her fingers brushed against the head, and he moaned low in his throat.

She wrapped her fingers around him and stroked him, loving the way his body trembled against hers, the way the low groans of pleasure slipped from his mouth.

She lifted her head and pressed a kiss against his chin before releasing him and reaching for the condom. He carefully moved to his back, and she handed the condom to him and then eased a pillow under his right knee.

"Thank you," he said.

She nodded and watched as he opened the condom and rolled it down over his cock. When it was in place, she knelt beside him and gave him a tentative look. "Ready?"

"Yes, are you?" he asked.

"Unbelievably ready," she said.

A smile crossed his face, and he patted his stomach. "Well, hop on then, cowgirl."

She giggled and straddled him, careful not to bump his right knee. She could feel his cock pressing against her clit, and she rubbed a bit experimentally. Connor moaned, and she grinned at him. "I think I'm going to like being on top."

He cupped her small breasts, flicking at her taut nipples with his thumbs. "I know I'm enjoying it."

"Okay, here we go," she said.

She supposed that wasn't a very romantic thing to say, but Connor just smiled at her and reached between her legs to lightly rub her clit. "Go slow, honey. Take your time, and if it hurts, don't feel like you have to keep going. We can stop as many times as you need."

Feeling awkward, she nodded and rose up on her knees, bracing one hand on Connor's chest. He put both hands on her hips and lifted her a little. She reached down and grasped his cock, guiding it to her pussy and pressing it against her entrance. The head slipped in, and she bit her lip at the new sensation.

"Okay?" His voice trembled with need, but his hands were steady as he gripped her hips.

"Yes," she whispered. She took a deep breath and lowered her body in a smooth motion. His cock slid into her, there was a brief, intense pop of pain, and then she was sitting on top of him, her pussy full of his cock and her knees digging into his ribs.

She stared down at him, and he caressed her hips and lower back. "How do you feel?"

"Weird. Kind of full and… weird," she said, then blushed a little. "It wasn't as painful as I thought it would be."

He rubbed her thighs. "That's good."

"Does it feel good for you?" she asked.

"Honey, you have no idea," he said with a strained smile. "It's pure torture to lie here and not move. Your pussy is so tight and wet."

"Is your knee okay?" She glanced behind her, her body twisting a little, and he groaned loudly.

"Yeah, it's fine. Do you think you're ready to move?"

She nodded and braced her hands on his chest before making a few experimental thrusts. He cried out, his hands tightening on her hips, and she watched in utter fascination as an intense look of pure pleasure crossed his face.

Already addicted to his reaction, she rocked and thrust a little faster, staring intently at Connor's face. He opened his eyes and met her gaze, his hands reaching up to cup both her breasts as his hips rose and fell in perfect timing with her thrusts.

"So good, honey," he whispered. "You feel so good."

A sweet warmth was starting up inside of her, and when Connor reached down and rubbed her clit, the warmth turned into a fiery burn.

"Oh!" She went stock still for a moment and then rode him harder and faster, finding the rhythm of their bodies with surprising ease. She didn't think she would come again, but as Connor thrust harder into her, one hand holding her hip to steady her, the other pressing against her pussy and rubbing at her clit, the familiar pleasure soared within her.

She let her head fall back, moaning and panting as they moved together, the bed squeaking with every thrust. Connor's fingers danced over her swollen, throbbing clit, and she cried his name, her fingers digging into his chest as she climaxed on his cock.

He shouted with pleasure, his body tensing and thrusting hard as she collapsed against his chest. He held her firmly and pumped in and out of her, his hot breath blowing in her ear and his low moans sending warmth through her body. He made one final thrust, his body stiff against hers and his hands pressing hard into her lower back before slumping against the bed.

She stayed where she was for a few minutes before easing off him and curling up next to him. He put his arm around her, and she rested her head on his chest as he threaded his fingers through her hair.

After a while, he said, "Are you okay, little Kira?"

"Yes," she said. "It was amazing."

He sat up and took off the condom, tying the end of it. She pushed into a sitting position and held out her hand. "Give it to me."

She tossed it in the garbage can beside the nightstand and pulled the covers over them before curling into his side. "Is your knee hurting?"

"A little," he said.

She frowned at him, and he kissed her forehead. "Totally worth it."

"I'll get you some meds."

He pulled her back into his arms when she tried to slide

out of bed. "In a little bit. For now, stay right where you are, little Kira. I like to cuddle after sex."

She giggled and threw her arm around his waist, snuggling close and kissing his chest. "You get fifteen minutes of cuddling, and then I'm getting your pain meds, Dr. MacMillan."

They lay quietly for a few minutes before Connor said, "Thank you, Kira."

She pressed another kiss against his warm skin. "I'm the one who should be thanking you. It was perfect. I'll never forget this night, Connor."

He kissed her forehead. "Me either."

CHAPTER 19

"I think I might be a sex addict, Gracie."

Grace choked on her sip of coffee before wiping her mouth with her napkin. "Honey, you're not."

"I might be," Kira said.

"You had sex for the first time on Friday. It's now Monday. You're not a sex addict," Grace said.

Kira glanced around the crowded coffee shop and lowered her voice. "Connor and I did nothing all weekend but have sex. My thighs hurt so much I could barely walk this morning. At work today, Rose asked me why I was limping, and I didn't know what to tell her. I just went bright red, mumbled something about a yoga accident and ran away. Well... limped away."

Gracie grinned at her. "How's your hoo-hah?"

"A little tender," Kira admitted. "But not enough to make me stop. Connor said we should take a break last night, but the minute we got into bed... we were all over each other."

"That's normal," Grace said. "You're not a sex addict."

"Are you sure?"

Grace nodded. "I'm happy for you, honey."

"Thanks," Kira said. "Sex with Connor is amazing."

"How's his knee holding up?" Grace asked.

"It's getting better every day. We're careful not to reinjure it. We've only had sex with me on top." Kira sipped at her coffee. "I like being on top, and Connor likes it too, but I also can't wait to try different positions."

"Variety is the spice of life," Grace said with a laugh. "I talked to Connor this morning at work, and he was in a damn good mood. I see he ditched the crutches for a cane."

"Yes. He only did a half day, but I called him at lunch, and he said it went well. He can put weight on his leg using the cane, and Grant ordered this special kind of stool that raises high enough for him to sit while he's looking at patients' teeth."

"Yeah, he was using it on the cavity filling this morning," Grace said. "It's good that he could return to work so soon."

"It is," Kira replied. "Connor was worried about letting Grant down, but he's been very understanding."

"So, now that you're dating for real, are you more nervous or less nervous about attending his cousin's wedding with him?" Grace asked.

"More, I think," Kira said. "I want to make a good impression on his parents, you know?"

"What about his ex?" Grace said.

"I'm not sure how I feel about it. I'm not worried that Connor is still in love with her or anything, but I don't know why they broke up."

"Connor didn't tell you?" Grace said.

"No. I asked when we were first fake dating, and he said he wouldn't talk about it with me."

"But you're actually dating now. Shouldn't that be something he shares?"

"Is it any of my business, though? They're over, and I assume it was messy and painful, which is why Connor won't discuss it. I won't push him about it."

"Well," Grace took another sip of coffee, "you're a better girlfriend than me. I'd be dying to know the details. Hell, I *am* dying to know, and he's not even my boyfriend."

"I think in a few more months, he'll tell me. Connor takes a while to open up, and I want to respect that. Not everyone can be an oversharer like me," Kira said with a small smile.

She glanced at her phone. "Half an hour until my showing. Can you believe I'm showing a house tonight? Two weeks ago, I couldn't find a client if my life depended on it. This morning, three different people called and asked me to show them some houses."

"That's awesome, Kira."

"Thanks. Can you keep hanging out with me, or do you want to go home to bed?" she asked.

"It's only six," Grace said.

"Don't take this the wrong way, but you look exhausted," Kira said. "Are you not sleeping again?"

Grace stared at her coffee cup. "My old friend insomnia might be knocking at the door."

"Oh, honey." Kira reached out and squeezed her hand. "Did you take your medication for it?"

"You know I hate taking it. It makes me sluggish and slow and doesn't feel like real sleep anyway."

"When was the last time you got a good night's sleep?"

"I don't remember," Grace admitted. "I slept a couple of hours last night at least."

"Well, you should go home and have a hot bath and do

your relaxation techniques," Kira said. "You don't need to stay here with me."

"I want to be here," Grace said. "Besides, none of that has been working, so what's the point? I might as well do something productive like sit in the coffee shop and discuss my best friend's sex life."

Kira laughed and pulled her phone out of her purse when it rang. "Hey, Gideon. What's up?"

She listened for a few minutes and then said, "I'm sorry, I can't. I have a showing in half an hour. Yeah, another one. Thanks, I'm excited too. But I feel bad for poor Tank."

She glanced at Grace. "Grace is here with me. I bet she'd be happy to stop at your place and feed Tank. What? No, she heard me… wait a minute."

She smiled at her best friend. "Gideon is working late. Would you mind stopping at his place, letting Tank out, and feeding him? Maybe hang out with him for an hour or so?"

Grace crossed her arms over her chest. "I don't have a key to his place."

"I'll give you mine," Kira said. "Please, Gracie? Poor Tank has been in the house all day. He's hungry, and he's gotta pee."

"Yeah, fine, okay. I'll go," Grace said.

"Great!" Kira smiled happily at her before saying into the phone, "Gideon? Grace will check on Tank. I'll give her my key to your place, okay? What? No, don't be silly. She doesn't mind. Why would she mind? Listen, I have to go. I'll talk to you later."

She ended the call and dug her keys out of her purse, taking off one of them and handing it to Grace. "This is Gideon's house key. Tank's food is in the pantry, lower shelf.

He gets five cups of dry food. Just let him out into the back-yard to pee. You don't have to take him for a walk or anything. Okay?"

"Okay," Grace said. She rubbed delicately at her temples, and Kira gave her a guilty look.

"I'm sorry. Are you sure you don't mind doing this? I know you're exhausted."

"No, it's fine. Tank needs to be let out, and it's not like I'll sleep anyway, right?" Grace took the key from her. "Good luck at your showing. Text me and let me know how it goes."

She was in Gideon's house. No big deal. She'd been in his house before. Sure, it was always with Kira, but so what? Gideon knew she was here. It wasn't like she was sneaking in or spying on him or something.

She opened the back door and looked for Tank. She rubbed her thigh where the flesh still stung. The minute she'd stepped into Gideon's house, Tank had come flying toward her. She'd gotten him to sit before he could knock her over, but as she was leading him to the back door, his madly wagging tail had whacked her a few times on the thigh. She'd be lucky if she didn't have a bruise tomorrow.

Tank was sniffing the fence line along the back of the yard, and she called his name. He snapped his head up, his big goofy grin making her smile as his wagging tail thudded a booming rhythm against the fence.

"C'mon, big guy," she said. "Time to eat."

The big dog bounded across the yard and straight into the house, knocking her against the wall as he rushed past her.

273

She followed him to the kitchen, where he sat beside his dog dish by the pantry door, his tongue lolling from his mouth.

She measured out the five cups of dog food, it filled the bowl to the brim, and set it in front of him. He stared at her, his tail thumping against the floor, and she made a go on motion. "Eat, Tank."

He chuffed happily and stuck his face in his food dish. She left the kitchen and walked past the living room and down the narrow hallway to the first door on the right. It was Gideon's office, and she studied his pin-neat desk, the books arranged by size and colour on his bookshelf, and the certificates that lined the wall behind his desk.

She liked her place tidy, but Gideon was a total neat freak. She'd never know how he kept his place so clean with a giant, slobbery, hairy dog.

The door on the left was a half-bath. She used it and washed her hands before hesitating at the bottom of the stairs. She could hear Tank still crunching away, and she climbed the stairs, walking past the guest room converted to a home gym and the guest bathroom before stopping at the end of the hallway.

Gideon's bedroom door was closed, and she cast a guilty look behind her before opening the door and stepping inside. Her gaze was immediately glued to the king-size bed between the two windows on the far wall. Although his bedroom was as tidy as the rest of his house, he, weirdly, hadn't made his bed.

She stared for a long time at his unmade bed before walking slowly toward it. She sat on the side of the bed, staring at the door to the attached bathroom before kicking off her shoes and lying in his bed.

Gracie! What are you doing?

She turned her head and buried her face into his pillow, inhaling deeply. It smelled like him, and her pussy immediately went wet. She clamped her legs together, resisting the urge to shove her hand down her pants, and inhaled again.

She turned on her side and reached down to grab the covers, pulling them up to her shoulders and burying her face in his pillow again.

Oh my god, Grace. Get out of his bed. Right now. Have you lost your damn mind?

She yawned and closed her eyes. It was so nice to be in his bed. It was stupidly comfortable, and Gideon's scent was oddly relaxing. She yawned again, tucking her hand under his pillow and wiggling into a more comfortable position.

For the first time in days, she felt sleepy. Hell, she was more than just sleepy. Her eyelids felt like bricks weighed them down, and every muscle in her body felt as rubbery as a noodle.

She would have a short nap. Gideon wouldn't be home for a few hours. She'd nap for an hour or so and then go home. He'd never know she was a weirdo freak who slept in his bed.

"Wake up, Grace."

Her eyelids fluttered open, and she stared blearily at Gideon. He was lying beside her on the bed, and a soft smile crossed her face. "Hi, Gideon."

"Hello, Princess."

Her insides quivered as liquid heat gathered at her core.

When she and Kira were seventeen, they'd had a brief obsession with Alfred Hitchcock movies. Gideon had been home from New Cassel, visiting his parents for the week, and he'd sat with Kira and Grace the night they watched *Rear Window*. The film starred Grace Kelly, an actress who would later become Princess of Monaco, and although Grace looked nothing like the actress, Gideon immediately gave her the nickname Princess.

A couple of months before that, the nickname would have annoyed her. She was the opposite of princess-like, and it was just another way Gideon acted like an irritating big brother. But that was before she'd begun noticing how good his ass looked in jeans or the way his body had filled out now that he was a police officer.

She was having decidedly un-sister-like thoughts about Gideon, and they both excited and confused her. Hearing him call her Princess in his deep voice had only heightened her newly discovered urges for him.

Of course, he hadn't called her Princess in years. Not since before his parents died.

"What are you doing in my bed?" She resisted the urge to reach out and touch him, afraid he would leave if she did.

"You're in my bed," he said.

"I am?"

He nodded, and she smiled sleepily at him. "Oh, right. Your bed. I haven't been sleeping well lately."

"Why not?"

"I don't know." She couldn't resist her need to touch any longer and slid her arm around him, resting her hand on his broad back. "I like sleeping in your bed."

"I like finding you in my bed." He smiled at her, and she licked her lips before studying his mouth.

276

"I want you so much, Gideon."

"I know, Princess."

"Do you want me?" She searched his dark brown eyes, looking for any hint that he still wanted her.

Brown eyes? Gracie... Gideon's eyes aren't brown. Wake up.

She ignored her inner voice, wiggling closer to Gideon and rubbing his back. "Kiss me, Gideon."

"I shouldn't," he said.

She rubbed his back again, using the tips of her fingers to smooth down the wiry hair that covered it. "You should."

Wiry hair? Wake up, Grace!

"Please, Gideon. Just one kiss?" she pleaded. "Just one, and then I'll wake up."

He made a low chuffing sound, and she squeezed him tighter before tilting her face toward his. "Gideon, please."

"Whatever you want, Princess," he whispered.

His mouth opened, and her eyes widened when his tongue, long and wide and definitely not human, licked her from her chin to the top of her forehead.

Gracie, wake up!

Her eyelids flew open, and she stared at Tank. The dog was stretched out beside her on the bed. Her arm was around the big dog with her hand resting on his back, and his head was lying next to hers on the pillow. He chuffed a second time before his tongue slurped across her face again.

"Tank, gross!" She jerked her head back and wiped the dog spit from her face. "Bad boy. *Bad boy.*"

She turned onto her back, staring at the ceiling and using one hand to block him from licking her face again.

"I've been kissed by a dog," she croaked out. "Boil some water, rip up some sheets."

She rubbed a hand across her face. Shit, what time was it?

The room was dark, and she fumbled for her phone in her pocket. How long had she slept? She had to get out of there before Gideon showed up and found her in his bed. She'd die of shame if –

Beside her, Tank made a low growl that turned into a whine of happiness. The bedroom light flicked on, and her stomach dropped.

She sat up, staring wide-eyed at Gideon standing in the doorway. For almost a minute, neither of them said anything. The only sound in the room was the thumping of Tank's tail against the bed.

"What are you doing in my bed?" Gideon finally said.

"I, um, I… fell asleep," Grace said. As Tank jumped off the bed and walked toward Gideon, she yanked the covers down and stumbled out of Gideon's bed. She shoved her feet into her shoes, her face a flaming tomato. "I'm so sorry. I was – I mean, I haven't been sleeping well, and I was tired and…"

She shut her mouth with a snap. Whatever she said would make her look like an idiot, and she hurried for the door. Before she could slip past him into the hallway, his big palm slapped against the doorframe and stopped her escape.

She backed up against the wall, staring wide-eyed at him as he placed both hands next to her head, his thick arms penning her in.

Trapped.

She was Goldilocks, and he was the bear who'd come home to find her in his bed.

She'd been a bad girl, and he would punish her until she was begging him for mercy, begging him to stop, begging him to make her come.

He stared down at her, his big body a hairsbreadth away but not touching her.

Never touching her.

"Do you know what I'll do to you if I find you uninvited in my bed again, Princess?" His voice was a low rasp that sent flames racing across her nerve endings.

Her tongue was stuck to the roof of her mouth, her heart was knocking against her ribs, and her lungs no longer worked properly.

She shook her head, her gaze never leaving those odd-coloured eyes. She could see her reflection in the pale blue of his right eye. The green of his left had darkened to jade.

"I'll put you on your knees, handcuff you to the head-board, pull your panties to your thighs, and," he paused, his gaze dropping to her mouth, "spank you."

Red hot desire exploded in her belly. Her pussy clenched uselessly around nothing, her nipples strained against her bra, and a noise that sounded embarrassingly like a whine slipped out of her mouth.

He dropped his arms and stepped back, one big hand resting on Tank's head. "Go home, Grace."

Legs trembling madly, she staggered out of his room.

———

KIRA STRIPPED OFF HER CLOTHES AND SLIPPED INTO THE BED beside Connor. It was only seven-thirty, but he must have been tired from his first day back at work. His eyelids flickered up, and he smiled at her. "Hey."

"Hi. Is your knee okay?"

"Yeah. I had a headache and decided to lie down for a bit. How did the showing go?"

"Good," she said. "They didn't like this house, but I

showed them a couple of others online, and they want to look at them tomorrow."

"That's great." He slid a little closer, running his hand over her naked hip before cupping her ass. "God, I love your ass."

She giggled and kissed his chest. "Are you hungry?"

"Not for food." He bent his head and kissed her. She wrapped her arms around his broad shoulders and returned his kiss, gasping into his mouth when he cupped her breast.

"We probably shouldn't do this," he said against her mouth. "I know you're sore."

"Not sore, more… tender," she said.

"We definitely shouldn't do this then," he said, but his hand was sliding between her thighs and gliding across her wet pussy. "Fuck, you're so wet already."

"I was thinking about you on the way home." She arched into his hand, moaning when he rubbed her clit. "I can't stop thinking about you. You've turned me into a sex addict."

His low laugh washed over her. "I think it's the opposite."

"Hey, I was sweet and innocent until I met you," she said.

He turned over and snagged a condom from the nightstand, ripping it open and rolling it on before facing her again. "I have enjoyed corrupting you."

"I've enjoyed it too." She traced her fingers along his inner thigh as she kissed his chest. "Lie on your back."

"Let's try something different tonight," he said.

He pulled her closer until her breasts brushed against his chest. He tugged on her leg until she draped it over his hip. He slid down a little, and she moaned when his cock brushed against her clit.

"Tilt your hips toward me, honey."

She tilted her hips, watching with breathless anticipation as he guided his cock into her wet pussy. He pushed and retreated, watching her face as he slowly filled her up until their bodies were pressed tight against each other.

She squeezed him with her leg, rubbing her foot against his ass as she smiled at him. "This feels good."

"Really good," he groaned.

He kissed her again, their tongues tasting and teasing as he fucked her with slow strokes.

"Knee okay?" she panted.

"Yeah, it's fine, honey." He cupped her ass, holding her tight as he thrust in and out. She ground her pussy against him, her hands digging into his back as he kissed her throat and upper chest. Her nipples brushed against him with every thrust, and she reached down and rubbed at her clit.

"Good," he breathed. "Touch your clit and show me how pretty you look when you come."

She moaned his name, her fingers rubbing at her swollen pink nub as he worked his cock in and out of her in a steady rhythm. He moved harder and faster, rocking their bodies together as he watched her caress and rub her clit.

Her soft cries grew steadily louder, drowning out his low groans of need, and she cried his name when she came, wetness flooding over her fingers. He gripped her ass harder, his cock impossibly thick and hard inside of her. She cupped his face, kissing him on the mouth and swallowing his cry of pleasure when he climaxed. They continued to rock against one another as they descended from their high. Connor peppered kisses across her face, and she smiled and stroked his back with long and lazy swipes of her palm.

He nuzzled her neck affectionately, and she tangled her fingers in his short hair. Her stomach growled, and Connor lifted his head. "Was that your stomach?"

She nodded, and he kissed her collarbone. "Come on, let's make something to eat."

"I've got some popcorn in the cupboard," she said.

He laughed and gave her butt a light slap. "Tempting, but if you're going to ride me again tonight, you'll need something more substantial."

She grinned at him. "In that case, get your butt to the kitchen and make me a sandwich."

CHAPTER 20

"Don't be nervous."

Kira took Connor's hand when he offered it to her. She could read his moods pretty well after spending practically all their time together in the last few weeks. The stiffness in his body, the tense line of his jaw, and the sweatiness of his palm indicated he was more nervous than her.

"Don't be nervous," he repeated as he locked the car.

She squeezed his hand. "Why are you so nervous?"

He glanced at the church. "I want you to like my family."

"I'm sure I will," she said. "It's going to be great."

He looked her up and down. "Have I told you how pretty you look?"

She smiled and smoothed her hand over her skirt. "Three times now, but thank you. You look very handsome."

He touched the tie around his neck before taking a deep breath. "Okay, let's do this."

They walked hand-in-hand to the church. Connor only had a slight limp, and although he was still wearing the knee brace, he hadn't used the cane in the last four days.

He opened the door to the church and pressed his hand on the small of her back, ushering her inside. People were milling around the foyer, and she felt the first tingle of nerves in her stomach when a few turned to look at them.

This is fine. Everything is fine.

Connor slipped his hand into hers as a tall man, his salt and pepper hair cut short and his eyes the same shade as Connor's approached them. "Hey, son."

He and Connor hugged briefly before Connor said, "Dad, this is my girlfriend, Kira. Kira, this is my dad, Rob."

"Hello, Mr. MacMillan. It's very nice to meet you." Kira held her hand out, and Connor's father swallowed it in his large grip.

"Nice to meet you as well. Please, call me Rob."

"Where's Mom?" Connor asked.

Rob studied the people in the foyer. "She's here somewhere. The last I saw her, she was talking to… oh, there she is. Gina! Gina, over here!"

Kira followed his gaze to a short older woman, her dark hair swept into a bun high on her head. She was talking to a tall, blonde supermodel wearing a dark purple dress that hugged her perfect body.

Connor's mother glanced over, and when she started toward them, taking the hand of the supermodel and tugging her along with her, Connor's hand tightened so hard around hers that Kira winced.

"Honey, too tight," she murmured.

"Sorry." Sweat beaded along his hairline, and she squeezed his hand.

"Okay?"

Before he could reply, his mother and the model stood

before them. Connor let go of her hand and gave his mom a hug and a kiss on her cheek. "Hi, Mom. You look great."

"Thanks, sweetie. You look very handsome." She tugged on his tie and smiled at him.

He stepped back and put his arm around Kira's waist, his hand digging into her hip. "Mom, this is Kira. Kira, this is my mom, Gina."

"Hi, Mrs. MacMillan. I'm so glad to meet you finally. I love your dress." Kira held her hand out, and after a moment's hesitation, Connor's mother shook it.

"Thank you. It's good to meet you as well."

There was an awkward silence, and when Connor didn't introduce the model to her, Kira smiled at her. "Hi, I'm Kira."

The woman smiled warmly, revealing perfectly straight, perfectly white teeth. "I'm Lisa. It's great to meet you. Your hair is amazing, and I love that necklace. Where did you get it?"

Kira's stomach dropped, but she kept the smile planted on her face by sheer willpower alone. Of course, Lisa would look like a goddamn model. *Of course, she would.* "Thank you. A friend loaned me the necklace."

"I love it," Lisa said. "It looks fantastic on you."

"Thank you," Kira said. "Your dress is beautiful."

Lisa smoothed her hands over her dress. "Thanks. I've had it for a while now, but I love the colour."

"Connor, aren't you going to say hello to Lisa?" Gina said.

"Hi, Lisa," Connor said.

"Hi." Lisa turned her perfect smile to Connor. "It's been a while. How are you doing?"

"Good, thanks. How are you?"

Connor's fingers were digging into her hip so hard she'd have bruises tomorrow.

"Really well." How Lisa stared at him made warning bells go off in Kira's head.

She took a deep breath and told herself not to be stupid. She didn't know exactly what happened between Lisa and Connor, but Connor didn't want to be with her. He'd been clear about that. It didn't matter how Lisa looked at him. It didn't matter that she was drop dead gorgeous with breasts twice the size of Kira's and an ass you could probably bounce quarters off. It didn't matter that she seemed genuinely nice. Connor wasn't interested anymore.

Are you sure about that?

She ignored her inner voice. She was feeling a little insecure, but who could blame her?

"Connor and Lisa used to date," Gina said to her. "They made the loveliest couple."

"*Mom*," Connor said.

"What?" Gina said. "You did."

"That was a long time ago." Lisa hooked her arm around Gina's and squeezed. "Connor's moved on."

"They were high school sweethearts," Gina said before smiling at Kira. "Your high school sweetheart always holds a special place in your heart. Don't you think?"

"I don't know," Kira said. "I didn't date in high school."

"What? As pretty as you are?" Lisa said. "I don't believe it."

She gave Kira another warm smile before releasing Gina's arm. "I'm going to find a seat before the church fills up. Kira, it was so lovely to meet you."

Gina grabbed Lisa's hand. "Honey, you have to sit with us."

"Oh, no, that's okay," Lisa said, glancing at Connor.

"You must," Gina said. "Rob, tell her."

"If Lisa doesn't want to sit with us, she doesn't have to, Gina."

"She's family," Gina said. "Kira, you don't mind if she sits with us, do you?"

"Not at all," Kira said.

"Then we're good," Gina said.

"Mom, I don't think -"

"Hush, Connor. Just because you and Lisa are no longer engaged doesn't mean she isn't our family anymore."

Engaged? They were engaged?

Bile rose in Kira's throat, and she swallowed it down, the burn in her esophagus making her feel nauseous. Okay, so Connor didn't mention that he was engaged to Lisa. No big deal. She didn't have to know every detail about his past with Lisa, right?

That's a pretty big fucking detail to omit, Kira.

"Are you all right?" Lisa gave her a concerned look. "You're suddenly very pale."

"I'm good. Just a little warm," Kira said.

Connor stared at her with a combination of guilt and worry. "Do you need to step outside and get some fresh air?"

Yes. She needed that badly. But if she was alone with Connor right now, the likelihood of her just bursting into tears was incredibly high, and she'd rather die before she let any of his family see that she was upset.

"No, I'm good." She made herself smile at him.

"I think we should get some fresh air," he said.

"We don't need to," she said.

"Mama G!" Lucas joined them, and he gave Gina an enthusiastic hug. "You're looking fantastic."

Gina laughed and patted his cheek. "You clean up rather nice yourself, Lucas."

"Don't I?" Lucas winked at her. "Ethel Borswell grabbed my ass not five minutes ago."

"Lucas!" Gina said. "Ethel Borswell is seventy-three years old."

"What can I say," Lucas said. "The ladies love me. All of them.'"

He shook Rob's hand, and Kira was weirdly grateful when he gave Lisa a decidedly cold smile. "Lisa."

"Hi, Lucas. It's good to see you again. How's the world of video games?" Lisa's smile had widened, but for the first time, Kira thought it looked fake and unnatural.

"Fine," Lucas said dismissively. He punched Connor in the arm. "I see you finally bought yourself a real tie instead of a clip-on."

"At least I'm wearing one," Connor said.

"Hey, gorgeous," Lucas smiled at her.

"Hi," Kira said.

"Lucas, this is Kira," Gina said. "Kira, Lucas has been Connor's best friend since they were kids."

"She knows," Lucas said.

"Oh," Gina said. "Have you two met before?"

Lucas put his arm around Kira's shoulders and tugged her away from Connor. "Of course we have, Mama G. I'm Connor's best friend, and Kira's his girlfriend. We've hung out like, what, five or six times now?"

He turned to Kira, who said, "Seven, I think."

"Right. I forgot about strip poker night," Lucas said.

Connor laughed, and even Kira managed a more natural smile. She barely knew Lucas, but holy hell, she was eternally grateful to him.

"We're practically besties, aren't we, Kira?" Lucas said.

"Practically," she said.

Lucas leaned down and planted a kiss on her cheek. "You're looking beautiful. Connor's a lucky man."

"Thank you." She gave him a huge smile that she hoped conveyed precisely how much she loved him.

"How about you, Lucas?" Lisa's voice had lost its warmth. "Are you seeing anyone special?"

"Does Ethel Borswell grabbing my ass count as someone special?" Lucas said. "Because I'm thinking it might."

"Oh, Lucas," Gina said with a sigh as Connor reached out, tugging Kira away from Lucas and up against him.

He gave her another worried look before leaning down and breathing into her ear. "I should have told you. I'm sorry."

She nodded but slipped her arm around his waist and gave him a squeeze and a reassuring smile. He definitely should have mentioned it, but now wasn't the time to discuss it.

"We should find a seat," Rob said.

Gina grabbed Lisa's hand. "All right. Follow me, everyone."

"You look like you could use this." Lucas sat down beside Kira and placed a drink in front of her.

"Oh, thank you, but Connor is getting me one," Kira said.

Lucas pointed to the far end of the room where an older woman with short, gray hair held Connor's arm and spoke animatedly to him. "Connor's been waylaid by his aunt. Trust me, he won't return for at least half an hour."

She smiled and picked up the drink. They clinked glasses,

and she took a sip, the burn of the whisky surprisingly helpful.

"So, how are you holding up?"

"Fine," Kira said. "I'm having a great time."

"Oh yeah?" Lucas gave her a skeptical look.

"Yes. The ceremony was beautiful, the food was delicious, and the music," she pointed to the dance floor where the bride and groom and a couple dozen of their friends and family were dancing, "is on point. I've enjoyed meeting Connor's family and friends."

He grinned. "Well, aren't you just a glass half full kind of girl."

"Thank you, by the way, for pretending to know me so well before the ceremony. It felt awkward, and you helped break the tension."

"Not a problem. I'm Connor's best friend, and it's my duty to help convince people his fake relationship is anything but fake."

The whiskey sloshed unpleasantly in Kira's stomach. "I'm sorry?"

Lucas studied her, a slight frown crossing his face. "Are you okay? I thought you knew Connor told me about this being fake. You're trying to make some firefighter jealous, right?"

"Oh, um, yeah, we were, but Connor and I decided to date for real," Kira said. "He didn't mention it to you?"

Lucas shook his head. "No, he didn't."

"Oh."

"I'm sure it's just because he was busy. Plus, he's not one to share much, you know?"

"Yeah, I know." Kira made herself smile at Lucas, but the nausea was growing. Why hadn't Connor told his best friend they were dating for real? Was he having second thoughts? Once the wedding was over, would he tell Kira they were over?

"So, I heard you found the perfect place for Stark's new office."

She blinked at him. "What?"

"Isaac Stark? He's my boss. You were the agent who found him the new office in Harmony Falls, right?"

"How did you know that?" she asked.

"Didn't Connor tell you? He called and asked me to recommend you to Stark."

"He did?" Kira said.

Lucas nodded. "He didn't say anything?"

"No, I ... he didn't." Warmth infused her entire body. Connor had helped her get her first sale.

A flash of purple caught her eye. Gina and Lisa stood together near the dance floor, talking to other wedding guests. She swallowed hard. Lisa was gorgeous and sweet, and she ran her own business. It didn't matter how many houses she sold, Kira would never be as successful or beautiful as her.

"Hey." Lucas touched her hand. He was also staring at Gina and Lisa and shook his head. "Don't let Gina's obsession with Lisa get in your head."

"He didn't tell me they were engaged," Kira said. "He won't even tell me why they broke up."

Lucas sighed. "Well, it's Connor's story and not mine to tell, so I can't say anything. But trust me when I say he has no interest in Lisa anymore."

"Why not?" Kira said. "She's smart, sweet, and beautiful, and his mother loves her."

"Lisa is not sweet," Lucas said harshly. "Don't let her fool you. She's a snake in the grass, and Connor dodged a fucking bullet with that one."

"If she's so terrible, why does Gina want them to get together so much? You'd think she'd want what's best for her son," Kira said.

Lucas drank the rest of his drink in two big swallows. "Gina is a wonderful person, Kira. She really is, and she loves Connor. He's her only kid, and she wants him to be happy. She believes Lisa is the one who will make him happy."

"Maybe she's right."

"She's not," Lucas said. "She's blinded by the fact that Lisa and Connor were together for so long, blinded by her belief that she knows what's best for Connor. She had Connor's life all laid out in her head, and when it went sideways, when nothing turned out the way any of them believed it would, she never really got over it."

He studied the top of the table, running his fingers over the soft white cloth that covered it. "Gina wants Connor to be with Lisa so much that she isn't seeing what everyone else in this damn room saw almost immediately."

"What's that?"

"The way Connor looks at you."

Warmth burned in her belly, and she took another sip of her drink. "Thanks, but you didn't even know we were dating for real. Connor isn't looking at me in -"

"I might have thought it was still fake, but it doesn't mean I couldn't see Connor looking at you like a love-struck puppy," Lucas said. "Truthfully, I am fucking relieved that you're actually dating. Connor's got it fucking bad for you, and he's been hurt enough in the past by a woman who was supposed to love him. I don't want to see it happen again."

"What did she do to him?" Kira said.

"I can't say," Lucas said with genuine regret.

"He won't talk to me about it."

"He will. Just give him a bit more time. You know how he is. It's hard for him to open up and be vulnerable," Lucas said.

"I know."

There were a few moments of silence before Lucas smiled at her. "Me, on the other hand? I wear my goddamn heart on my sleeve. The ladies can't get me to shut up about my feelings."

She laughed and took another sip of whiskey. Lucas grabbed his glass as a woman with tightly permed, violet coloured hair and wearing a billowing leopard print caftan clumped her way toward them. "Shit, here comes Ethel. I gotta run, beautiful. She's grabbed my ass so many times since the ceremony, I've got bruises from cheek to cheek."

He left just as Ethel approached the table and eased into the chair beside Kira. She studied her silently before saying, "You seem all right for a Falls girl."

"Thanks?" Kira said.

Ethel grunted in reply as she stared at the dance floor. Connor had escaped his aunt and was now dancing with his mother, and Ethel watched them for a few minutes. "I've been watching the two of you tonight. He seems real happy with you. That's good. After what he went through, he deserves to be happy."

Kira wasn't sure what to say. Ethel glanced at her before looking back at Connor. "Real shame about that boy's career."

Kira frowned. "There's nothing wrong with being a dentist."

"I ain't talking about that," Ethel said. "I'm talking about his baseball career."

Kira didn't know how to respond. Luckily, Ethel went on like she wasn't even there. "I wasn't surprised when he moved away, even if it did break his mama's heart. Hard to live in a place where you ruined so many people's hopes and dreams."

"What do you mean?" Kira asked.

"Of course, it was a real shitty thing for the town to do to him. He might have been the best baseball player Willington had ever seen, but it wasn't right the pressure they put on him. He was just a kid, you know?"

Kira nodded and clenched her hands tightly in her lap as she watched Connor dance with Gina. She prayed Ethel would continue, releasing her breath in a soft rush when the old woman did.

"He was the town's golden boy. Top athlete in the school. We had scouts come and watch him play. Scouts! To our little town. The mayor nearly shit his pants he was so giddy. I tell you what, the entire town showed up to that ball game. Connor was only seventeen, and you'da thought the pressure would have gotten to him, but it didn't. He played his best game that night. He was planning to go to college in New Cassel and play some college ball while he got his degree. But rumour was after they watched him in that game, they was gonna draft him right out of high school. That's how good he was."

Ethel stared moodily at the dancers. "He was good too. Like a dancer out there, you know? Moved fast and was a natural leader. And his batting? Shit, you ain't never seen someone hit so many home runs. He still playin' ball in the Falls?"

Kira nodded. "Yes. He plays for the local league."

"Figured he would. Baseball is in his blood. He wouldn't

be able to give it up for good. It's a damn shame the accident ruined everything."

"The quads?" Kira whispered.

"Yeah," Ethel said. "He and some of his friends went out on their quads a few days before graduation. They weren't drinkin' or anythin' like that, but they were being reckless and stupid. But that's how teenage boys are, aren't they? Can't think of nothing at that age but baseball and the balls between their legs."

Ethel shook her head. "Anyway, Connor got into that accident, tore his knee to hell and just like that, his career was over. The town's golden boy was tarnished."

Kira stared at Connor. He was smiling at his mother, and something in her chest tightened until she could barely breathe. He didn't deserve what happened to him.

"His parents were disappointed," Ethel went on as if she didn't even notice Kira's heart falling right out of her damn chest. "Real disappointed. They had high hopes for their boy and believed he would be a famous baseball player. Hell, everyone did. When he became a dentist, it sucked the life right out of most of the townsfolk. Most believed he'd still make it as a ball player even with his knee messed up. They was ready to name a goddamn street after him, and then… hell, it was like he didn't even exist."

"That's awful," Kira whispered. She wanted to march across the dance floor and tear Connor away from his mother. She wanted to take him home to Harmony Falls where he belonged, where no one looked at him like he was a failure.

"Sure was," Ethel said. "His girl broke up with him, and I think that was the straw that broke him. He didn't have his career or his girl, and every day he had to face the disappointment of an entire town. I don't blame him for leaving. Do you?"

"I hate this town," Kira said.

"We ain't all bad," Ethel said with a shrug. "Besides, it looks like it worked out all right for him. He's got you now, don't he?"

Kira gripped her knees when Gina pulled Connor to a stop next to Lisa, who was dancing with Connor's father. Gina said something to Connor before practically pushing Lisa into his arms. She took Rob's hand and tugged him away as Connor stared down at Lisa. She said something to him, and he nodded before putting his arm around her waist and taking her hand. As the music turned soft and slow, they started to dance, and Kira looked down at the table.

Her pulse was thudding, and the whoosh of blood in her eardrums muted the music.

He doesn't love her anymore, she reminded herself fiercely. *He doesn't love her anymore.*

"Ain't no need to be jealous now." Ethel patted her hand in an almost comforting way. "He ain't hot for her anymore. Besides, just between you and me, his mama might be pulling for him and her to get back together, but I ain't never thought that Lisa was after him for anything but the fame. Why, the minute his ball career was done, you could practically see the light dying in her eyes. She wasn't nearly as taken with him after that. He worshipped the ground she walked on, and after years of saying she loved him, she tossed him aside just like the rest of the town did."

Ethel made a sound of disgust. "Why Gina can't never see that, I don't know. She thinks Lisa walks on water, and she ain't ever gave up hope that the two of them will get back

together. Just because she married her high school sweetheart don't mean that everyone will."

Kira didn't want to look at Connor dancing with Lisa, but
she couldn't help it. She glanced at them again, her stomach
tightening. Even from here, she could see how upset Connor
was. His face was red, and he was staring at Lisa with anger
and hurt.

She jumped to her feet. She had no idea what was wrong,
but she wasn't about to sit here and watch Lisa upset the man
she loved. She didn't care if it made her look like a jealous
shrew. She was breaking up their damn dance.

Before she could move, Connor tore away from Lisa. His
face still red and his shoulders hunched, he walked away
from Lisa and straight toward Kira.

CHAPTER 21

"You look terrific, Connor," Lisa said.

"Thanks." He glanced across the dance floor to the table where Kira sat. Ethel was sitting with her, and he groaned inwardly. Ethel was the biggest gossip in town. Who knew what the hell she was telling Kira.

"Hey? You still with me?" Lisa touched his face, and he jerked his head back.

"Don't, Lisa."

"I can't touch you now?" Hurt was written across her face. "We were together for years, Connor."

"And now we're not," he said.

"We're still friends."

"Since when?" His tone was blunt, but she gave him a soft smile.

"I've missed you, Connor."

"Why?"

She sighed. "What do you mean, why? Look, I know things didn't end well between us, but I've been doing a lot of thinking in the last year. We used to be good together, didn't we?"

He shrugged, his gaze returning to Kira. They'd been here long enough. After this dance, he'd take her back to the hotel room and try to give her an acceptable answer for why he hadn't told her he was engaged to Lisa.

The truth would be better.

"Kira seems nice." Lisa squeezed his shoulder.

"She is," he said. "She's amazing."

"How did you meet?"

"She's a client."

"How is dentistry treating you?" Lisa asked.

He sighed. "Do you actually care? You hate that I'm a dentist."

"I don't hate it," she insisted. "I was young, and I was stupid and disappointed."

"You were disappointed? It was my dream that ended," Connor said.

"Both of our dreams ended," she snapped. She breathed deeply, arranging her face into a calm mask again. "Look, what's done is done, okay? We both made some mistakes that we regret. But that doesn't mean that how we felt – *feel* – for each other is over."

"What are you talking about?" Connor said.

"Us," Lisa said. "I'm talking about us."

"There is no us. You ended it two years ago when you couldn't stand the thought of being a dentist's wife."

"Can you blame me?" she said. "I thought you were going to be a famous baseball player. I thought we were going to leave this stupid town and we were going to make something of ourselves. And then the accident happened, and every-thing changed. You changed."

"Well, sorry that I couldn't be all sunshine and happiness after my career was destroyed," Connor said.

"Look, I don't want to fight, okay?" Lisa said. "I'm sorry for what I said and did. I really am. I know it isn't an excuse, but I was young, immature, and really sad."

He could see the tears in her eyes and familiar guilt inched from his belly and into his chest. "I didn't mean to hurt you, Lisa."

"I know you didn't," she said. "I forgive you for that, Connor, I do. I miss you a lot. In the last year, I've realized just how much. I want to try again."

She smiled at him, her face soft and warm, and rubbed his back. "Let's try again, sweetheart."

"I'm with Kira now," he said.

"You've known her what? Two months? She doesn't know you the way I do. She never will. She hasn't been through what we have. Don't let an infatuation with her ruin our chance to try again."

"It's too late," he said.

"It isn't. Think about how happy your mom would be if we started dating again. You can make up for disappointing her the way you did. Don't you want that, Connor? I know how much it hurts you that your parents are unhappy with how your life turned out. You can fix that. Come back to me and make your parents proud of you again."

He stiffened, his hand squeezing onto hers until she gasped. "Connor, ouch."

He released her hand, staring down at her as the back of his neck grew hot and a fire burned in his belly. "You think I can only make my parents proud by dating you?"

"They love me," Lisa said. "They know that I'm good for you. You could move back home and open a practice here in Willington. We'll get married and give your mom a couple of grand-children. We'll be happy together, just like before the accident."

"I don't love you anymore," he said.

Anger flashed in her eyes. "You don't mean that. You've loved me since you were fifteen, Connor MacMillan."

"I don't love you now." His voice was slow and deliberate. "I have a life outside of this town, and maybe it isn't the life I planned, but it's *my* life, and I'm happy. I'm happy with Kira."

"She's isn't right for you," she said.

"She's perfect, and I love her," he said.

She froze in his arms, the sneer transforming her face from beautiful to cold and ugly. "Fine. Be with your stupid Falls girl. Let's just hope that you don't fuck up her life the way you fucked up mine."

Heat flooded his face, bile bubbled in his belly, and for one brief moment, he thought he would throw up. He swallowed thickly, staring at Lisa as she gave him a defiant look.

"There you are," he said. "I wondered when the real Lisa would make an appearance."

He pushed away from her and headed toward Kira. She was standing at the table, and he held his hand out to her. "Time to go."

"All right." She took his hand, and he led her toward the door.

"Connor? Where are you going?" His mother was hurrying toward them.

"We're leaving. I'll call you later," Connor said.

He walked faster, ignoring the pain in his knee. He pushed open the door of the rental hall and stepped out into the cool night air. Holding Kira's hand, he walked away from his past without a second look back.

"I'M SORRY I DIDN'T TELL YOU I WAS ENGAGED TO LISA." Connor paced in the hotel room as Kira sat on the edge of the small loveseat.

They'd decided to rent a room for the night rather than drive back to Harmony Falls, and he regretted that decision. He wanted to be back in Kira's home, in her bed and between her legs, not thinking about his hometown, Lisa, or his parents' disappointment. The guilt was always stronger when he was here. He could feel it in the very molecules in the air, threatening to drown him.

"It seems like there's a lot that you didn't tell me," Kira said. "Or your best friend. Why didn't you tell Lucas we were dating for real now?"

He sat beside her, relieved when he reached for her hand, and she didn't pull away. "I'm sorry. Not telling Lucas wasn't intentional. It just slipped my mind."

He studied their linked hands. "I have a lot of baggage regarding this place, and I didn't want to burden you with it. Especially since Lisa doesn't mean anything to me anymore, and our engagement was just a stupid mistake I'd like to forget."

"Ethel told me about your baseball career," she said.

He muttered a curse and stared down at their linked hands.

"You should have told me that," she said. "Why didn't you?"

"Because I fucked up," he said. "I had a chance to be somebody, and I fucked it up. I'm ashamed of that."

She cupped his face and made him look at her. "You are

somebody, Connor. Just because you're not a famous base-ball player doesn't make your life meaningless."

"I'm a dentist, Kira," he said.

"A damn good one. Being a dentist takes brains and deter-mination, and don't you dare let anyone make you feel less for being one. If my parents were alive, you have no idea how thrilled they'd be that I was dating a dentist. They would have loved you, Connor. They really would have. Hell, my brother likes you. Do you know how rare that is? Gideon is hard to win over, and you did it in a single conversation."

She reached up and cupped his face. "I know it's hard being back here. I know it has terrible memories for you, but do not let it make you feel less. You are amazing."

He kissed her gently before resting his forehead against hers. "You're the amazing one."

"I am pretty great," she said.

He laughed and kissed her again. "I'm sorry I didn't tell you about my past. It's just… it's still difficult."

"I get that," she said. "But you know that you can tell me anything, right? I'm not going to judge you for anything."

"I know," he said as guilt seeped into his belly. "I'll try to be more open with you."

"Good. What did Lisa say that upset you?"

He hesitated, and she gave him a gentle poke in the chest. "This is an excellent time for you to work on being more open with me."

He smiled a little. "She wanted to get back together with me."

"What?" Her look of indignation was adorable. "She said that to you?"

"Yes."

"With me right there?"

"Yep."

"I thought she was so sweet," Kira said, "and then she tried to steal my man right out from under my nose. She's lucky we're not still at that wedding. I'd punch her right in her gorgeous face."

He laughed, and she wrinkled her nose at him. "I've got a cop for a brother. I know how to punch someone."

"Fine, but what do you think Gideon would say if I called him and told him you were sitting in a jail cell in Willington for assault."

"She would be the type to press charges, wouldn't she?" Kira said.

"If you messed up her face, yep."

Kira sighed. "I hate that she's so beautiful."

"She's not nearly as beautiful as you." He stroked his thumb across her bottom lip. "She's dog food, and you're prime rib."

She burst into laughter. "Seriously? You're comparing my looks to meat? Connor, I love you, but you have got to work on your compliments."

He sucked in a breath. "You love me?"

Her face flushed, and she stared at her lap. He cupped the back of her neck and tugged her head up, staring intently at her. "Do you love me, Kira?"

"Yes," she whispered. "I do."

His chest tightened, and happiness flowed through him like a tsunami. "I love you too."

Her smile lit up the room, and she mashed her mouth against his. He angled his mouth over hers, licking the seam of her lips until she opened her mouth, and he could taste her sweetness with his tongue.

She pulled back, gasping a little, and tore at his tie. "Get naked, now."

He grinned and shrugged out of his jacket. "Whatever you say, little Kira."

"YOU WANNA GRAB A DRINK AT THE BEAVER?" GIDEON ASKED. "It's still early."

"Sure." Connor pulled out his phone. "Just let me text Kira and tell her I'll be a little while. I told her we were just going to the movies."

He sent a quick text to Kira as Gideon drove toward the pub. "How's work going?"

Gideon shrugged. "Fine. Lots of domestic calls this weekend. How was the wedding? I haven't talked to Kira since you got back."

"It was a wedding," Connor said. "My cousin was happy, so that's what matters."

"You and Kira pretty serious now?" Gideon pulled into the parking lot and parked before staring at Connor.

"We are." He didn't look away from Gideon's gaze.

The big man nodded. "I'm glad. You're good for her. Let's get that drink."

Connor followed him into the Thirsty Beaver. He had a feeling that would be all the praise he'd get from the sheriff, but oddly, it was enough.

The pub was packed for a Wednesday night, but they found a table easily enough. They sat down and ordered a couple of beers. Connor glanced around the pub, scowling a little when he saw Daniel sitting at the bar. He was drinking a beer and staring at the television behind the bar.

"Is Daniel drinking alone?" he asked Gideon.

Gideon just shrugged. "Don't know, don't care. The guy's an idiot. I'm gonna hit the head. I'll be right back."

As Gideon walked away, Connor's phone buzzed. He read the reply from Kira and, smiling a little, texted her before stuffing his phone into his pocket. He reached for his beer, pausing when he realized Daniel stood in front of his table.

"Hey, doc." The firefighter was swaying, and his eyes were bloodshot. He took another drink of beer before gripping the back of the chair for support.

"Hello, Daniel."

"How's it going?"

"Fine," Connor said. "You?"

Daniel shrugged and took another drink of beer. "Where's Kira?"

"She's at home."

"You living with her now?"

Connor didn't reply, and Daniel cocked an eyebrow at him. "Why so quiet, doc?"

"I guess I have nothing to say to you," Connor said.

"Is there a reason you hate me?" Daniel asked.

"You mean other than because of the way you used Kira for years?"

Daniel snorted loudly. "You don't know shit about me and Kira."

"I know you took advantage of her kindness. I know you used her and didn't think once about her feelings."

Daniel leaned forward, swaying unsteadily. "Kira and I have a special relationship. One that worked just fine until you showed up."

"It wasn't special," Connor said. He was trying not to be

pissed, but something about Daniel poked every one of his buttons.

"Yeah, it was. Maybe you don't like the fact that your girl loved me before she ever loved you."

"It wasn't love. It was a crush, and you didn't mean that much to her," he said.

"No?" Daniel straightened. "'Cause just this morning, I heard Addie talking on the phone to Harper. Guess they haven't talked for a while because she had a lot to say. Especially about Kira. "

Connor's nostrils flared as Daniel gave him a drunken grin. "Turns out that sweet little Kira was holding on to her virginity for me. For years she waited, doc. That kind of sounds like I meant a little something to her. Don't you think?"

Connor stood, his hands in tight fists at his side. "Shut your fucking mouth, Daniel."

"I'm just sayin' if a woman is waiting for a man to be her first, it means something. Of course, according to my sister, you came along and convinced her to give up her v-card. Pretty bold move, doc."

His urge to punch Daniel was almost too great to ignore. Afraid he would act on it, he shoved past the firefighter, his body tensing when Daniel grabbed his arm.

"Let go of me, Daniel."

Daniel leaned closer, the scent of beer clinging to him. "How did it feel, doc? Taking something that belonged to me."

Connor snarled with anger and punched Daniel in the face. There was immediate pain in his hand, so strong it made him feel sick, but he ignored it as Daniel fell backwards onto the table. Blood gushed from his nose that now canted to the left, and there were startled shouts and cries from the people closest to them.

Connor leaned over and grabbed Daniel by the collar. More pain flared in his hand. It felt like the bones were grinding together, and he grunted with pain before glaring at the bleeding firefighter.

"Get off me," Daniel's voice was thick from the blood that flowed into his mouth.

"If you say one more word about her, if you even say her name, I'll knock every one of your goddamn teeth out. Do you hear me, you son of a bitch?" Connor said.

An arm hooked around his throat and dragged him back. He clawed at the arm with his good hand and was shaken roughly for his trouble.

"Enough." Gideon's voice spoke into his ear. Connor relaxed, and Gideon released him before stepping between him and Daniel. "What the fuck is going on here?"

"He started it." Daniel spit out some blood and pressed his t-shirt to his nose.

"Fuck you," Connor said. He shook out his hand, wincing when it sent pain flaring straight up his arm.

Gideon stared at Connor's rapidly swelling hand. "Well, that's broken."

"It's fine," Connor said.

"It isn't," Gideon said. "Trust me, I've seen enough broken hands to know." He turned and studied Daniel's face. "And your nose is definitely broken. Come on, both of you need to go to the hospital."

"No fucking way," Connor said.

"I'm not going with him," Daniel said.

"Both of you shut the fuck up and get in my car," Gideon said as he threw some bills on the table. "You're fucking lucky I'm taking you to the hospital and not a damn jail cell. Move your asses, now."

"You should have called me earlier, Gideon." Connor could hear Kira's voice even over the noises in the ER.

"He didn't want me to," Gideon protested.

The curtain whipped open, and Kira hurried to the bed, staring at Connor's hand. "Oh, Connor."

He looked at the ceiling as Kira pressed a kiss against his mouth. "Honey, your poor hand."

"It's fine," he said.

Kira glanced at Gideon, who said, "Pretty sure it's broken. He had an X-ray about twenty minutes ago. We're just waiting for the results."

"The results are in." Jack ducked behind the curtain, and Connor's throat tightened as the ER doctor gave him a grave look.

"Is it broken?" Kira asked.

"Spectacularly," Jack said. "You're gonna need surgery, Connor."

"Fuck," Connor spat.

Kira squeezed his good hand as Jack said, "If it makes you feel any better, that firefighter's nose may never be the same."

Kira stiffened. "What firefighter?"

When Connor didn't reply, she glanced at Gideon. "What's going on?"

Gideon sighed. "Connor and Daniel got into a fight. Connor punched Daniel in the face."

Kira stared at Connor. "Why did you punch him?"

"He pissed me off," Connor said.

She closed her eyes and took a deep breath. "Okay. We'll circle back to that later." She glanced at Jack. "When will he have surgery?"

"Lucky for him, the orthopedic surgeon had a cancellation tomorrow morning." Jack stuck Connor's chart into the holder at the end of the bed. "We'll keep you here overnight, fast you and prep you for surgery."

"I'd rather go home and return in the morning," Connor said.

"Yeah, well, I'd rather be sitting on some beach with a drink in my hand, but here we are," Jack said. "We'll move you to a room in about half an hour. Until then, sit tight."

Jack left, and Kira smoothed her hand over Connor's forehead. "Can I get you anything?"

He shook his head. "No, you should go home."

She frowned. "I'm not going home. I'll stay with you until –"

"I'd rather you just go," he said. "I need to call Grant and somehow explain to him that I won't be able to do my fucking job for the next six weeks."

"Connor, it's okay. Grant will understand."

"Please, I don't want a pep talk right now," Connor said. "Can you just go? I'm tired and in pain and don't feel like being around anyone."

Kira glanced at Gideon before nodding. "Yeah, okay. I'll text you later."

She pressed a kiss against his mouth. "Are you sure you want me to go?"

"Yes." He couldn't look at her. If he saw the hurt in her eyes, he'd ask her to stay, and what good would that do? She didn't need to watch him stress and panic over fucking up

311

yet again. If she stayed, he might say or do something to drive her away.

"All right. I love you."

"Love you too." He closed his eyes, only opening them when he was sure she was gone.

He stared down at his swollen hand, panic swooping through him and stealing the air from his lungs.

He really was fucked.

CHAPTER 22

Panic.

Panic, thick and heavy in his belly like a stone.

He sat on the couch in his living room, staring blankly at the wall as Kira flickered in and out of his peripheral vision like a nervous butterfly.

Her soft hand lifting his cast and sliding a pillow under it. Warm breath as she kissed his forehead before disappearing again. The muted sound of her voice as she spoke to him.

He couldn't hear it. Not past the panic.

He dropped his gaze to his hand, the thick, heavy cast concealing the sutures under it. Three pins and a metal plate in his hand. Six weeks in a cast and physical therapy afterward.

May lose dexterity.

May experience numbness.

The surgeon's voice in his head egged the panic on. Made it bigger. Brighter.

"Connor? Look at me."

Kira's soft voice dampened the edge of panic enough for

him to take a deep breath. Enough so he could almost think normally. Almost.

"Yeah?"

"Honey, is the pain terrible?"

He shook his head. It wasn't. The pain meds had taken care of it. His hand felt numb, nothing more. Maybe that was the panic's work, though.

"I wish you would have stayed at my place," she said.

He shrugged. He knew what he had to do, and it would be easier on her if he did it here. He didn't want to break her heart in her own goddamn home.

"Everything will be fine," she said.

He stared at Kira's sweet face. She actually believed that even though she was there when Connor woke up after surgery this morning. Even though she had heard what the surgeon said. She believed it.

The bitter laughter spilled out of him, harsh and horrific and unstoppable. "You can't be serious."

"I am," she said. "Your hand will heal, and you'll return to work in no time."

"You heard what the surgeon said. It's bad, Kira. Really bad. Even with physical therapy, I may be unable to move my fingers. I can't exactly be a dentist if I can't move my fucking fingers."

The panic was making him shout. Kira didn't flinch. She sat beside him and rested her hand on his thigh. "It's okay. That was a worse case scenario. He thinks it'll be fine."

"He thinks. That's just great. The surgeon *thinking* I'll be fine makes me feel much better," he said.

"I know you're scared, but I promise it will work out."

"I can't work for six weeks, Kira. And after the cast comes

off... I may never be able to work as a dentist again. What part of that is working out? I have fucked my life."

He took a deep breath. Even worse, he had fucked Kira's life. Just like he'd fucked up Lisa's. He'd done something incredibly stupid, and now Kira would pay for it.

"You haven't," she said. "Grant is a good guy, and he won't end the partnership just because of an accident."

More bitter laughter spilled out. "It wasn't an accident, Kira. I fucked up because I'm an idiot. You'd think I would have learned, but apparently, I'm a goddamn moron. I've ruined my life and yours."

"Mine?" Kira blinked at him. "How on earth have you ruined my life?"

"Don't act dumb," he snapped. "If I can't work as a dentist, what the hell will I do? Work at goddamn Walmart? You really want to be with a guy who can't keep a career? What do you think your friends, your *brother*, will say when I'm working at a gas station because I blew my chance at a career *again?*"

"They don't care what you do for a living. I don't care," Kira said. "I love you, and I'll love you whether you're a dentist or not. It doesn't matter to me, Connor. People make mistakes and -"

"I won't drag you down with me. Lisa spent years with me being miserable because I made a dumb mistake and because I was too weak to let her go. I won't do the same thing to you."

"I am not Lisa," Kira said. "Don't compare her to me, Connor. It isn't fair."

"What isn't fair is expecting you to live with the consequences of my stupid mistakes."

"Stop it," Kira said. "I love you, and I'm with you through the good and the bad. That's the way love works."

He shook his head, staring numbly at the cast. "I'm not destroying your life the way I destroyed Lisa's. You should go."

"No," she said. "You need me."

"Please, just leave, Kira," he said. "I don't want to date you anymore."

"You're lying," she said.

He looked away from her, the bile churning in his guts, the air like soup as he tried to drag it into his lungs. "I'm not. I won't saddle you with my fucked-up life. We're done. Please leave."

"Connor, you don't mean that."

"I do."

"You asshole," she said. "You think that by driving me away, you're doing the right thing, the *noble* thing, but you're not. You're just being a damn coward. Do you hear me, Connor MacMillan? You're a coward!"

She stood and stomped out of the living room. The door slammed, and he pressed the back of his head into the couch, staring at the ceiling as depression descended over him like a heavy shroud.

"JESUS, YOU LOOK LIKE HELL." LUCAS UNWRAPPED THE GARBAGE bag from Connor's cast and tossed it in the garbage. "I thought getting your ass into the shower would help, but nope. Still looks like you've been marinating in a pile of shit for a few days."

"Thanks," Connor said. His hand was aching, and he

rubbed his arm above the cast. "You know, I asked you to come by this weekend to help me, not insult me."

"You have a perfectly lovely girlfriend who could be helping you, and I'm pretty sure she would have kept the insults to a minimum," Lucas said. "Why don't I call her and ask her to come by."

"Give it a rest," Connor said wearily. "I told you, Kira and I are over."

Lucas stirred the soup in the pot on the stove. He tasted it and added some more salt before stirring it again. "Tell me again why you did the stupidest thing in the world and broke up with Kira. I love hearing how you're a goddamn idiot. Truly. It warms my cold, black heart."

"I'm glad this is all a joke to you," Connor said.

Lucas sat down across from him. "It's not a fucking joke to me, Connor. I hate seeing you this way, but also... you need to grow a fucking pair. You push Kira away, a lovely girl who, for whatever reason, thinks you're amazing, just because that bitch Lisa convinced you that you ruined her life."

"I did."

"You didn't," Lucas snapped. "Listen, your parents and Lisa did a real fucking number on you, and truthfully, I kind of hate them for it. You didn't ruin anyone's life, including your own, and you have got to stop being such a sad sack of shit and move the fuck on."

"Your pep talks are the fucking worst," Connor said.

"Yeah, I know." Lucas stood and returned to the stove to stir the soup again. "But you need someone to hit you with the truth hammer. Was punching that smarmy firefighter in the face a stupid idea? Yeah, maybe, but it happened, and now you have to deal with it. Maybe you've fucked your hand, and maybe you haven't, but either way, you've got to man the fuck up and live with your actions. Call Kira, tell her you're an idiot, and ask for forgiveness. You need her, Connor. She's the best damn thing that's ever happened to you."

"What do I have to offer her?" Connor said. "I make mistake after mistake after mistake. I've most likely ended my career. I'm a disappointment to my parents, hell, an entire fucking *town*, and I suck at relationships. How many times did Lisa call me cold? How many times did she beg me to open up to her, and I never would? I'm not meant to be with someone, Lucas."

"Oh, boo fucking hoo," Lucas said. "You think you're the only one with baggage? Everyone has it. The trick is finding the right person to handle your particular baggage. Maybe that's Kira, or maybe it isn't, but you won't know if you don't give this thing a fucking chance."

"She called me a coward."

"You're not, but you sure as hell are acting like one," Lucas said. "So, you're not good at expressing your feelings. That doesn't mean you're not worthy of a relationship. Maybe you didn't open up to Lisa because you knew deep down that she was a stone-cold bitch. Christ, dude, get over yourself. This emo shit you have going on is not a good look for you."

"Again – your pep talks are the worst," Connor said.

"Call Kira and apologize," Lucas said. "Ask her for a second chance."

"It's too late for apologies." He stood and headed for the doorway.

"Where are you going? It's almost lunch." Lucas said.

"I'm not hungry. I'm going to lie down for a while."

GRACE STARED WORRIEDLY AT KIRA. THE LAST TIME SHE'D SEEN her best friend looking so pale and sad was in the weeks after her parents died. Fear trickled into her belly, and she leaned forward and took Kira's hand. "Honey? You're taking your meds, right?"

Kira sighed and stared out the living room window. "I am. Stop worrying, Gracie. I'm not depressed. I'm just... sad and angry and... I miss him."

"I know, honey."

"I'm worried about him. He can't use his right hand at all. How is he showering, or cooking, or driving? He's trapped in his little apartment and has no close friends here."

"He's okay," Grace said. "He took an Uber to the clinic on Friday. He didn't look or smell all that great, but I heard him telling Grant that he had a friend coming down for the weekend to help him."

"What did Grant say? Do you know?" Kira asked. "Is he angry with Connor?"

Grace shook her head. "No, he isn't angry. He's remarkably level-headed about it. He's bringing in a friend of his – some semi-retired dentist - to cover Connor's work while he heals."

"That's good," Kira said with relief. She stared out the window again as Grace studied her. Despite what Kira said, fear still gnawed at her belly. Maybe she should call Gideon. Grace didn't *want* to call Gideon, not when she couldn't get the sound of his low voice promising to spank her out of her head or her dreams, but she was worried about Kira.

The doorbell rang, and when Kira made no move to get up, Grace stood. "I'll be right back, honey."

She walked down the hallway and opened the front door, staring at the man standing on the porch. "Can I help you?"

"I'm looking for Kira," the man said. "My name's Lucas. I'm a friend of Connor's."

"What do you want?" She blocked the doorway with her body, not failing to notice when his gaze lingered for a moment on her breasts.

"I was hoping to talk to her." He gave her an admittedly cute grin. "I promise I'm harmless."

"She's upset. She's not up for visitors right now," Grace said.

"I get that. But I just came from Connor's place, and if she's anywhere half as miserable as he is, then I think you should let me talk to her," he said.

"Gracie? Who is it... Lucas?" Kira peeked over Grace's shoulder. "What are you doing here?"

"I came to talk to you," Lucas said.

"Let him in, Grace," Kira said.

She stepped aside, giving him a little scowl when he winked at her as he slipped by. "I like your shoes, Gracie."

"It's Grace, and thank you," she said.

She followed them to the living room, sinking into one of the recliners as Lucas sat on the sectional. He stared at Kira, who was pacing the room and said, "Connor is an idiot, but he loves you."

"He broke up with me," Kira said.

"Because he's an idiot. But he is miserable without you."

"Then maybe he shouldn't have broken up with her," Grace said.

Lucas grinned at her. "Oh, he absolutely shouldn't have, but you know us guys, we do stupid shit all the time."

She didn't reply, and Lucas shifted his gaze back to Kira.

"Go see him, Kira. I guarantee you the minute he sees you, he'll be begging you for forgiveness. He knows he made a stupid mistake."

"If he wants her back, why are you here and not him?" Grace said.

"He's sensitive," Lucas replied. "He thinks Kira hates him now, and he's afraid of being rejected."

Grace snorted. "Connor is not sensitive."

"He is," Kira said. "He just hides it well."

"Yep," Lucas said. "He loves you, Kira. He loves you and made a stupid mistake that he now regrets. But you have to understand that Lisa – and, to a certain extent, his parents – messed with his head. They made him believe he ruined his life, and Lisa let him think he ruined hers. She's an asshole who was only with him because she wanted all the perks of being a famous baseball player's wife. Her true colours emerged the second she knew that wasn't a possibility. She fucked him up by refusing to admit that she didn't love him and kept him hanging for a few years. She should have done him a favour and just walked away as soon as his ball career ended."

He leaned forward, clasping his hands together and giving Kira an earnest look. "It's not an excuse for him breaking up with you, but it explains why he made such a dumb decision. Can you go and talk to him? Please?"

Kira nodded. "Yes."

Grace could see the relief sweeping across Lucas' face. "Great. That's really great. You won't regret it, Kira."

"Okay. I'll change quickly, and then I'll go." Kira ran upstairs, and Grace studied Lucas.

"If this goes bad, I'm blaming you," she said.

"Fair enough." He gave her another flirty grin, his gaze

lingering on her breasts and then her hips. "So, you know this is totally going to work out for those two lovebirds, right? That means they'll eventually get married, which means we'll eventually be at the wedding together. The best man and the maid of honour, staring at each other across a crowded church while our best friends pledge to spend the rest of their lives together."

He stood and moved a little closer, giving her another appreciative look. "Later on, you'll have a little too much to drink, I'll have a little too much to drink, and we'll probably end up in your hotel room. Both of us knowing we're making a mistake, but neither of us able to resist this simmering sexual tension between us."

A small grin crossed her face. "Sexual tension, huh?"

He stepped closer and tugged lightly on one curly strand of her hair. "You're feeling it, too, right?"

"It feels more like indigestion to me."

He laughed and took a step back. "Oh, I do like you. I'm starting to see the appeal of Harmony Falls girls."

"Took you long enough," she said.

Lucas grinned at her. "Want to have drinks with me while our best friends get back together?"

She reached up and brushed an imaginary piece of lint from his broad shoulder. "Sorry, handsome. Willington boys aren't my thing."

"You think I'm handsome?" Lucas said.

She rolled her eyes and headed out of the living room. "You're moderately appealing."

"I'll take that as a compliment."

Kira stepped inside Connor's apartment. Her stomach was churning, and she couldn't remember the last time she was this nervous, but she forced herself to move forward. God, she hoped Lucas was right. If he wasn't, she was about to make a right fool of herself.

She checked the living room before walking down the hallway to Connor's bedroom. She knocked and opened the door. Connor was sitting on the edge of the bed, staring at his cast, and her heart squeezed tight. It'd only been forty-eight hours since she'd seen him last, but she missed him terribly.

"Connor?"

He jerked and winced, his hand pressing against the cast on his right arm as he stared wide-eyed at her. "Kira? What are you doing here?"

"I miss you," she said.

He swallowed hard. "I miss you too."

She crossed the room and sat down beside him on the bed. He studied her face. "I'm sorry. I'm so goddamn sorry. I'm an idiot, and I know it's asking a lot for you to forgive me, but I'm asking anyway."

She slipped her arm around his shoulders and kissed him. "I forgive you for being an idiot and trying to break up with me."

He smiled a little. "Trying?"

"It didn't stick," she said. "I let you think it did because I'm a nice girl."

He rested his forehead against hers. "I shouldn't have tried to break up with you, but I was panicking. I didn't want to mess up your life."

"You didn't, and you won't," she said. "You didn't ruin Lisa's life either, no matter what she says. And as far as your parents go – it's a real shitty thing for them to make you think you're not good enough."

"They just wanted what's best for me," he said.

"Maybe, but they went about it the wrong way," she said. "You're a good man, Connor. You don't need to be a world-famous baseball player to live a happy and fulfilling life. I'm sorry your parents can't see that, but I can."

She cupped his face. "Being a dentist isn't something to be ashamed of. You are good at what you do, and you help people. Be proud of who you are. I am."

"I love you," he said.

"I love you too. So much. If it turns out that you can't be a dentist, then we'll figure out something else. Together. I'm in this with you no matter what because I love you for who you are. A wonderful, thoughtful man who deserves the very best in life," Kira said.

He kissed her again and slid his left arm around her waist, holding her tightly against him. "You are the best thing that's ever happened to me, Kira Walker. I love you."

"I love you too, Connor MacMillan."

Keep reading for an excerpt from Book Two in the Harmony Falls Series, "Perfect Harmony".

PERFECT HARMONY EXCERPT

Grace cursed and yanked viciously at her bra. The wires were poking, and the band was digging into her soft flesh.

"Fuck it!" she muttered. She was almost home, but she absolutely couldn't wear this hellish torture device one minute longer. Holding the steering wheel with one hand, she arched her back and stuck her hand down the back of her dress before clawing at the bra's hooks. The car weaved into the other lane, and she cursed again before steering it back to her lane. The hooks finally released, and she moaned happily when the band loosened.

She pulled the bra straps off her arms, yanked it out from under her dress, and tossed it into the back seat just as a siren went off behind her. She jerked, her hands tightening on the steering wheel as she stared in the rear-view mirror.

"No, no, no," she said. "Are you fucking kidding me?"

For one crazy moment, she thought about just stomping

on the gas before she came to her senses. She turned off the main road onto a quiet side street and parked before shutting off her car. Maybe it wouldn't be him, maybe it would be Ian.

Either way, get your bra on, dumbass!

It was too late. The door of the police vehicle opened, and Gideon Walker's big body stepped out. He wore jeans with his shirt and police vest, and the denim clung to his thighs.

"Fuck, fuck, fuck," she whispered. She stared frantically at herself. The sun had set, but it wasn't very dark yet. The streetlight she had parked under provided more than enough light to see the way her heavy breasts pushed at the thin material of her dress. It was more than evident that she was braless, and she quickly clamped her arms over her tits as Gideon stopped next to her window and leaned down.

"License and registration."

"Gideon," she said. "Seriously?"

He raised one eyebrow at her. "License and registration."

She sighed in irritation, and keeping one arm across her chest, she yanked her wallet from her purse and fumbled it open. She pulled out her license and handed it to him before unbuckling her seatbelt and reaching into the glove box for the registration. He took it from her and perused both as she scowled at him.

"Why did you pull me over?"

He ducked his head into the car, and she had to fight her sudden urge to lick his neck. Being arrested for sexually assaulting the sheriff wasn't her idea of a good fucking time. He studied the interior of her car before moving back a little.

"Where are you coming from tonight?"

"Your sister's house."

"Were you drinking?"

"No," she said.

He stared at her, and she cleared her throat. "I had one beer, Gideon."

"Just one?"

"Yes. You know I wouldn't drink and drive. Why did you pull me over?" she said.

"You weaved into the other lane." He stepped back and straightened.

She stared at his gun and the handcuffs hooked to his belt before her gaze dipped to his crotch. Her face flushed, and she hurriedly looked away. Was now the time to be thinking about his cock?

No, it definitely wasn't.

"Step out of the car."

"Are you kidding me?" she said. "Gideon, c'mon. You know I don't drink and drive. Just give me a warning for distracted driving and let me go."

"Step out of the car," Gideon repeated. "Don't make me ask you again."

She hesitated a moment longer. Gideon made a low noise of disapproval and opened her car door. Keeping her arms crossed over her chest, she climbed out of her car and glared at him.

"You're a real dick, Gideon."

His gaze narrowed. "You might want to think twice before insulting a police officer."

"You gonna arrest me for hurting your feelings?" she said. "Does the big bad sheriff hate it when a woman makes fun of him?"

"Enough," Gideon growled. "You're doing a sobriety test."

"Like hell I am!" she nearly shouted. "I am not drunk."

"Either do a sobriety test or park your car and walk home," he said.

She glared at him. "Fine, I'll walk."

A brief look of shock crossed his face. She poked him hard in the chest, and he grunted in surprise as she said, "Get out of my way so I can start walking."

He didn't, and she poked him again. He scowled at her. "Don't do that again, Grace."

Slowly and deliberately, she poked him for a third time in the chest. His nostrils flared, and she squeaked in surprise when he grabbed her arms and turned her around. He pulled her arms away from her chest and pushed them onto the top of her car as he pinned her against the car with his hard body.

She stopped squirming immediately, her nerve endings lit on fire by the feel of Gideon's body against hers.

"Let go of me," she said in a trembling voice.

"You assaulted a police officer," he said into her ear. "You're lucky I don't arrest you right here."

His breath tickled her ear, and she supposed she should have been freaking out about the possibility of spending a night in jail. Instead, she was consumed by all sorts of images of Gideon and his handcuffs and just how he might use them on her.

Her pussy throbbed, and her nipples tightened, and if she were any wetter, she'd be fucking drowning in her own come.

"I – I poked you," she squeaked out and then cleared her throat. "It was hardly an assault."

"How much have you had to drink?" he said again. "You were weaving."

"Oh, for God's sake. I was taking off my bra."

"What?"

"My bra." He was still holding her arms on the top of her car, so she thrust her chin toward her back seat. "My bra's in the back seat. I was taking it off while I was driving, and that's why I weaved, okay?"

"Keep your hands on the top of the car," he said. He released her hands and shone his flashlight in the back window. Her bra was lying on the seat, and her cheeks burned as Gideon studied it before flicking off the light.

"Happy?" she said. "It was just a bit of distracted driving. If you don't mind, I – oh God! Gideon, wh-what is that?"

<hr/>

The moment he saw the lacy pink bra in the back seat, all of the blood drained from Gideon's head to his dick. It went from half-hard to fully erect in less than five seconds. Grace wasn't wearing a bra. She was wearing a thin dress and no bra. If he wanted to, he could tug down that dress and lick and suck on her nipples. He'd finally know what colour they were, finally know how they'd taste, and how she would sound when he sucked on them.

Grace was speaking to him, but it was lost in the haze of lust that had descended over him. The sensible part of his brain screamed at him, but it was muffled and barely louder than a whisper. He stepped closer and let his erection press against Grace's lovely ass.

"Oh God!" she said. "Gideon, wh-what is that?"

He stepped back. This was madness. He needed to tell Gracie to get into her car and drive home. He opened his mouth and said, "Spread your legs."

She stared over the top of her car as her fingers curled into tight fists. "Why?"

"You assaulted a police officer. I need to check you for weapons." He pressed his cock against her ass again. His pulse pounded when her back arched just the tiniest amount at the contact. He stared at her upper back and shoulders. The thin straps of her dress were flush against her skin, and he pictured sliding them down her arms. He placed his hands on her wrists and lowered his mouth to her ear.

"Spread your legs for me, Gracie," he said in a low voice.

She moaned and spread her legs. Gideon stepped between them and rested his dick against her ass. She moaned again, and he nearly came in his fucking pants when she ground her ass against him.

"Don't move," he said harshly.

She stiffened, and he slowly slid his hands up her forearms to her upper arms. Her skin was satin soft, and he breathed in her delicious scent as he gently patted her upper arms.

"Gideon," she whispered. "What are you doing?"

"Checking you for weapons," he said.

He curved his hands around her shoulders and stroked her upper chest. She twitched when he ran his fingers over her collarbone.

"Stay still, Princess," he said.

She shivered all over when he said her nickname. He ran his hands down her back to the generous curve of her waist. He cupped her waist and squeezed lightly before moving his hands to her stomach. He felt her suck it in as he stroked her round belly. He made a noise of disapproval and traced his finger along the curve of her lower belly.

"That tickles," she said.

He moved his hands to her hips and cupped them. She inhaled sharply. "Gideon!"

"You're not carrying anything that will hurt me, are you, Princess? Nothing concealed that will poke or stick me?"

"Where would I have it concealed?" she said.

He bit back his laughter as she said, "You're one to talk about poking. I know that's not your damn gun digging into my – oh my God!"

He had crouched behind her and slid his hands up her calves. She started to close her legs, and he slapped her right calf lightly. "Keep them open, Princess."

She stopped moving, and he murmured, "good girl" under his breath. Her delightful ass was right in his face, and it took all of his willpower not to bite one plump cheek. Instead, he slid his hands up both her calves to her knees.

"Gideon?" Her usual self-confidence had disappeared, and she sounded nervous and unsure.

"Stay still, Gracie," he said.

She trembled as he ran his hands up the outside of her thighs under her dress. He moved his hands to the back of her thighs just below the swell of that delectable ass, and she made a low moan of need when his fingers slipped to her inner thighs. Her legs widened automatically, and he groaned inwardly before sliding his hands down her inner thighs to her knees.

He stood, and she hitched in a shaky breath as he said, "Turn around, Princess."

She turned and stared at him. He loved how tall she was. It would be so easy to lift her dress, pull down her panties, and fuck her against the car. Just lift her to her tiptoes and a quick twist of his hips, and he'd be inside of her.

His cock throbbed, and he clenched his hands into fists as she said, "What's wrong?"

He'd deliberately avoided looking at her chest, but Christ, a man only had so much willpower. He dropped her gaze to her tits.

"Fuck," he muttered.

Her breasts strained against the thin fabric of her dress. He could see the hard outline of her nipples against the cotton fabric, and he was itching to suck on them through the material.

"Turn back around, Princess," he ordered before he could succumb to his madness.

"Gideon, this is ridiculous."

"Do what I say."

He could see the desire fading in her eyes to be replaced by impatience as she swung around to face the car again. He smiled to himself. God, he had always loved her short temper.

"Don't move," he said, placing her hands on the top of the car again. He reached down and rested his hands on her hips. She shuddered when he stroked the swell of her tummy.

"What are you do – oh, hell," Grace moaned.

He cupped her breasts and leaned forward until his dick pressed hard against her ass. She arched her back, filling his hands with her warm flesh. He kneaded her heavy breasts before pinching both her nipples. She made a delightful moan that went straight to his cock. Fuck, could he be that lucky? Did Gracie like a little pain with her pleasure?

He took a quick look around as Gracie rubbed her ass against his cock. The side street she'd parked on was quiet, with no one outside on their porches or walking their dog. Still, it didn't mean that they weren't watching.

But the car hid Gracie's upper body. If anyone were watching from inside their house, they'd see what looked like him doing a routine stop and body check. Nothing more.

He wouldn't be able to see Grace's tits or taste them, but he could at least touch them. Before his rational mind could tell him to stop, he slid his hands into the bodice of Grace's dress and cupped both her tits. Her skin was warm and silky smooth, and her reaction made him want to lift the back of her dress, yank down her panties and slam his cock into her pussy.

She cried out, her hands digging into the top of the car as her head fell back to rest on his shoulder. He pulled on her diamond-hard nipples. She made another cry of pleasure, and with regret coursing through him, he said, "Lift your head, Princess."

"Gideon, please," she moaned.

"Head up," he said.

With effort, she lifted her head and stared across the car with a glazed look of need as he rubbed and caressed her incredible breasts. He took another look around them and made a quick decision when he didn't see anyone. He would regret it tomorrow, but right now, he would take what he wanted for once.

"Distracted driving is a substantial ticket, Princess," he whispered into her ear.

"I – what?" she said.

He pressed his dick tight against her ass, smiling at her groan of need.

"Distracted driving gets you a ticket," he said. "But I'll be nice to you."

"Just a warning?" She ground her ass against his dick.

"I'll give you a choice," he breathed into her ear as his gaze roved the neighbourhood. "You can get a ticket for distracted driving, or you can climb into the back of my car, take off your panties, and watch as I eat out your pussy."

She moaned, her ass grinding against him again when he pinched her nipples. "Well, Princess? What will it be? Ticket or pussy eating?"

"Pussy eating," she said. "Definitely pussy eating."

ABOUT THE AUTHOR

Elizabeth Kelly was born and raised in Ontario, Canada. She moved west as a teenager and now lives in Alberta with her husband and a menagerie of pets. She firmly believes that a person can survive solely on sushi and coffee, and only her husband's mad cooking skills prevents her from proving that theory.

For more information about Elizabeth, check out her website at

www.elizabethkelly.ca

facebook.com/EKellyBooks
instagram.com/elizabethkelly_author
amazon.com/Elizabeth-Kelly/e/B00EOHZ0MS
bookbub.com/authors/elizabeth-kelly

ALSO BY ELIZABETH KELLY

Tempted Series

Tempted

Twice Tempted

Forever Tempted

Breathless

Tempted Trilogy (Books 1-3)

Red Moon Series

Red Moon

Red Moon Rising

Dark Moon

Alpha Moon

Pale Moon

The Recruit Series

The Recruit (Book One)

The Recruit (Book Two)

The Recruit (Book Three)

The Recruit (Book Four)

The Recruit (Book Five)

The Recruit (Book Six)

The Shifters Series

Willow and the Wolf (Book One)

Ava and the Bear (Book Two)

Katarina and the Bird (Book Three)

Porter's Mate (Book Four)

Bria and the Tiger (Book Five)

Rosalie Undone (Book Six)

The Dragon's Mate (Book Seven)

Rise of the Jaguar (Book Eight)

The Assassin and the Bear (Book Nine)

Elora and the Crow (Book Ten)

The Draax Series

Reign (Book One)

Rule (Book Two)

Rebel (Book Three)

Surrender (Book Four)

Survive (Book Five)

Salvation (Book Six)

Harmony Falls Series

Sweet Harmony (Book One)

Perfect Harmony (Book Two)

Forbidden Harmony (Book Three)

Redeeming Harmony (Book Four)

Absolute Harmony (Novella)

Beautiful Harmony (Book Five)

Reckless Harmony (Book Six)

Seasoned Romance Series

Bet Your Heart on Me (Book One)

Take a Chance on Me (Book Two)

Place Your Trust in Me (Book Three)

Individual Books

The Necessary Engagement

Amelia's Touch

The Rancher's Daughter

Healing Gabriel

The Contract

A Home for Lily

Saving Charlotte

Shameless

The Fairy Tales Collection

Broken

An Unlikely Seduction

Holiday Romance

The Christmas Wife

The Christmas Rescue

The Christmas Nanny

The Christmas Boss

Sordid Games

www.ingramcontent.com/pod-product-compliance
Lightning Source LLC
Chambersburg PA
CBHW070534260626
47161CB00002B/375